D1555553

BEAST CHARMING

First Paperback Edition: March 2015

For information on subsidiary rights, please contact the publisher at rights@jollyfishpress.com. For information, please visit our website at www. jollyfishpress.com, or write us at Jolly Fish Press, PO Box 1773, Provo, UT 84603-1773.

Printed in the United States of America

THIS TITLE IS ALSO AVAILABLE AS AN EBOOK.

Library of Congress Cataloging-in-Publication Data

Wardell, Jenniffer, 1981–
  Beast charming : a novel / by Jenniffer Wardell. — First paperback edition.
     pages cm ISBN 978-1-939967-38-1 (pbk.)
  I. Title.
  PS3623.A7356B43 2015 813'.6—dc23
                            2014036950

10 9 8 7 6 5 4 3 2 1

To everyone still searching for their own fairy tale.
Never be afraid to write the story yourself.

Also by Jenniffer Wardell:

Fairy Godmothers, Inc.

BEAST CHARMING

JENNIFFER WARDELL

JOLLY
FISH
PRESS
Provo, Utah

CHAPTER 1

Of Frying Pans and Fires

Beauty held up the mangled gauntlet, ready to fight. She'd spent most of the afternoon yanking the thing out from between a dragon's teeth, and said dragon would probably approve of her using it to beat her father's head in. "Get. Out. Of. My. Way."

"Not until you've returned to your senses and come back home." Noble Tremain—whose birth certificate still identified him as Frank—folded his arms across his brocade-covered chest and tried to stare her down. Her father sincerely believed he was an important and powerful man, even though he'd spent most of Beauty's formative years being kicked out of rich people's houses. "This *ridiculous* job is an insult to the family name."

Beauty shoved her shaggy brown hair out of her eyes with her free hand, glaring at the man who was technically responsible for her existence. She'd told herself only a few months ago that she needed to move again, just in case her father finally tracked her and Grace down, but she was sick of letting the man ruin her life. Besides, she couldn't leave her sister to face this alone.

"So sedating princesses and sneaking your daughters into secret ballrooms is what, creative parenting?" She gritted her teeth to keep from shouting, furious he'd insisted on doing this where she worked. The only good thing about all this was that he'd caught her before she'd made it inside. "Or how about that time you knocked us unconscious and left us in an ogre's cave, hoping a questing hero would just *happen* to rescue us?"

Her father's brow lowered at the reminder of that last incident. "You could have *tried* to be a little more in peril with that ogre," he snapped, his round face tensing up with annoyance. Behind him, Beauty could see the front doors open a little, giving whomever was on the other side a shield to continue listening behind. "I found you the largest, most terrifying-looking creature in the region, and you and your sister come back looking like you'd been out making a social call."

"It's not our fault we're more competent than you thought."

The ogre, horrified at the sight of the two girls collapsed in what turned out to be his living room, had promptly woken them both up and given them herbal tea and berry cookies. Both Beauty and Grace had immediately sworn never to tell their father what had actually happened, though Grace still sent the ogre a card every year on his birthday. "Now get out of my way or I'll call security. I know the concept is foreign to you, but I actually have a job to do."

His eyes flared with a fresh burst of offended fury. "You're related to nobility!" His face started to turn red as his volume increased, only adding to the certainty that every *single* person in the building would know about this in the next few minutes. "How *dare* you work at a temp agency!"

Beauty pulled her arm back, already visualizing the spot on his forehead where the gauntlet would make contact. Around them, the birds chirped merrily in encouragement. "Are we really dragging Mother's second cousin into this?" she warned him quietly. "Particularly after Mother ran off and left you for the royal tax collector?"

This time, it was her father's turn to grit his teeth. "You are *still* related to nobility, you ungrateful brat, no matter how it happened," he hissed. "And if you and your sister would just come home and start behaving like *reasonable* daughters, I could get you married to a desperate royal somewhere and *finally* get some use out of you."

Beauty threw the gauntlet, pleased when it careened off his head with a definite *thunk*. While he was still reeling from that, she advanced on him. Despite her short height, she was intimidating enough that her father backed up a step. "You tried to shove us into any ridiculous fairy tale situation you could for *years*, Father, and all you have to show for it is two daughters who hate your guts. If you want your happily-ever-after so bad, *you* go put on a dress and lock yourself up in a tower. Grace and I are done."

"Don't you dare tell me what your sister will and won't do!" Unfortunately, her father's thick skull had helped him recover far too quickly. "*She* at least has the decency to speak to her father with a civil tongue!"

"That's because she's a kind and reasonable human being," Beauty snapped back, fury rising. If he'd started harassing Grace again . . . "I, however, seem to take after *you.*"

If she'd tried, she couldn't have come up with a better insult. The red surged back all at once, making him look like an evil sorceress had turned him into a beet, and sheer rage made him seem to grow just a little as he gathered his breath for a rant that would undoubtedly be heard all the way back into town. "You miserable, ungrateful—"

Fortunately, whatever else he'd been about to say abruptly choked to a halt when he was dragged several feet into the air. Beauty forced herself to take a deep breath, giving the red in her own vision a chance to clear as she looked up at the extremely tall man who currently had Noble by the collar. "Hi, Steve," she said after a moment, trying to sound as if having a shouting match with her father in front of her work was a normal, everyday occurrence. If you take out the part about work, it used to be absolutely true. "Did Manny send you out to help quiet things down again?"

Steve nodded, completely unconcerned about her father's

increasingly frantic struggling. "He said that you need to be better about pest control, or you'll scare off customers." Steve was nine feet tall, gentle as an enormous bunny rabbit. He served as the agency's yard and outdoor maintenance man since he was too tall to comfortably fit through the doors. Rumor had it that his mother was a giantess, which had led to no end of speculation about his father. "Besides, he needs your report about the dragon job."

"Pest control?" Noble shouted, swinging an arm upward to hit at Steve. The impact had no more of an effect on Steve's placid expression than the struggling had. "How dare you say such a thing, you impudent . . ."

"Don't listen to him, Steve. He's cranky." Beauty hoped her father didn't make enough of a fuss to accidentally choke himself on his own shirt or something. Not that she would have minded, personally, but she didn't want Steve to get into trouble. "Any chance you can drop him in the compost pile as soon as I go inside?"

Steve considered this, giving Noble a single experimental bounce that made him squawk like an extremely angry chicken. "I could do that," he said thoughtfully, then gave Beauty a faintly chiding look. "You know you could have asked me for help, right? You didn't have to wait for Manny to tell me."

Beauty blinked, startled, then blushed as Steve wagged a finger at her. A few feet overhead, her father was attempting to light them both on fire with the heat of his most disdainful glare. Ignoring him, Beauty smiled at Steve. The expression made her round face far prettier than it normally managed to be. "Thank you." She patted him on the hand as she went by, then grabbed the gauntlet from where it had fallen. "Feel free to bounce him a few more times if you want."

She went inside, her smile widening at the one last squawk that followed her in as the doors closed behind her. Then, deliberately ignoring the sound of rapidly scurrying feet that signaled her audience hurrying to look busy someplace else, she exchanged nods with the woman at the front desk and headed straight back for Manny's office.

He didn't look up when she pushed open the door, smoke puffing placidly up from his nostrils as he scanned the current assignment list on his magic mirror. Mandrake Kent was a three-foot-tall dragon, complete with tiny, useless wings and a blanket refusal to talk about anything he'd done before starting the temp agency that bore his name. "Well, now I know where your temper comes from," he said blandly.

Beauty took a deep breath, grateful for the knowledge that her boss was prepared to let things go at that. "Sorry about that," she sighed, fixing the collar of her shirt and absently running a hand through her hair to straighten it. The dress code at the agency wasn't nearly as strict as it would have been at Fairy Godmothers, Inc. if she would've taken the secretarial job they'd offered her, but she didn't want Manny to think she wasn't trying. She already flouted tradition enough by being the only woman in the office to wear pants. "The last I heard, he was over in Far Away trying to convince some earl to take him on as a personal advisor."

Manny made a small dismissive gesture with his claw, finally looking up at her. "He scares off my customers, and I'll sue his velvet-covered rear end into the next kingdom." He paused briefly, raising a scaly red eyebrow at the sight of the gauntlet Beauty dropped into his trash can. "Tell me that's not from the guy I sent over to Percy before you."

Beauty gave a small smile. "No. Apparently, our client went over to his brother-in-law's house for dinner and didn't ask enough questions about the ingredients list. He knows he could have gone to a dentist to have it removed, but he likes us better."

"I would, too. Dragon dentists tend to use swords or claws instead of toothpicks." He blew out one more puff of smoke. "Let me see it." He held a hand out as Beauty fished the gauntlet out of the trash and handed it to him. He studied it a moment, then bared his teeth in an expression that everyone in the office had decided was probably a dragon grin. "I'll call Percy back to tell him this is from a pre-packaged destroyed armor set. He didn't blow his diet."

She folded her arms across her chest, finally relaxing for the first time in what felt like hours. "I'm sure he'll be happy to hear it." When Manny looked up again, she tilted her head in the direction of his magic mirror. "I'm not really in the mood to go home right now. Any chance I could pick up one more assignment before I call it a day?"

He set down the gauntlet, double-checking the list. "Unless you've changed your mind about kissing that enchanted public relations guy, there's nothing right now that you could finish in a couple of hours. Want an overnight job?"

Beauty hesitated, weighing the likelihood of her father deciding it would be worth his time to try to harass her at home, then sighed. "Sure." She sat down in the chair opposite his. "What have you got?"

"Let's see." He tapped his claws against the desktop as he mulled over a few selections. "You don't know Dwarvish, so that one's out. That one I'm saving for Steve . . ." Manny looked up. "The agoraphobe in the tower called again. Swears she just wants some company for a few days, and promises the person won't have to move any furniture or hear about how lonely she's been since the evil sorceress died."

Beauty groaned, covering her face with her hand. "Please, Manny, no." Pretty much everyone with the agency had taken a turn with the woman by this point, and most swore they'd have rather spent a day off cleaning up after a hydra than go back. "You really should put her on some sort of 'will no longer sacrifice temps to this' list."

"Never. As long as threat of death isn't actually involved, I'm always willing to take people's money." Still, she was relieved to see reluctance flash briefly across his face. "I'll save it for the next person who pisses me off." He scanned down through a few more assignments. "Some butler's looking for a general assistant. The timeline's open-ended, and though I make no promises I'm pretty sure the most complicated thing you'll have to do is clean something."

Beauty's brow furrowed. "Why would a butler need an assistant? Don't people rich enough to hire one have an entire houseful of staff ready to do all that?"

Manny shrugged. "How should I know? Maybe he wants someone to keep his shoes shined." He held the mirror up, wiggling it a little. "You want the job or not?"

She hesitated again, less than thrilled with the idea of spending the next week helping someone tackle their monthly cleaning list. But if she saw her father again today things would end with one of them getting arrested for assault, and she wasn't above running and hiding in order to keep that from happening. "Sure. Give me the info, and I'll stop by my place and pack a bag before heading over there."

"Think of it this way." He made a few quick taps on the mirror, then handed her the printout. "At least there's less of a chance you'll accidentally get eaten on this one."

THE HOUSE, AS it turned out, was surprisingly normal for an ancient manor in the middle of nowhere. Sure, there were spikes in various places, and some stone things leering down at her from the upper ledges, but the entire place was generally clean and well cared for.

Of course, the shattered statue in the middle of the front walkway put something of a damper on the overall look. Beauty moved closer to it, peering upward at the spot of ledge just overhead before glancing back down at the wreck of stonework sitting at her feet. The rest of it was scattered over a surprisingly wide portion of the otherwise immaculate front lawn, and all Beauty could think was how hard the statue would have had to hit the ground in order for the pieces to spread out that much . . .

Her head snapped upward at the sound of the front door

opening. A lean, impeccably dressed older man stood in the doorway, looking at her as if she intended to sell him something. "If you've come here to break the curse, it would be wisest of you to leave now and find something more useful to do with the rest of your evening. You are, of course, fully within your rights to persist in your initial venture, but if that's your decision I insist you remain outside while you speak to him. I grow weary of replacing the carpeting, and won't be able to hire a reliable serviceman to perform the task until Monday."

Beauty narrowed her eyes at him, the tone superior and dismissive enough to set her teeth instantly on edge. Then what he actually said finally filtered through her brain. "Wait." She blinked at him, the first flickers of panic flaring to life in her stomach. She could deal with dragons, ogres, witches, and the evilest of evil sorceresses without a problem, but put an enchantment or a member of the nobility anywhere near her and she turned straight back into a fumbling, mortified sixteen-year-old. "What curse?"

He studied her a moment, then his expression eased as he gave her a small nod. "Ah. Pardon my presumption. How may I help you?" His eyes flicked downward to the broken statue at her feet, and something that looked almost like parental disapproval flashed across his face for a moment. "I must apologize for the mess. Normally such matters don't escape my notice." He lifted his hand a fraction, then hesitated. "If you would be so kind as to take a step back."

Having seen enough in her life to know when to take that kind of advice, Beauty did what he asked. The man made a brief gesture with his hand, and what felt like a sudden gust of wind ruffled Beauty's clothing as it circled the pile of stone and lifted it like a small, gentle tornado. It hung in the air for a moment, waiting, until the man swept his hand to the right. "Put it with the others, then you may return to your previous duties." The wind sped off with the stone like a herd of obedient puppies, and the man's attention returned to Beauty. "Now, you were saying?"

Panic now tamped down under a very firm desire to know

exactly what she was getting herself into, Beauty pulled the printout Manny had given her out of her pocket. "You are Richard Waverly, right?" she asked carefully, making sure she had a route open in case she suddenly needed to retreat. "And you did hire a temp from the Mandrake Agency, despite the fact that apparently you've figured out how to get the wind to do your bidding?"

"I am indeed Richard Waverly, though I would prefer it if you referred to me simply as Waverly." He studied her for a moment, expression suddenly penetrating enough that Beauty would not have been at all surprised to learn the man was capable of reading minds. "I presume you're the woman they've sent over to fill the position?"

She nodded. "Beauty Tremain." When his brow furrowed slightly, she reached into her pocket again. "Do you need to see my ID?"

"No." Brow still furrowed, he shook his head. "It's of no consequence. Come inside, and we can discuss the details of your employment."

"There are a few things we need to discuss out here." Firmly aware of the fact that nothing short of potential death would be enough of an excuse for Manny to let her out of this job, Beauty lifted her chin and pretended like she had options. "If you can get the wind to help you do all your cleaning, I need a better idea of exactly what sort of work you're expecting out of a human assistant."

"Wind is a close enough description of my support staff for the moment, though technically speaking, not accurate in the slightest." He smiled slightly, which annoyed her. The annoyance was almost a relief, the emotion steadying her in a way little else could have. This, she was used to. "As to what your other duties will be, I believe that would be best discussed after you've met the master of the house."

She glanced down at the disturbed patch of grass where the broken statue had been, remembering her earlier thought about how hard it would have needed to hit. Then she looked back up at Waverly, raising an eyebrow. "You mean the same master who was apparently playing lawn darts with stone sculptures earlier today?"

The faint disapproval from earlier flickered back across his face.

"Yes, unfortunately. And while I admit that the particular example you saw was no loss to the art world even before James had finished with it, the habit will need to be stopped. Hopefully that will be a side effect of your current duties."

Beauty's eyes narrowed. "And how exactly am I supposed to stop someone who can toss a statue around like an egg?"

This time, it was his turn to raise an eyebrow. "If I were to hazard a guess, I would say by being cleverer than he is."

That stopped her short, particularly when she realized she had no snappy comeback. After five minutes of conversation she felt shaky, confused, annoyed, and just defiant enough to not have the sense to back down. On top of all that, she really needed the money if she wanted to keep eating on a regular basis.

She took a deep breath, hoping she wasn't about to get herself into the kind of trouble she'd spent most her life trying to get out of. "I know what you said before, but I want to make absolutely sure you know that there will be no fairy tale endings whatsoever if I'm involved. No curse breaking, no handsome princes, nothing."

Waverly smiled again. "Then you should fit in wonderfully." He took a small step to the side, holding the door open wide enough that she could get through it as well. "Now will you come inside so we may discuss the details, or should I have dinner brought out to you on the lawn?"

With a sigh, Beauty went inside.

CHAPTER 2

Pest Control

Something stirred in the decorative hedge.

James Charlton Hightower, who had been known as "the Beast" long before he'd ended up furry, froze at the small sound it made. The noise was too loud to be from either a bird or small animal, both of which usually knew better than to take shelter in the extremely thorny witches' nails bushes. Clearly, it was time for a little more pest control.

He waited, claws flexing, for a second sound to help him pin down the exact spot where his prey was hiding. Then he pounced, grabbing the girl's foot and dragging her out from the hedge without any concern over the cuts and scrapes he was adding to her already impressive collection.

When she shrieked, he yanked her up so she was hanging in the air by her ankle. "Maybe I should eat one of you," he growled, letting his voice climb slowly into a full roar. When she looked up, eyes wide, he peeled his lips back enough to give her the full effect of his long, sharp canines. "Indigestion would be worth finally managing to pound the message into your tiny little minds that *I'm not interested in having the curse broken!*"

"I just . . . I . . ." He'd barely done anything to her, and the girl was already trembling so hard she could barely speak. "I was . . . my family is in the area, and I know the guidebook had a warning about you but I thought maybe they just didn't understand . . ."

"Stop. I don't care." His eyes narrowed as she went silent, wishing for a moment that he really did eat people. It was about the only vengeance suitable for the company behind the enchanted nobility guidebook that had included his name in last year's edition as part of a misguided attempt at expansion. He'd had Waverly threaten them with a lawsuit, using a legal team rather than claws to emphasize that he wasn't even titled, but that still left an entire year's worth of guidebooks the company hadn't been able to recall. "Burn the book this second and I'll decide whether or not I let you live."

The girl made a whimpering sound, nodding frantically. "I didn't really think I was your true love or could break the curse or anything, but I've had the guidebook for months now and I haven't even used it *once.*" She was crying now, tears streaming down her forehead, though he couldn't tell whether it was due to terror or to the blood dripping pretty steadily from the cut on her shoulder. "I . . . I was just going to wait in the bushes and see if you were really as scary as everyone said . . ."

Hating the guilt he could feel threatening to overtake him, he dropped the girl and watched while she scrambled into a sitting position. "Did you get the answer you were looking— Not that way, you idiot . . ." James cut off the rest of the threat to reach forward and grab the girl again, stopping her panicked retreat straight back into the middle of the thorny bush he'd yanked her out of. He picked her back up, and looked for a place he could put her back down without having to rescue her again. When she started sobbing, he shook her a little. "Stop it. I'm trying to help you run away without your collapsing in the woods and dying of blood loss." He pointed toward the front of the house, hoping Waverly wasn't anywhere near a window at the moment. "Do you think you're capable of escaping that way without doing any more injury to yourself?"

She bolted the second he let her go. Once she'd disappeared from sight, James sighed and ran a hand through his hair. The encounter had been both frustrating and deeply unsatisfying, leaving him even more restless than when he'd come out hunting for home invaders. He could head upstairs and smash more statues, but he doubted it would do much to relieve the pressure building inside him. The last one certainly hadn't . . .

"That was stunningly compassionate." James flinched a little at the dry voice behind him, hesitating a moment before turning to see Waverly standing on the walkway. When their eyes met, the older man raised an eyebrow. "Should I be concerned?"

James narrowed his eyes, pointing a claw at the man who had been his only family since he'd turned fourteen. "That wasn't compassion," he insisted, knowing that protest was futile but unable to stop himself. "It's just useless to torment them when they can't even see me through their flood of tears. And how long have you been standing there, anyway?"

"Long enough." Waverly smiled slightly. "If you're rethinking your choice of the witches' nails, I would be happy to have them removed and replaced with somewhat less predatory bushes."

James glared at him. "The bushes are *fine*. After this, I'll start chasing the girls into them on purpose." He stopped, catching something in the other man's expression. "Were you looking for me? I thought you'd decided to spend the afternoon working on the financial reports while the elementals swept the walkways." They were lesser air elementals—Waverly had always been infuriatingly vague about the details, but apparently he'd won them off a djinn in a poker game and they needed constant supervision on any task in which there was a chance of breaking things.

For a second, Waverly's normally serene expression looked almost solemn. "I would be more than happy to turn the reports back over to you the moment you say the word," he said quietly.

They'd had this discussion several times already since he'd been cursed, half in the form of fights and half in tense, heavy silences. This time, James felt the quiet weigh down on him as he slowly shook his head. "No." His voice was flat, making it clear he didn't want to discuss the matter. "I know you think it would work, but for once in your life you're wrong about something."

Waverly narrowed his eyes. "Name me one thing you have ever truly wanted to have happen that you didn't achieve through sheer bullheadedness."

"Juliana." He felt the growl rise up at the memory of the delicate blond he'd proposed to. They'd never been able to prove the curse was her fault, but if she wasn't the cause, the coincidences were a little too ludicrously convenient. "I wouldn't call that an achievement, would you?"

"I said *truly* want," Waverly shot back, "and you and I both know this has nothing to do with whether or not you would be accepted by the people you used to do business with. What you are truly doing by hiding out here and refusing to see anyone is making some sort of ridiculous point to the universe, without giving even a *moment* of thought as to whether or not you will survive the experience!"

The silence that fell was heavy enough to make it difficult to breathe. Waverly never shouted, and seeing him upset enough to break that rule shook Beast in a way the words themselves couldn't have. He wanted to apologize, even though he didn't think he was wrong, but that would start a conversation about feelings that he sincerely doubted either of them wanted to have. They were far more comfortable caring about each other without actually having to discuss it.

"So," James asked finally, the gruff edge in his voice the only visible sign of the argument they'd just had, "Did you need something, or did you just come out here to torment me?"

The other man, his own expression once again restored to its usual implacable serenity, inclined his head back toward the house. "We have a visitor. She'll be staying here for the foreseeable future, and as such I insist you introduce yourself without the shadows or skulking you've become so fond of."

James just stared at him, stunned. No matter what else they

fought about, Waverly had always chased the curse-breaking hopefuls away just as quickly and thoroughly as James had. Even the possibility that he might be trying to spring one on him felt like a betrayal. "Unless you have some sort of female relative you've never told me about, this had better be a joke."

Waverly's expression didn't even flicker. "I assure you, it's no joke. She's a temporary employee, and will serve as my personal assistant while I feel such a thing is necessary."

That was marginally better, though James had no doubt there was far more going on than the other man had just told him. Still, he needed to get as much information as possible before whatever plan Waverly was cooking up went into effect. "Fine," he snapped, stalking toward the house. When he got to the stairs, he turned back and pointed another claw at Waverly. "But this is the only time I ever have to see her. If she even *thinks* about trying to save me from myself, I promise you I'll eat her without compunction."

Waverly's expression didn't change. "Do let me know when that happens. I won't bother making dinner that night."

Growling at the sarcasm, James shoved his way inside and went to find this woman of Waverly's. If he was lucky, he could eat her before the older man caught up.

SHE WAS WAITING in the library, perusing the books he hadn't touched in almost a year with a wide-eyed interest that made him envious and annoyed all at the same moment. He watched her from a shadowed corner of the upper walkway, studying her entirely unremarkable face for any sign of what Waverly might be up to. She looked vaguely familiar, as if he'd met her once several years ago, but if so, she clearly hadn't made enough of an impression to help with whatever scheme Waverly was cooking up. The fact that she was wearing pants was somewhat unusual, but he had to give her credit for dressing more sensibly than most of her gender.

Waverly was nowhere in sight, despite having had plenty of

time to catch up. It was a clear sign that this was a test, and he was waiting to see how he and the girl would handle each other without the aid of a referee.

James smiled grimly, wondering what she sounded like when she shrieked.

He watched her carefully slide a book back into place on the shelf, and he tensed as he waited for the right moment to pounce. She turned around, her dark brown eyes scanning the room as if she were looking for something. Then they shifted upward to peer into the shadows of the upper walkway. Startled, James withdrew a little, eyes narrowed with sudden wariness as he followed her visual search. When she found nothing, she folded her arms across her chest. "I know you're up there, so you might as well come down and interrogate me or whatever else you were planning on doing. Waverly said he was going to look for you, which means he clearly considers this part of the hiring process."

James was pretty sure she was bluffing, but the fact that anything he did would prove her right limited his options considerably. He briefly considered staying silent until she let her guard down again, but he was far too stubborn himself not to recognize the same trait in the set of her shoulders. He had no doubt she would play the waiting game as long as she needed to, and there was a pretty good chance he'd lose.

He growled, letting the sound reverberate low in his throat, and he had the satisfaction of watching her freeze for a second. "Who said I wanted to ask you questions? I might just be figuring out what part of you I'm going to eat first."

She turned in the direction his voice had come from with an "Are you kidding me?" expression. "I've known Waverly less than five minutes, and I already know there's no way he'd let you get blood on these carpets."

The corner of his mouth twitched upward without any conscious decision on his part, which only made him more annoyed. Clearly, he was going to have to reclaim the upper hand in this situation.

With a full-throated roar, he aimed his leap to land almost on top of the girl's head. She stumbled backward, just like he'd expected, and it gave him the few seconds he'd needed to straighten up to his full seven feet in height. He lifted his claws, curving them inward slightly so they glinted in the lamplight, and gave her a smile that was all teeth and no humor. "I think what you know has very little bearing on the situation," he said, voice a dangerous purr.

Her eyes slowly lifted to meet his, going wider by the second as she took a step back. He was certain she was about to shriek, or at least start shaking, but all she did was let the air out of her lungs in a rush. Then she squeezed her eyes shut, muttering something low enough under her breath that he couldn't catch much more than the word "stupid." It was a confusing enough reaction that he didn't press his advantage, and by the time she opened her eyes again her expression had cleared completely. "Hi," she said calmly, holding out a hand. He had nearly two feet on her, but the size difference didn't seem to make her at all nervous. "I'm Beauty Tremain from the Mandrake Agency—yes, I know I have a ridiculous name—and I'm pretty sure I'm going to be Waverly's new assistant for the foreseeable future. I presume you are the master of the house? James, is it?"

He ignored the hand and allowed himself a moment to just glare at her, seriously considering risking Waverly's wrath for getting blood on the carpet. The other man would deserve it, and it seemed like the only way to get the reaction he expected out of *someone* before the day was over. "Don't get comfortable," he snarled. "You won't be here long."

"Okay, then," she said after a moment, dropping her hand. "I'd expected something more imaginative out of you, but I guess we all have our off-days."

"It's not my imagination you need to be worried about." James took a step closer so he could loom more effectively. "You're the one who apparently volunteered to be part of Waverly's latest master plan. Did he give you even a hint of what was going on, or did he dupe you into it?"

Beauty winced at that, continuing the annoying habit she was developing of surprising him. "I *knew* it was a bad idea to get anywhere near an enchantment again," she muttered, rubbing a hand across her eyes like she could feel a headache coming on. When she lifted her head again, her expression was apologetic. "Look. Whatever you think is going through Waverly's mind right now, I promise you I want absolutely nothing to do with any kind of scheme or master plan. When my office got the work assignment, all it said was a butler needed an assistant."

Suddenly, he realized where he'd seen her before. "Is your father named Noble? A short man, with slicked-back hair and a ridiculously trimmed goatee?"

She went instantly pale at the mention of the man's name. "Please don't tell me you've met him," she said quietly, the sudden pleading edge to her voice more unsettling than anything else she'd done. "And if you have, please accept my sincere and deeply felt apologies for whatever extremely embarrassing thing I'm sure he did."

James felt an entirely unexpected pang of sympathy, deciding then and there not to tell her that he'd seen the man get kicked out of a ball once. Beauty and a woman who must have been her sister had followed behind, he remembered, chins held high and making as graceful an exit as was humanly possible. "I was warned about him by some business associates, back when I . . ." He stopped suddenly as he realized what he was about to say, clearing his throat as his eyes slid away from hers. "A while ago."

"Ah." She moved closer, lightly touching his arm, and when he met her eyes again there was understanding in them. "Whatever Waverly's cooking up can't be that bad, right? I mean, he clearly cares about you, and if we're both pretty sure something's coming we can probably head it off at the pass."

His brow lowered. "If we see it in time," he said darkly. "With Waverly, life's a chess game and he's always three moves ahead of you."

"Which won't help him much, if you knock the board off the

table." Beauty smiled a little. "Though if you'd figure out a way to do that without eating me, I'd appreciate it."

The corners of James's own mouth twitched upward again, and this time he didn't fight it. "I think I can manage that."

At the sound of the library door opening, both of their heads snapped around like they'd been caught at something. Waverly was standing on the other side, and James had no doubt he'd been monitoring the entire conversation so that he could choose precisely the right point to make his entrance. "Excellent. I was hoping the two of you could become acquainted without screams or bloodshed of any kind."

James narrowed his eyes at the almost cheerful edge to the other man's voice. "I've always wanted to know—can the elementals tell you what people are saying, or do you just stand with your ear pressed against doors?"

Waverly just raised an eyebrow at him, clearly unwilling to dignify that with a response, then turned his attention to Beauty. "As my assistant, Miss Tremain, your duties are simple." He pointed at James without looking at him. "Find James a hobby, and force him to participate in it."

Beauty's eyes widened at the exact same moment his did. "A hobby?" she said faintly, glancing over at Beast before returning her attention back to Waverly. "Seriously?"

"He can't be," James snapped, glaring at the older man. "I'm not a child, Waverly. I don't need a babysitter."

Waverly met his glare with one just as fierce. "What you need is someone to shake you back into living, and I no longer have the energy to beat my head against your obstinacy and still keep the house and accounts in proper order." His gaze snapped over to Beauty. "I don't care what the hobby is. Hunting, botany, needlepoint . . . as long he does *something* other than brood and destroy unattractive statuary."

Beauty's brow furrowed as she attempted to regroup mentally. "What standards are you using to determine a hobby? Does he have to do whatever it is for a certain amount of time, or will it be enough if he starts looking more . . ." She glanced over at Beast again, a silent apology in her eyes. ". . . cheerful?"

"I will accept less brooding, though I draw the line at the statues." Utterly composed again, he smoothed his hands down the front of his jacket as if straightening an imaginary wrinkle. "His family's taste was abhorrent, but eventually we'll run out of statuary and he'll start moving on to the good furniture."

"I could start in on the furniture immediately, if that would help matters," James cut in, flexing his claws. He could have handled some kind of complicated plot in which Waverly attempted to out-strategize him for his own good, but this was just insulting.

Waverly ignored him, attention still focused on Beauty. "You will have a room, meals, and the previously agreed upon salary for as long as you need to fulfill your duties." When she didn't say anything, he raised an eyebrow at her. "Are we agreed, or shall I have the agency send over someone else?"

She took a deep breath, eyes fixed on James. He refused to meet her gaze, glaring at Waverly in disgusted defiance of the entire mess. Waverly looked right back at him, expression serene in the misplaced certainty that he was right.

Next to him, he heard Beauty sigh. "We're agreed."

Without another word, James pushed past Waverly and slammed out of the library.

CHAPTER 3

The Easy Way Out

Three hours later, there was still no sign of him.

Since that time had included a dinner featuring Waverly's melt-in-your-mouth roast, Beauty took the continued absence as a clear sign that James was an idiot. Of course, since she was the one who'd gotten herself lost in the middle of the rapidly darkening woods trying to find him, it was probably a case of the gnome calling the gremlin short.

She muttered insults at both of them as she pushed aside a low-hanging branch, ducking out of the way before it could snap back and smack her in the face. She'd had the genius idea of following the trampled undergrowth, completely ignoring the fact that she could have been following a very angry bear for the last twenty minutes who would now have every right to sue her for stalking. That, or she was walking in an enormous circle, and James was hidden somewhere watching and laughing his head off.

Clearly, this was the universe's way of telling her she should have never said yes to any of this. She should have just gone home this afternoon, and if her father had shown up she could have dumped a load of Pegasus poop on his head from the stable next door and called the city guards on him. Or, if she hadn't been that smart, she could have said no after Waverly had told her exactly what her duties would be and gone back to deal with Manny. He would have made her take the agoraphobe job, but she probably would have survived the experience.

Or she could have stayed inside the manor house like a sensible person, because if *Waverly* didn't seem worried about James hiding in the woods for hours on end then there was absolutely no reason for her to be. Just because he seemed like he—

Beauty heard a sharp crack above her head a split second before something large and furry shoved her sideways and to the ground. Her shoulder hit the undergrowth the same time that something crashed down right where she'd been standing, and she opened her eyes just enough to see what looked like the entire top half of a tree filling up her makeshift path.

She shifted around to stare up into James's absolutely furious eyes. She was momentarily breathless by his sheer proximity and the fact he had probably saved her life. He was a lot more intimidating this way, large and angry and radiating warmth like he was a walking fireplace. The stupider parts of her brain pointed out that he would probably be really nice to curl up against, and Beauty *really* wished he would start shouting so she could remind herself just how frustrated she was with him.

Thankfully, he obliged almost immediately. "You idiot! This isn't some safe happy little princess forest, where birds come when you sing to them and deer stand around waiting to bat their eyes at you!" He shoved himself to his feet with a growl, slamming his hand into a nearby trunk like he wanted to bring another tree down. "If you're going to insist on tromping through the forest like some hare-brained giantess, the least you could do is pay attention and make sure you don't get yourself killed!"

Eyes narrowed, Beauty scrambled to her feet. "*I'm* the idiot?" she yelled back at him, fists clenched. "I'm not the one who ran off like some enormous five-year-old just because I hit *one* little problem I couldn't shout my way out of!"

He whipped his head around to glare at her. "You're right," he snarled, baring his teeth again. "If I eat you, though, I take care of my problem."

"Oh, stop with the threats to eat people. I don't care how big and scary you look—curses don't change people's diets." She stepped forward, shoving aside a branch. "And if you've been eating Waverly's food for years, there's no way you'd be happy with gnawing hunks of bloody meat."

James's brow lowered for a moment, and Beauty wondered if he'd just realized that he'd missed dinner. She smirked inwardly at the thought, and something must have shown on her face because his eyes flared. "Don't think you suddenly understand the situation because you've been here for a couple of hours. He has no right to try to manipulate me like this!"

Beauty opened her mouth to fire something back, then closed it when she realized she had no idea what to say. She knew better than almost anyone how miserable it was being stuck in the middle of someone else's scheme, and though she was sure Waverly cared a lot more than her father it might not make enough of a difference. Even if it did, she didn't have the right to make that decision for him.

He narrowed his eyes, suspicious at her sudden lack of response. "What? Don't tell me I've finally stunned you into silence."

Annoyance surged back to swamp any vestiges of sympathy that had threatened. "Can we be mature about this for at least a few minutes?" she snapped back. "Even if Waverly is manipulating you, just beat him at his own game! All we have to do is convince him that you've found something non-destructive to do with your free time, and we'll both be out of each other's hair for good!"

He held his hands up in front of her, claws glinting in the twilight. "Can you imagine *these* building furniture or slapping paint on a canvas?"

There was an edge to his voice that suggested she'd scraped against a serious conversation that needed to be had at some point, but she couldn't imagine it would end up being with her. "There's always gardening," she said sarcastically. "I'm sure you'd do very well with begonias."

"I don't want to putter around in the blasted garden!" he roared, hands clenching into fists. "I want to be left alone!"

"Then lie!" Exasperated, Beauty threw her hands up in the air. "Just *pretend* to pick up some stupid hobby! It's not like he asked for proof that you'd found inner peace and enlightenment!"

He stopped for a minute, brow lowering again, and she wondered for a second if she'd actually gotten through to him. Then he shook his head. "It would never work. He may not have asked for proof of inner peace, but that's what he's looking for."

"But that's not what he *asked* for. He's set the rules, now all you have to do is follow them specifically enough to counter his play." Beauty folded her arms across her chest, wishing things seemed this simple when she was dealing with her own father. "Together I'm sure we can fake it well enough he won't have any room left to argue."

His eyes narrowed at the word "together." "Why are you siding with me on this? Most women would be arguing that I'm desperately in need of some emotional healing."

"And volunteer themselves up to be the doctor?" She made a dismissive noise. "Don't flatter yourself. Not that you're not cute, but I have things I'd much rather do with my life than take on the impossible job of trying to make you sweet and charming."

His glare sharpened even further. "Sarcasm isn't helping your case any."

Beauty furrowed her brow, not sure what he meant. "If you want to take honesty as an insult, that's your problem."

Something flashed in James's eyes that she couldn't quite read, and it took a moment for his usual surly expression to snap back into place. "Then you still didn't answer my question. Why are you offering to be so helpful?"

She watched him for a moment, trying to decide how honest she was willing to be with him. The complete truth would require more of an explanation of her childhood than she was willing to share with anyone, but a small piece of it would probably keep her from getting into too much trouble. "It *is* my job," she reminded him, letting every bit of annoyance come out in her voice. "Getting you to go along with this is my best chance of not only getting paid, but keeping my boss happy enough that I'll be able to remain gainfully employed when this fiasco is finally over."

James watched her intently, which suggested that he was giving her response far more thought than she'd dared hope for. "What if I took care of the entire fee you and your agency would have gotten for this job?" He folded his arms across his own chest, echoing her stance, and there was an undeniable challenge in his voice. "You get your paycheck for the week, your boss can't get mad at you, and we both get out of each other's hair without going through the effort of lying to Waverly."

It seemed like the perfect solution, which made her immediately suspicious. "How do I know you'll actually do it? For all I know, you'll kick me out the door and that's the last I'll ever hear from you."

His jaw tightened briefly, and if she didn't know any better she'd say he looked almost disappointed. "I'll make sure you have the money in hand before you walk out the door. Waverly will be annoyed, but they're my accounts and I have final authority over what's done with them."

She still wasn't happy with his answer, which was starting to worry her just a little bit. "That won't keep Waverly from complaining to my boss. I could still get in trouble."

James raised an eyebrow. "As the job didn't start until a few hours ago, I can't imagine Waverly's actually paid anyone yet. If nothing else, I've never met a supervisor who wasn't willing to look the other way after a little financial encouragement."

Beauty didn't have the slightest doubt that a bribe would work on Manny, at least for something stupid like this that wouldn't end up hurting anyone. James had answered all of her concerns and cut her off from making any new ones—if she had any sense at all, she'd take his offer and head straight home. If they started wrapping things up now, she might even be able to grab a carriage in time to spend the night in her own bed.

She'd never have to even talk to this idiot again, let alone get the chance to explain that there were people in the world who might have some idea of what he was going through. And she'd never have to risk giving in to the ridiculous temptation of actually trying to make the man smile occasionally.

It was the perfect solution.

"You are the most stubborn, idiotic, blind man I have *ever* met!" she shouted at him, suddenly furious for reasons she refused to think about. "I should have just left you to wander out here for eternity!"

She stalked past him, heading back the way she'd come. In the mood she was in, the forest had better not *dare* get in her way.

AFTER FOUR WRONG turns and plenty of time retracing her steps, she finally made it back to the manor. The walk had given her anger more than enough time to settle, leaving a combination of frustration, misery, and embarrassment that drained all the energy out of her. It slowed her steps across the darkened lawn, and instead of going inside she dropped down onto a bench near the back door and leaned forward to rest her forehead against her hands.

A moment later, she heard the sound of the door opening, followed by quiet footsteps heading in her direction. She lifted her head as Waverly approached, stopping precisely at the polite conversational distance for someone you hadn't known a full twenty-four hours yet. "I take it your search did not have a successful resolution," he said quietly, and in the faint light from the manor windows his expression seemed almost gentle.

She let out a long breath, deciding she probably needed years of therapy in light of the fact that she was letting herself get emotionally affected by any of this. Yet another thing to blame on her father. "He wants me out of here badly enough that he's going to throw money at my boss to make me go away." She looked up, meeting Waverly's eyes. "It will work, in case you're curious."

"Interesting." Waverly smiled a little, as if he'd heard something encouraging. "I presume from your demeanor that you did not find the idea quite as clever as James did?"

She narrowed her eyes at him, deciding he sounded far too pleased about the news. "No," she said finally. "I don't like other people telling me what to do."

"I believe I'm familiar with that particular character trait." There was something careful about the words, and Beauty had a sneaking suspicion he was humoring her. "Which is why I will merely suggest you come inside for the night. Though you've made an excellent start, there will be nothing more to do on your assignment until tomorrow morning at the earliest."

Beauty just stared at him. "'Excellent start?'" she said in astonishment, sure one of them must have missed something. "Whatever you thought you were doing by hiring me, it's not going to happen—as soon as Manny and I get paid, he's going to order me back to the agency office. I won't have any reason to fight him."

Waverly just looked at her for a moment, studying her expression with the same calm thoroughness he'd used when she'd first arrived. "Where did you find him?" he asked finally. "Though his forestry skills have only recently achieved any real level of proficiency, James is remarkably skilled at avoiding people when he's determined to brood."

She hesitated, not wanting to answer but caught without a lie that would be even remotely believable. When she realized there wasn't going to be another option, she cleared her throat. "I . . . wasn't looking where I was going." Her gaze slid away from Waverly's, and she focused on keeping her voice as expressionless as possible. "A huge tree branch fell, and he pushed me out of the way before I got flattened. Then we yelled at each other for a while."

There was only silence in response, which was surprising enough that Beauty risked a glance back over at Waverly. The distance in his eyes made him look like he was lost in thought, and it was deep enough that it took a second before he realized she was looking at him. He blinked, refocusing on her, and his expression softened. "For what it's worth, that is the best news I've heard in quite some time."

She couldn't deny the love in the other man's voice, which even on its own was more than enough to make Waverly different from her father. She sighed, knowing the realization wasn't going to help her be any more sensible. "I still don't see what you were trying to do by hiring me. He's a little old for a babysitter, not to mention big, but if bringing me here is the first step in some more complicated plan I'm not sure it's going as well as you think it is."

His expression turned rueful. "I'm afraid that my larger purpose in hiring you isn't nearly as intricate as James undoubtedly believes it to be." He moved closer, smile flickering again. "Though I must admit to being flattered that he's overestimated my genius in such a manner."

"Any chance you could let me in on what that larger purpose is?" she asked, lifting her hands in a helpless gesture. "If I know where we're supposed to be going with this, it might help me restrain the urge to hit the man with something heavy."

Waverly raised an eyebrow, the gesture so much more expressive than when she did it that Beauty was briefly tempted to start practicing the look in front of the mirror. "If either of you had paid proper attention in the library, you would realize I've already explained the complete extent of my 'secret plot' to both of you."

Her brow furrowed as she tried to remember. "I don't think either of us believed you," she admitted finally, voice quiet.

His expression softened. "James has a habit of never believing anyone, I'm afraid. Generally, sheer stubborn will has been enough to compensate for that deficiency, but the curse . . ." Shadows filled his eyes as the words trailed off, and he had to take a breath before starting again. "He needs to be poked, prodded, and harassed until he has no choice but to live again. And you, my dear, have already made an excellent start in that direction." Briefly, he squeezed her shoulder in an almost fatherly gesture. "Thank you."

Beauty's throat tightened and she cleared it in an attempt to get the emotion out of her voice. "You might want to wait on that until you see if I can actually do anything."

This time, his smile was serene. "Unlike James, I have learned to believe." He straightened his shoulders. "Now, however, I fear I have duties to return to inside. Though you're welcome to follow me whenever you see fit, it would be completely understandable if you wished to linger out here for a little while longer." He tilted his head in the direction of the forest. "It is a lovely night."

Catching his message, Beauty stayed outside as he'd implied even though she didn't believe anything would come of it. He'd been right about it being a nice night, and as the minutes ticked by, she closed her eyes and took a deep breath of the nature-scented air. She had no desire to go tromping through the woods again, but the trees made for a wonderful view. "You're not packing, I see."

Beauty's eyes flew open at the sound of James's voice behind her, heart kicking once against her chest in what she would swear to her dying day was nothing more than surprise. Taking a deep breath, she tilted her head back to meet his glare. "No, I'm not," she said calmly. "Like I told Waverly, I don't like other people telling me what to do."

His brow furrowed. "You can't be that masochistic." When she just smiled, his eyes narrowed. "I'm trying to make your life easier, you idiot," he snapped, frustration and something she couldn't quite identify shading the words. "The least you could do is work with me on this."

"I don't want my life to be easier. Besides, I think you're trying to make *your* life easier, and you frustrate me enough that I have absolutely no interest in helping you do that." She twisted around to the other side of the bench so that she could look at him without making her neck sore. "I wanted to help you with Waverly, but you already missed out on that opportunity."

He watched her with an intensity that suggested he was trying to develop telepathic powers by sheer force of will. "So you're on his side now?"

Beauty folded her arms across her chest, not sure whether that was the edge of hurt or petulance she could hear in his voice. Since it didn't matter in the long run, she forced herself to stop thinking about it. "Well, you certainly didn't want me on yours."

James's eyes narrowed again. "You said it was just a job."

She hesitated a moment at that. "I never said 'just,'" she corrected him, knowing she was arguing semantics but determined not to give any more than she absolutely had to. She was making a big enough mistake by listening to the tangle of emotions tugging at her—actually admitting them to someone would be beyond stupid. "It is my job, but that doesn't mean I can't decide who I'm doing it for."

He just looked at her, clearly weighing whether or not he could believe what she was saying. She held his gaze, pretty sure he would see further argument as the sign she was trying to con him. Finally, he huffed out a breath. "I'm not going to make it easy on you," he snapped, then turned and stalked into the manor. Beauty stayed where she was, watching James slam his way inside.

When he was safely out of sight, she let herself grin.

CHAPTER 4

The Breakfast Trap

Since it was Beauty and Waverly's fault he couldn't fall asleep in the first place, James smashed three more statues just before dawn. Annoyingly, neither of them seemed sufficiently bothered by the noise to actually wake up, and the manor stayed utterly silent until a much more dignified hour.

When he stalked downstairs, wearing his habitual scowl and the same dirt-stained pants he'd had on the day before, Beauty smiled at him from her seat at the dining room table. It was exactly three seats away from his, just a little too far away to be within arm's reach but close enough she was clearly prepared to annoy him all through breakfast. "Ah, there you are. Coffee's still hot, but I should warn you that there's cream and sugar on the table. Waverly mentioned that they offend your sensibilities—his words, by the way—but he's compassionate about the fact that I'm a terrible addict."

James just glared at her, wondering if she was really this chipper in the mornings or just pretending to be because she could see how little sleep he'd had. If it was the former, he might end up having to kill her purely in self-defense. "It sounds like you're certainly enjoying being on Waverly's side," he snapped. He had only overheard the tail end of their conversation the night before, not nearly enough to give him any kind of logical explanation for what she was still doing here. If it was simply because she liked Waverly . . .

Annoyed by the thought, he scowled as he sat down.

She took a sip of coffee before answering, brushing aside the hair that had fallen across her forehead. It seemed even less organized than it had yesterday, as if the soft-looking mass was as willfully defiant as she was. "It's nice having someone want me on their side," she said quietly, then her smile widened. "Besides, I'm willing to think kindly about any man who makes me pancakes in the morning." She turned her head towards the kitchen, raising her voice so Waverly could hear her over the sound of cooking. "Any chance you'd be willing to marry me? I'd be a terrible wife, but you'd never find a bigger fan of your food."

Even though he knew the proposal wasn't serious, James's claws were digging into the table by the time Waverly came out. "Sadly, my dear, I don't believe we would suit," he told her, clearly amused as he set the pancakes and a pitcher of syrup down in the center of the table. "Though you may want to hold off on any proposals of marriage until you actually taste this morning's meal. For all you know, the masterful nature of my roast was merely a fortunate fluke."

She smiled up at him as she served herself a small stack of pancakes, and James had to swallow a growl at the glow of affection on her face. It made her prettier than he'd given her credit for, which didn't help his mood any. "I've learned to believe."

Waverly returned the smile before turning his attention to James. "Good morning." Without asking, he poured James the cup of coffee he had been too tormented to get himself. "I made extra, since I presumed you'd be particularly hungry after missing dinner last night."

Hearing the forgiveness in the words, James felt like a teenager again. "Thank you," he said gruffly, deliberately ignoring Beauty until the urge to break something had faded. He took a deep drink of the coffee, then took his own serving of pancakes as Waverly headed back into the kitchen.

Beauty cut a careful forkful and made a little pleased sound as she took her first bite. "You must have amazing self-control," she said after she swallowed. "If I spent years eating like this, I'd be fatter than those gingerbread witches."

Ignoring her, he leaned forward for the syrup. When the pitcher met his outstretched hand, he lifted his head to meet Beauty's eyes over its top. "I didn't know I couldn't tease Waverly," she said quietly, settling back into her own chair. "I won't apologize, but I will stop if it upsets you."

He was used to Waverly being able to make him feel guilty, but the fact that Beauty had already picked up the talent was probably a bad sign. "It's not that," he said finally, not quite able to meet her eyes. "Just stop being so annoyingly cheerful, and we'll get along fine."

She laughed, surprising him into looking up. "That I will apologize for," she said easily, taking another drink of her coffee. "My father never got up before noon, so my sister and I learned to wake up as early as possible. It was the only way we ever had any peace and quiet."

He watched her, wondering if the slip about her life was a calculated move to try and get him to open up. Beauty, however, didn't even seem to notice she'd done it, and after a moment he let himself relax. "I don't hate mornings," he said finally. "I just didn't sleep well last night."

She took another bite of her pancakes. "I heard."

James's gaze immediately snapped back to hers. "I knew it!" He pointed an accusatory finger at her. "No one could sleep through that."

"I didn't know whether to be sympathetic or annoyed with you for causing such a racket." Her lips twitched in amusement. "So I stayed in my room and read."

He narrowed his eyes at her. "If you'd actually come and found me, I might have stopped causing the racket," he snapped, realizing what the words sounded like only after they'd already left his mouth. Beauty just looked at him for a second, brow furrowed in confusion, and James scowled as he tried to tell himself that he'd simply wanted proof that he'd kept her awake. That was all he'd meant. "Besides, they were ugly statues."

"I know." She shrugged at his questioning look. "Waverly had mentioned how terrible they were, so last night I went upstairs to see for myself. When I caught sight of the pile you'd made this morning, I recognized the trollish goddess of love from the east hallway." She shuddered. "You should have smashed that one years ago."

"Believe me, it wasn't the worst one up there." He took a bite of pancake, pretending that he didn't feel the slightest bit self-conscious about how tiny and fragile the fork seemed in his huge, hairy hands. As long as she didn't seem to notice, he could keep pretending. "The one of my grandmother as a fairy queen was a thousand times worse. It gave me nightmares when I was younger." When he saw her smother another laugh, he felt the corners of his mouth threaten to sneak upward. "It wasn't just me. Three of my nannies burst into tears and quit at the sight of it."

Beauty shook her head, the laugh finally escaping. "Why didn't your parents get rid of it? No matter how bad their taste was, I would think proof they were emotionally scarring people would be enough to convince them."

"My grandmother lived with us until I was almost ten, and both my parents were terrified of her. By the time she died, they no longer needed to worry about nannies." Another memory hit, this one enough to bring the smile out whether he wanted it there or not. "When Waverly showed up at the front door, he insisted that getting rid of the statue was a condition of his accepting the job. As soon as he'd gotten them to agree, he'd set his little wind elementals on it."

"Your mother was never quite comfortable with me after that," Waverly added, sweeping in with biscuits and a tray of ham. "Though it hadn't been my precise intention at the time, her lingering fear of me proved an invaluable tool during your formative years."

James snagged a piece of ham, then passed the tray to Beauty so she could do the same. "You can sit down and have some of this yourself, you know," he told Waverly. "If you wait too long, the food will get cold and offend your refined palate."

Waverly picked up a biscuit, then deftly split it open and spread a light layer of jam on each side. Putting it back together, he took a refined bite as he carried it into the kitchen with him.

Staring after him, Beauty's brow furrowed again. "He does eat, doesn't he?" she asked, turning back to James for confirmation. "I mean, I know some butlers take the whole 'seen but not heard' thing seriously, but I didn't think it was like that with the two of you."

James shook his head. "Waverly's no more a butler than I am a prince, and he only pretends to be one when it suits him." As the thought sank in, he realized what was going on and scowled. "He's trying to get us alone together."

Watching him, Beauty sighed. "I don't suppose it would help to point out that we have been eating alone together for at least a few minutes now without any actual bloodshed."

Realizing she was right, he shifted his glare in her direction. She'd gotten him *talking,* of all things, and within only a couple of minutes he'd been happily sharing facts about his childhood like they'd known each other for years. True, they were mostly inconsequential facts, but they'd only been talking for a few minutes. Who knew what she'd have him saying after an hour? "You're much more dangerous than you look."

She narrowed her eyes at him. "I don't know whether I should be flattered or suggest that you get help for your raging paranoia." Taking a bite of ham, she hesitated as if getting the matter some thought. "Lucky for you, I'm willing to be distracted by food."

He watched her, still trying to figure out why she had stayed. She liked Waverly, but she hadn't tried particularly hard to get him to sit down and eat with them. He'd found the perfect loophole to take care of any lingering sense of responsibility to her boss, and she didn't have either the mercenary zeal and delusional idealism that alternated in the eyes of the women who showed up trying to break the curse.

Unfortunately, he had no idea what else was left. "Aren't you supposed to be thinking up hobbies for me to try?"

"I was sort of hoping you could give me some ideas on that front." Her voice was light as she spread butter on one of the biscuits. "While I'm sure I'd have fun torturing you with whatever random activity struck me at the moment, there has to be *something* you enjoy doing besides brooding and destroying unattractive statues."

James took a bite of ham, eyeing her carefully. "Even if there were, it's none of your business." It was enough to imagine the looks on people's faces if he went around checking on his investments, or the damage he would do to his books if he tried to turn the fragile pages with his claws. He had no interest in discovering yet another activity that was no longer an option for him.

Beauty pointed her butter knife at him, annoyance sharpening her features. "All 'none of your business' means is the person saying it doesn't have anything at all intelligent or persuasive to add to the argument. You might as well just say 'neener neener neener' and get it over with."

She had a point, which was enough to send his own annoyance level spiking. "What about you? Shouldn't you be smart enough to figure out the perfect torment without needing me to give you clues?"

She started shaking her head before he'd even finished speaking. "Only through experimentation, which means forcing you to suffer through various activities until you find one you loathe slightly less than the others. And if you try to resist, I'm pretty sure Waverly will help me bully you into it." She gave him a challenging look. "Are you sure you wouldn't rather take the easier route?"

"I offered *you* the easier route," he shot back. "And you said no. Why should I be any smarter than you are?"

Beauty sighed again. "True." She set down her fork for a moment, leaning forward a little as she studied him. "Are you going to make

Waverly bully you into doing everything? Because if you do, that will be one way of making sure we're never alone together."

It was a good point, which should have made the possibility sound a lot more appealing than it actually did. Instead of dwelling on why that might be, he raised an eyebrow at her in challenge. "Are you saying you can't handle me on your own?"

She made an exasperated noise. "Physically, of course not. I may be stubborn, but I'm not delusional."

"Fine." He spread a hand out, palm up. "We won't make size or strength an issue. If you can talk me into it, I'll try any ridiculous hobby you throw at me at least once."

That caught her attention. "So can I talk you into all of them now, or are we going to have to start the battle all over again with each new idea I come up with?"

"Oh, no." He shook his head. "I'm not going to let you lock me in to something before I find out exactly what I'm getting myself into. You'll have to convince me one hobby at a time."

She pointed a finger at him. "But you'll give me a fair shot at convincing you, right? And if I do, you'll actually put enough effort into the hobby to see if you might really like it?"

He hesitated, realizing suddenly that he was letting himself be backed into a corner. "No matter what it is, I'm not going to like it."

"I'll only believe that if I see you actually trying." She lowered her brow at him, managing to look surprisingly stern and parental for a moment. He wondered if she'd needed to discipline children at some point. "It's only a fair game if I genuinely have a shot at winning."

"A game?" He set down his own fork, surprised at how right the words sounded. "Is that what we're setting up here?"

She shrugged again. "Well, you *could* call it a fight we're planning to stretch out for a week or so, but that would force us both to stay angry and tense for a lot longer than I really want to." She smiled a little. "We're both too young to have heart attacks, and I have no desire to make my father's life easier by dying."

James's gaze stayed steady on Beauty, studying her as he considered the offer. He still hadn't found a satisfactory answer that explained what she was doing here, but going through with this would give him plenty of time to find out why. Besides, a little competition would help mitigate the fact that it was proving frustratingly hard to stay mad at the woman. He kept trying to remember she was the enemy, and she just kept distracting him with conversation.

Even now, he couldn't decide whether he was annoyed or impressed by that. "Okay, we'll call it a game." He leaned forward slightly. "But that means the winner deserves some kind of prize. What do I get when I prove just how wrong you are?"

"That's easy." She made a dismissive noise, waving the question away with her hand. "If you win, you get the unrivaled joy of never seeing me again. The real question is what I'll get when *I* win."

"That depends on what you want." He knew he couldn't pin her into an answer this quickly, but it might at least give him the chance to eliminate a few more possibilities. "If you're looking to get me out of *your* life, all you'd have to do is say the word."

"Like I said, that would be too easy." She paused a moment in thought, absently picking up a chunk of ham from her almost completely forgotten meal. "And you already promised me money, so that's not going to work either."

Watching Beauty eat reminded James of his own food, and he felt an odd jolt of embarrassment as he took a quick swig of his rapidly cooling coffee. Food, in his experience, had generally proven to be more interesting than other people. "If you don't know what prize you want, there's no point in playing the game."

She raised her eyebrows in what looked like genuine surprise. "Who says?" she shot back. "I've always thought the joy of winning was enough of a prize for anyone."

His agreement was instant enough he had to stop himself from saying it out loud. When you played the investing game, it was rarely because you wanted to get richer than you already were. The money was really more of a way of keeping score, of showing that you were clever enough to see three steps ahead of everyone else.

He hadn't felt that way in a very long time.

"Fine." He kept his voice as flat as possible, hiding the interest he could feel flickering inside him. This was tragically the closest thing he had to excitement in his life, but right now he wasn't sure he could say no to even this much. "If you win, then you'll have the joy of being right."

The corners of her mouth curved upward a little, suggesting a competitiveness that made his interest spike just a little sharper. If he'd seen her like this at that ball, he suspected he wouldn't have forgotten her even for a moment. "I'll want to hear you admit that I'm right. Maybe even put it in writing, so I can cherish the memory forever."

"Only if you'll do the same thing when *I* turn out to be right. No matter how much effort either of us put into it, there is *no* hobby out there that I'll enjoy."

"That's what you think." She stood up just enough to lean across the table, holding a hand out towards him. The challenge in her expression was far more appealing than it should have been. "But I agree to your terms. Do we have a deal?"

James didn't move, his eyes still on hers. He might be no closer to knowing why she had persisted in going along with Waverly's plan, but the last twenty minutes had proven just how truly sneaky his plan was turning out to be. The fact that he was tempted to say yes to her at all meant that Waverly's plan had already succeeded on at least one level, and the truth was that saying no wouldn't lessen the temptation any.

Hopefully, he'd never have to admit that to anyone.

"Two weeks," he said firmly. There would be plenty of time to go back to brooding after she was gone again, he reminded himself, and there were still several more unattractive statues waiting for him upstairs. "If you haven't found a hobby I'm willing to tolerate by then, you go home and I win by default."

She considered this, then nodded. "Two weeks. And if we snap and try to kill each other before then, the survivor wins by default."

He glanced down at her hand again, then looked around the room on the off chance he could see the elementals hiding in a corner somewhere. When he met Beauty's eyes again, she lifted her eyebrows in question. "Expecting something to leap out of the corner at you?"

Beast shook his head. "Just promise me you'll help me find out whether Waverly really does stand listening at doors."

She laughed. "We'll put that on our to-do list."

"Okay, then." He reached for her hand, wondering if he was going to regret this later. "We have a deal."

CHAPTER 5

Shaking the Dust Off

Beauty had been in some terrifying attics because of the temp agency—witches tended to keep failed experiments in theirs, some of which were still alive and sentient—but James's had a shadowy, maze-like quality that reminded her of the cursed forest she and Grace had been left in when they were kids. You almost didn't want to lift your lantern, because seeing the details somehow only made it worse . . .

"If you get yourself killed up there, I'm not bringing your body down."

Making an exasperated noise, Beauty walked back over to the open trapdoor and glared down at the man who was glaring up at her. "You should be relieved at the possibility," she snapped, swiping at the thick dust that was already starting to cling to her pants. Clearly, this was where it all went to hide from Waverly. "If I die, you win by default."

"But I'd have a dead body in my attic." The clouds of dust she'd shaken off had drifted down toward James, making him sneeze. She stifled a grin. "There's not a cleaning spell in the world strong enough to take care of that smell."

She opened her mouth for a snappy comeback, then stopped.

"Wait." Her eyebrows lifted. "How do you know what a dead body smells like?"

"My grandmother tried to go the zombie route for a few weeks after she died. It didn't end well." Beauty's eyes widened at the mental pictures contained in those two simple sentences, and James winced at her expression. "Stop getting me to talk about my family and just get down from there."

"No," Beauty said automatically, defiance renewing her determination. When his eyes narrowed, lips curling upward like he was getting ready to growl, she put her hands on her hips and stared him down. "You're interfering with the bet. Waverly said I could use anything I find up here, and I need some resources if I'm going to come up with two weeks' worth of hobbies to torture you with."

He made a disgusted noise. "If this is your idea of getting ready for the bet, you might as well just concede defeat. I can promise you I won't have the slightest interest in anything up there."

Beauty smiled in temporary victory. "Then you won't mind if I poke around up here, will you?" Before he could respond, she stepped away from the doorway and out of his immediate sight. Setting her magically-protected lantern on the attic floor, she decided over-thinking her quest wouldn't help matters and opened the nearest box. When it turned out to be completely full of tiny shoes, the largest of which was no bigger than her thumb, she sighed and pushed it aside before opening the next box. It was baby clothes this time, including one very brittle dress that seemed to be made out of dried flower petals . . .

She was just opening a third box when she heard a loud scraping sound coming from the floor below, along with some muttered cursing that had a definite growl to it. She tensed, trying to decide whether going over to see what was happening would somehow encourage him, then took a deep breath and made herself focus on the box. If she'd annoyed him enough to destroy another one of those hideous statues, it could probably be considered a community service . . .

"Boo."

Beauty jumped at hearing James's voice in the absolute last place she'd expected it, and immediately scrambled around to glare at him and deny that he'd startled her. His head and shoulders were poking up above the trapdoor opening, kicking up even more dust clouds as he shifted around enough to get his arm up into the attic. Despite the fact that he was going to have to go through a pretty intensive fur-cleaning session later, he smirked at her like he knew exactly what she was about to say. Refusing to give him the chance of being right, she raised an eyebrow at him. "That was a remarkable amount of fuss just to climb a simple ladder."

His brow furrowed as if she'd just said gibberish, and as the rest of her brain caught up she realized she should have spent a little longer thinking of a good comeback.

"If I'd tried the ladder," he said flatly, the "You idiot" not spoken but clearly implied, "I would not only have stranded you up here when I shattered it—I'd probably be on the floor bleeding to death from a massive head injury."

She knew that, or would have known if he hadn't insisted on being so frustrating and distracting all the time. "How's Waverly going to feel about your moving the furniture around?" Beauty shot back, her voice a little too sharp as she pushed her hair out her eyes. Somehow, he was much easier to deal with when there were several feet between them. "I can only imagine what those heavy armoires would do to Waverly's nice hardwood floor."

He winced a little at that, but he wasn't about to let her flip things that easily. "It's fine," he said shortly, eyes narrowing slightly as he looked past her toward the boxes she'd been investigating. "You're definitely wasting your time in that corner."

"And how would you know that?" Beauty asked, deliberately turned back to the box she'd been looking at before James had interrupted her. The wildly gaudy, hopefully fake jewelry that was piled inside only helped his argument, so she grabbed another box and hoped James's family had saved *something* that wasn't quite so obviously useless. "As you so colorfully explained, I can't imagine you spend much time up here."

"That was my mother's corner." There was something odd in his voice that made her turn back to look at him, but by the time their gazes met she could only see dry amusement in his eyes. "And from the look on your face, I can see you've already opened enough boxes to get a pretty clear idea of what she was like."

Beauty just looked at him for a minute, feeling the same entirely irrational tug that had made her decide to stay and dig herself even deeper into this whole mess. If he didn't get so annoyed every time he was the slightest bit vulnerable, she'd almost be willing to swear he was doing it on purpose just to make her life harder.

His eyes narrowed when he realized she was staring at him. "What?"

For once, honesty actually seemed like a safe enough answer. If he got mad, the worst that he could do was stomp off and leave her far less confused. "I was just wondering whether I should point out that you just brought up your family again without any kind of prompting or secret magical coercion on my part."

James blinked, then swore softly and scowled at her. "It's still your fault," he said darkly. "You get me *talking.*"

Beauty swallowed a sudden laugh. "You mean there's a way to get you to *not* talk?"

The scowl, unsurprisingly, deepened. "I don't know. Is there a way to get *you* to not talk?"

This time, the laugh didn't have a chance of staying in. "Not that anyone's found."

He kept glaring at her for a few seconds, but then his expression eased as the corners of his mouth curved upward. "At least you're honest."

"There is that." Suddenly feeling far more cheerful—a fact that the more sensible part of her brain considered a very bad sign—she gestured to the boxes she'd already opened. "You do have a point about your mother, though. Do I want to know about the tiny shoes, or is it anything like the zombie story?"

He lifted an eyebrow. "I didn't even give you any details on the zombie story. Are you really that much of a wimp?"

She shrugged. "An excellent imagination can look a lot like wimpiness in certain circumstances."

He thought about that, then actually grinned. "You're going to be fun to tease."

She gave him a mock scowl, waving him on. "Evil scheming later. I want to hear about the shoes."

James leaned forward slightly, clearly settling in. "Father was happily destroying the family fortune on such exciting prospects as dwarvish tanning salons and dragon dental schools—"

"Actually, you probably could make money on a dragon dental school. It depends on who comes up with the curriculum."

He gave her an amused look. "Duly noted. As I was saying, Father's side projects made Mother decide that mere shopping was no longer draining the coffers fast enough. After a visit to a fae shoe store, she decided that they would be perfect accessories for ladies' pets."

Beauty's brow furrowed. "You mean like those tiny dogs?" When he nodded, her eyes widened. "She wasn't stupid enough to try to put a set on one of those miniature gryphons, was she?"

He nodded. "In a way, though, it was for the best. After that she wasn't willing to even think about tiny shoes, and the stock she had already bought went up here."

"Not nearly as bad as the zombie story, but I sympathize. If we'd had any kind of family fortune, I'm sure it would be gone by now." She stood, brushing off her pants again, then looked up at James again as a thought hit. "Did Waverly save the rest of the family money, or did you do it once you got old enough?" When he opened his mouth, she held up a warning finger. "And before you ask how I know one of you did, you are *way* too cocky to actually be poor."

His mouth closed, and this time his smile was completely self-satisfied. "We both did. Waverly showed up when I was eleven, and he took over the family finances almost immediately. He started teaching me the basics after my parents died a few years later, and I discovered that I not only had a talent for it but loved proving I could work the system better than everyone else. When I was eighteen, I took full control of the family finances and Waverly became my right-hand man."

She could read the rest of the story on his face. "And together, you made mountains of money."

He nodded. "And together, we made mountains of money." He smiled suddenly, caught up in some happy memory. "Other investors used to call me 'the Beast' because I was ruthless about stalking the perfect investment opportunity. If anyone tried to get in my way, I'd utterly destroy them."

She couldn't help but smile back at him. "Sounds like you were a force to be reckoned with."

"Oh, I was." Then his expression dimmed. "Waverly's essentially running things at the moment."

There were a thousand different losses in that single sentence, all of them still fresh enough to cut deep. The sound of them hurt Beauty's heart, and for a second she wanted nothing more than to wrap her arms around him and try to offer what comfort she could. Since that would result in a near-fatal level of embarrassment, she took a deep breath and offered the only comfort she could be certain he'd accept. "You know, you really owe it to me to show me around up here," she said matter-of-factly, moving the boxes she'd already tried back into the same general position she'd found them in. "You were right about the fact that I could get lost and die up here, and though you'd technically win we both know it would be cheating."

He gave her another "You're an idiot" look. "So falling through the floor would be better than breaking the ladder on the way up?"

She made a dismissive sound, moving over to pound her foot against a specific spot of floor. "These support beams are sturdy enough to support a giant. If they can't hold you up, it's only because you're eating too much of Waverly's cooking."

He looked at her through narrowed eyes. "If I die because of this," he said finally, "I'm coming back to haunt you."

Beauty smiled. "Fair enough." When he shifted, clearly trying to figure out the best way to haul himself up to the attic, she held out a hand. "Need some help?"

He glared at her. "The day I need help climbing up anywhere is the day I hire myself out as a monster-skin rug." And he did indeed get himself up through the trapdoor, with only a minor amount of straining and one awkward moment it would have been rude to point out. Honestly, Beauty barely even noticed it, as most of her brain had gotten caught up in the sight of watching sleek, fur-covered muscles move. The sight was . . . mesmerizing, enough so that her brain was fogging over slightly by the time he made it all the way up to the attic.

The part of her head still capable of being sensible tried valiantly to stop her appreciation, knowing what this meant. She'd tried to argue that her desire to take care of him was nothing more than sympathy for their mutually damaged childhoods, but staring at him like this was only a step away from dreaming of hearts and songbirds. Only an idiot would develop a crush on a man who kept threatening to eat people every time he got annoyed.

Watching him, Beauty had a sneaking suspicion that she was exactly that kind of idiot.

James took a second to steady himself on the beams, then looked up in time to catch Beauty staring. His eyes narrowed again, expression darkening. "I'm not any more horrific-looking up here than I am in the rest of the house. You already missed your chance to be shocked."

Beauty blinked, suddenly realizing how James had interpreted her staring at him. "I'm not . . ." The denial stuck in her throat when she realized she'd have to explain the real reason she'd been checking him out, at which point the only sensible option would be to pitch herself out one of the attic windows. If the man would put on a shirt more often, they wouldn't have this problem in the first place . . . Of course, she couldn't say *that,* either, which meant her brain was left to grab for the closest alternative. "Who does your tailoring?" she asked a little desperately. "I have a friend at work whose mother is a giant, and he has hardly any nice clothes because it's so much trouble finding ones that fit right."

James's glare sharpened, though he suddenly seemed far more annoyed than offended. After the last few minutes, it was probably the best response she could have hoped for. "So you were staring at me because of my pants?"

As her brain slammed down on a *really* inappropriate answer to that question, Beauty lifted her chin in defiance. The stupider the lie, the more you had to commit to it. "Because of Steve. The pants just made me think of him."

He glared at her some more, then turned and muttered something that sounded like it included Steve's name and at least a few surprisingly colorful curses. Beauty, not entirely certain what to make of the response, stayed silent while he made a visual sweep of the room and pointed at a shadowy corner that looked no different from all the others. "Over there," he said shortly, sneezing when the dust on his fur got a little too close to his nose. Swearing again, he swiped his arms clean and sneezed again at the resulting dust clouds.

Beauty, in what she considered to be a very kind gesture on her part, continued to be silent.

Once the vicious cycle seemed to have settled down somewhat, he squeezed his eyes shut for a moment and gave a long-suffering sigh. "Remind me again why I agreed to let you stay?"

She couldn't help but smile. She seriously had to figure out how he kept making her do that. "My guess?" she responded. "We're both secretly masochists."

THEY ENDED UP searching slightly to the right of where James had pointed, since their original route was blocked by what appeared to be a small but complete one-room cabin made of petrified gingerbread. When she asked about it James actually winced. "My grandmother's sister used to live in the thing. It seemed like a bad idea to ask for too many details."

Luckily, the other section of attic was much more accessible. Of course, that didn't make it any more useful for James's list of potential hobbies, since the rest of his family proved to either have no taste whatsoever or an unhealthy attachment to disturbing personal mementos. A sensible person would have undoubtedly known better than to keep asking for the accompanying stories, especially after the gingerbread house, but Beauty had never been particularly sensible.

"Is this thread?" she asked him, brushing more dust out of the way as she leaned over a bag full of fine golden strands. She couldn't imagine getting James to sew or embroider even on pain of death—she hated it too—but someone in his family must have really been into needlework. The bag was almost as tall as her waist, and even bigger around than her father. "Because that tailor of yours would probably kill to get his hands on gold thread this delicate."

He turned, curious, then shook his head when she held up a handful of strands. They'd fallen into a relatively easy camaraderie while they'd explored, somehow going almost half an hour without fantasizing about braining the other person with something heavy. "My great-great-uncle dated one of Rapunzel's daughters for a while. That was her version of giving him a lock of hair to remember her by."

She looked back down at the bag, trying to imagine how much hair the woman must have held on to. "And future generations have held onto a bag of magic hair for what, making emergency wigs?"

James thought about it a moment, then grinned. "Actually, that's not a bad idea. They'd sell well in the tourist areas." Then he caught sight of something across the room, and the humor instantly slid off his face. She stayed silent, watching, while he leaned forward and picked up the painting that had been leaning against the wall.

It was a portrait of a man and a woman, posing together in the classic "we're painting this so our great-grandchildren will have to hang it on the wall" pose. The woman looked like some kind of fairy princess, with porcelain skin, waves of pale blonde hair, and a softly pointed chin that made Beauty hate her instantly. The man standing next to her was just as nicely dressed as the woman, with broad shoulders and rich, dark brown hair barely long enough to curl underneath his ears.

Slowly, she stepped closer, trying to figure out why the man seemed so familiar. She might have run into him at one of the balls her father had dragged her to, but those parties tended to be blurs of mortification that kept her from remembering anyone who might have been able to recognize her later. Though it would be hard to forget that expression—an almost-glare that seemed to be ordering the artist to hurry up so that he could get back to something more interesting . . .

Her eyes widened as realization hit, and she swallowed back a gasp of astonishment as her gaze flew upward to James's face. He didn't even seem to have registered the fact that she was standing there—he was just staring down at the painting with a look that she could only describe as lost. It hurt to see, to imagine him wishing that the woman from the painting were up there with him instead of Beauty, and she took a silent step backward in an attempt to return to her corner and pretend she'd never been there at all.

Then he lifted his head, the lost expression disappearing as he set the painting back down where he'd found it. "You're not going to ask?" he asked quietly, and she realized he hadn't been as unaware of her watching him as she'd thought.

She took a deep breath, telling herself it didn't matter. "Your eyes haven't changed at all." When he turned to look at her in surprise, she put every ounce of will into keeping her voice and expression even. "I was wondering about the woman, though."

There was only silence for a moment. "Juliana," he said finally, a world of tension in his voice. "My ex-fiancée."

She reached forward, wanting to touch him but not quite brave enough to cross the entire distance. "Did she leave after the curse?"

He continued in silence long enough that Beauty had nearly decided he wasn't going to answer. When he finally spoke, he half-growled, "I think she's the one who cursed me." It was an admission he clearly hadn't wanted to make. Beauty wanted to pretend it was anger, since she herself now wanted to hit the woman on the head with something heavy, but she was pretty sure she'd heard every shade of James's anger in the short time she'd already been there. And this . . . this sounded like so much more than that. "As I had thought we were in love, I clearly made some sort of profound error."

They just looked at each other for what seemed like a small eternity, then Beauty took a deep breath and made a confession that not even her sister had ever heard. "I've been rejected by thirteen princes, nine dukes, four counts, and seven earls. No matter what my father thinks, I tried with at least half of them." She hesitated, jaw tightening. "I actually thought I was in love with one of them."

After a moment, James's expression softened. "If I remember correctly, there's a 'build your own torture chamber' kit up here somewhere. I'm pretty sure we could find it if we looked together."

Slowly, Beauty started to smile. "Have I mentioned how much I like the way you think?"

INTERLUDE

Scheming for the Greater Good

Waverly stared up at the ceiling, listening carefully to the sounds filtering down from the attic. Occasionally the low murmur of voices rose, and one particular thump was loud enough that he half expected the survivor to call him for medical assistance. No such call came, however, and there was even a sound that seemed suspiciously like laughter.

Waverly smiled, pleased by the thought.

Taking advantage of the window of privacy, he turned to the magic mirror at his desk and tapped out the sequence for the mirror he intended to connect with. Most mirrors responded to voice commands, but Waverly generally preferred to keep his business as discreet as possible.

The magic clouds in the mirror swirled, and after a moment a red, scaly face appeared with the narrow-eyed expression of someone who'd just been interrupted. "If you're about to ask me for someone else, Waverly, call back in twenty-four hours. You've got to give the kid a little more time."

"Mandrake, your optimism continues to astound me," Waverly said dryly, leaning forward a little. "If you have so little faith in your selection, why did you send her in the first place?"

Smoke puffed out of the dragon's nostrils. "You know that's not what I meant, you card-counting, Medusa-loving—" The incipient rant cut off abruptly as his glare sharpened, and he gave the other man a long, evaluating look as his claws clacked against his desk. Waverly, patient as always, simply sat there and let him look.

Finally, Manny made a disgusted sound, blowing a puff of smoke out of his nostrils. "You could have just told me thank you, you know. No need to be so flaming annoying about it."

The corners of Waverly's mouth curved upward. "If I'd simply said it, you would have been certain I was lying."

"True." Manny's expression relaxed into a slightly predatory amusement, which like most draconic expressions was easily mistaken for the desire to munch on someone's internal organs. "So things are working out with Beauty and that boy of yours? I know she wasn't exactly what you asked for, but I know how you appreciate a little pro-active thinking in a business associate."

"Unless they're attempting to kill me, of course." It was an old joke between them, nearly as old as James was himself. "And if I recall correctly, I believe I left the details up to your discretion. I will admit, though, when Miss Tremain first arrived I mistakenly thought she'd come hoping to break the curse."

Manny's eyes widened. "You didn't actually *tell* her that, did you?"

Waverly paused briefly, surprised at the dragon's reaction. "Yes, but her confusion rapidly made me aware of my error. And if it was a sensitive subject, you had ample opportunity to warn me about it in advance."

"Didn't think I had to. Of the two of us, you're generally the tactful one." He sighed, shaking his head. "Kid had a bad history. Her dad threw her and her sister at every member of the nobility within fifteen feet of a fairy tale situation, and the only reason he stopped was that they brained him with an enchanted prince one night and made a run for it while he was unconscious."

Waverly's brow lowered a fraction, searching his memory for

the faint echo of recollection he was feeling. When he found it, his eyes widened. "You partnered Noble Tremain's daughter with the one man who refuses to finish his fairy tale. I don't know if that was brilliant or utterly malicious of you."

Manny shrugged. "As long none of you are bleeding yet, I'll go with brilliant." He paused, pointing a claw at the other man. "Keep an eye out for her old man, though. Your left toe is probably smarter than he is, but he's kept himself alive this long by causing trouble for everyone else."

Waverly considered this, then gave the dragon a small nod. "I'll make a note of it." He briefly regretted the impracticality of having the man killed, though if Beauty remained with them long enough he would consider asking whether she would want it done as a gift. "And on a similar but somewhat unrelated topic, have you made any progress on that other matter we discussed?"

"Couple of rumors out of the southern provinces, but nothing I'd bother getting out of bed for." The dragon's brow lowered. "You sure this Juliana didn't have some witches or evil sorceresses in her family? This is a pretty substantial disappearing act for a rich little airhead hanging on to her daddy's coattails."

"I know," Waverly said darkly, having come to a similar conclusion some time ago. Anyone who could evade his connections this thoroughly was not to be lightly dismissed, and the fact he had made the mistake of underestimating her was an error that galled him still. He had considered her nothing more than the useless arm decoration she'd appeared to be, and therefore had allowed her to hurt the only person he'd ever been willing to claim as family.

"Unfortunately, whoever put the curse together appears to be either a complete imbecile or a deranged lunatic. Not only did the experts James and I consulted fail to find the deactivation trigger in the hideous mess, they're not sure if one even exists at all."

Manny nodded, knowing Waverly wouldn't appreciate any outward sign of sympathy. "I've seen True Love's Kiss undo even the cheapest curses. If you can believe what little testing has been done, it's pretty much a universal trigger." He paused, growing thoughtful. "The patched-together look of the curse could have been this Juliana sticking her nose in some concoction of her daddy's so that she could save her boyfriend once she found him again." When he saw Waverly's eyes narrowing he shrugged, the gesture almost apologetic. "A girl who could pull off something like this probably has a daddy who could do her one better."

After a moment, Waverly inclined his head in acknowledgement, though it took a moment longer before his expression eased again. "As I said before, Mandrake, your optimism continues to astound me."

Manny snorted in amusement. "If Beauty and James get hitched, I get to be the one who walks her down the aisle."

Waverly smirked in response. "It's lucky for you she isn't particularly tall, then. You should just barely be able to reach her hand."

Manny flipped him off. "Watch yourself, buddy, or I might just forget my promise and give old Snake-bangs the code for your mirror. She's been asking about you."

Waverly chuckled. "What I want to know is why she still has the code for *your* mirror."

Manny just grinned. "You know what in-laws are like."

CHAPTER 6

A Little Light Disarming

It was the attic's fault, James decided. There was something about being in dark, dusty space full of old memories and potential deathtraps that made people agree to things they knew they'd regret later.

He hadn't even *liked* fencing, at least until they'd kicked him out of that particular private school for finally making that little snot bleed all over his fancy gold shirt. Trying to teach Beauty, particularly when he suspected she'd consider the rules about as important as he had, would clearly be a disaster.

The next morning, he'd planned on logically explaining that to her—or failing logic, give her a few extra days on the bet as a bribe—as soon as they'd finished breakfast. Then she told him she'd be heading straight into the library for the next few hours, without even *mentioning* fencing, and all logic immediately vanished from his brain.

"I thought we were starting the bet," he snapped, hating how annoyed he sounded. It felt suspiciously like he was jealous of his own library, which was not at all an acceptable precedent to be setting up. "I gave you the rest of yesterday to plan, but from now on you'll use up your time whether or not you do anything."

She raised an eyebrow, clearly not sure where this was coming from. "The attic was no help, so I planned on looking through your library to get a better idea of what you like."

"It won't help you. Most of it was my grandfather's."

Her eyes narrowed. "Maybe some of the books on the upper floors are, but pretty much everything I saw was published in the last twenty years or so. And before you try to lie again and tell me they belonged to your parents, I'd like to remind you that you've already told me way too much about them for me to believe you."

The handful of times he'd lied to Juliana, she'd never called him out on it. Looking back, he wasn't sure if she hadn't cared or if she just hadn't known him well enough to tell he'd been lying. "Fine. But it's old information anyway." He held up his clawed hands. "I haven't touched anything in there in since I got these."

Beauty just looked at him for a moment, frowning. Then her eyebrows lifted in sudden realization. "You've been avoiding the library because you don't want to hurt the books?" He didn't respond, but she must have seen the answer on his face because her expression instantly softened. "And I can't even tell you how sweet that is, because you'll just growl at me."

That threw him. "You think it's sweet?"

"Someone loving books that much? Given the fact that I barely restrained a happy dance of joy when I saw your library, I'd *have* to approve." She leaned forward a little, her expression turning impish. "Of course, I also approve of the fact I get to prove you wrong."

This time, it was his turn to narrow his eyes. "Oh, really?"

She stood, moving close enough to gently take one of his hands. His skin tingled everywhere it made contact with hers, highly sensitized even through the fur. James told himself to ignore the feeling, an order his brain utterly failed to follow.

With her other hand, she touched a fingertip to one of his claws, then shook her head and looked up at him. "Unless you start sharpening them, I'm quite sure you won't rip through the paper if you are careful. I know a manticore who actually runs his own library, and his claws are almost as long as yours." She studied his hand, as if taking mental measurements of his claws. "You'd just have to find a slightly different way to turn the pages."

James just stared at his hand, knowing he should be embarrassed but was still a little too stunned to pull it off properly. *He* should have been the one to figure that out, and the fact that he hadn't made some of Waverly's accusations echo uncomfortably in his ears.

What you need is someone to shake you back into living.

He looked back up at Beauty, not able to see even a trace of sarcasm or derision in her expression. "All it'll take is a little practice, and then you can have your books back," she said softly.

He stared at her another moment, feeling the world open up just a little. He still wasn't sure Waverly was right, but right now seemed like the perfect time to give the theory a shot.

Decision made, he gave her a firm nod. "Practice later. Now, I'm teaching you how to fence."

"I DIDN'T WANT to ask this where Waverly could overhear, but are you sure we should use real swords?" Beauty asked, giving the sword a test swing that was more graceful than he'd expected. They were in the backyard, far enough away that the furniture wouldn't be at risk but close enough that ice packs and bandages would be on hand if someone got a little over-enthusiastic.

Not that either event was particularly likely. The swords he'd chosen were technically too heavy for fencing—he'd left his rapier in the wall about an inch from the instructor's head—but they were old and dull enough that not even the local Hero's Pawnshop would take them.

He gave her a friendly smirk. "I thought you'd see the chance to injure me as an incentive."

She grinned. "True."

Seeing the smile blossom on her face, James suddenly realized he'd said the comment hoping to make her smile. It was a dangerous thought, and he tried hard to pretend that it had never occurred to him. "Just how much experience have you had with swords, anyway?" She paused, brow lowering as she considered the question. "Are we talking about actually *fighting* with one, or does chasing someone while you're waving a sword around and screaming at the top of your lungs count?" She paused. "I've also hit someone over the head with one, but that was technically a decorative sword. It broke."

It was James's turn to grin. Not only could he picture both circumstances, but he had no doubt whomever she'd terrified had deserved it. "Unfortunately, neither situation is really applicable here."

She shrugged. "Then I think you could safely say I have no experience."

"Fair enough." He was a little careful as he lifted his own sword, adjusting his grip to take the claws into account. This was another reason they weren't using rapiers, which were much tinier. "You do know that fencing won't actually help you kill anyone, right? I'd teach you real sword fighting, but I never learned it. When you're rich, it's generally not considered an applicable skill."

She just looked at him for a moment, expression torn between amusement and sudden distrust. "You know, most people try to dissuade me from doing unusual things, not apologize that they can't teach me more of them."

He shifted into a proper fencing stance, decided he looked like an idiot, and moved into a more relaxed position. "Weren't you the one who said, 'Not that you're not cute, but I have things I'd much rather do with my life than take on the impossible job of trying to make you sweet and charming'?"

She blinked at him, eyes wider than they had been, and Beast realized belatedly that he probably shouldn't have included the first part of the quote. A second later, he realized he'd included it because he genuinely meant it.

Hot on the heels of that thought was the realization that there was a chance she had genuinely meant it, too. His cheeks warmed, and for the first time in a long time, he was glad he was covered in fur.

Shaking the thought away, he immediately began pushing the conversation forward. "Besides, I'm a huge, hulking monster with anger management issues. I'm contractually obligated to encourage violence and anarchy on principle."

She made an exasperated noise as she held up her own sword, trying to mimic his fencing position. "Speaking of anger management issues, I'm wondering if I should be worried about the fact that you've been remarkably agreeable about this. Shouldn't you be grumbling more?"

"It's part of my evil plot," he said easily, a little surprised himself. He'd almost say he was feeling cheerful, but he generally tried to avoid admitting things like that under anything but pain of death. "If I distract you long enough, the two weeks will be over and I'll have won my bet."

Beauty smirked. "Of course, your plot could merely be part of *my* plot, which is both dastardly and magnificently complex. Waverly helps me with it when you're not paying attention." She grinned. "Besides, you could always fence as a hobby. Maybe today will help you remember all those joyous times you had waving a sword around and make you fall in love with it all over again. Then *I'll* win the bet."

"I'm hoping for your sake that was sarcasm." Deciding that he should probably work some actual teaching in at some point, he showed her some basic footwork. "When you advance, lead with your front foot. When you retreat, lead with your back foot. It keeps you from tripping over yourself."

Beauty took a few test steps forward, then carefully touched the tip of her sword to his chest. "If you dislike it so much, why did you start fencing?"

"My parents were big on having me develop useless skills. It kept me out of the way and gave them something to show off at dinner parties." She'd been here only two days, and it was already safe to say Beauty knew more about his childhood than any person alive except Waverly. He'd given up trying to fight his instinctive urge to tell her everything, but the fact that he had no idea why it kept happening still bothered him. "I also learned Dwarvish, and got through some basic Elvish before my tutor's anti-aging magic wore off completely and she collapsed into a pile of dust."

Sudden interest lit her eyes. "You know Dwarvish? Is there any chance you could—" Just then a thought hit and her expression immediately slid into one of horrified realization. "Is that why you were so upset about me being hired to find you hobbies?" she asked, immediately lowering her sword arm and staring at him with such guilt that he got the ridiculous urge to hug her. He slapped the thought away. "Because I'm sure Waverly wouldn't have phrased it like that if he'd known, and the last thing I want to do is dredge up someone else's bad childhood memories . . ."

He stared at her for a second, not entirely sure what had just happened to make her so concerned. He was definitely not comfortable with the suspicion that he'd somehow caused it, whatever it was. "Beauty, it's okay. The thought honestly never occurred to me."

She just looked at him for a minute, then swallowed as embarrassment chased away the apology in her expression. "Which means I just had a panic attack for absolutely no reason."

Still not the reaction he'd been looking for. He'd had no trouble with her wanting to kill him or her fuming at his argumentative genius, but seeing her look this fragile was just wrong somehow. He dropped his hands from her shoulders. "What happened to harassing me? You've screwed up every good sulk I've tried to have for the last two days."

The disgusted look she shot him was a vast improvement on her former distress, marking that moment the first and hopefully only time in his life he'd been relieved to have someone annoyed with him. "It's different when you deserve it." She moved away from him, taking a deep breath as she retrieved her sword. "But some parts of a person's life hurt more than others."

He picked up his own sword, the moment suddenly as solemn as the one the day before when she'd seen the picture of him and Juliana. The portrait had been painted just after they'd gotten engaged, a process as easy and elegant as their entire relationship had appeared to be. She'd always been so soft-spoken and delicate that she had calmed him merely by being in the room, and though they'd never had much to talk about it hadn't really seemed to matter. Her presence had been the important thing, right up until their first, last, and only fight.

He chuckled suddenly, realizing he'd passed that particular milestone with Beauty about thirty seconds after they'd first met.

When he looked up, he noticed her watching him. Her brow raised for a second in question, and he just shook his head and held up his sword. In some ways, it was easier when he'd only wanted to yell at her. "Let's see if we can get back to some actual teaching, shall we?"

FOR MOST OF the next hour, they did considerably better at staying on task. They went through what basics James remembered, slowly and carefully enough not to injure each other and imprecisely enough his old instructor would have shuddered to watch them.

"Take the bottom half of your sword blade and push it against the top half of the other person's blade." He laid his blade against hers to demonstrate. "Push downward really hard if you want to try and knock the sword out of their hand, or curl it around like this if you want to twist it out of their hands." Slowly, he used his sword to push hers a little bit in both directions so she could get the feel for it. "If all else fails, you can knock their blade sideways and out of the way so you can attack."

They switched sword positions so she could try the moves, clearly more comfortable at knocking the blade out of the way and lunging than either of the other two options. "When you do this, what's to keep the other person from stabbing you with the dagger they've got hidden in their other hand?"

He tightened his grip as she tried again, knowing she'd be annoyed if she thought he was letting her win. "One, the fact that points and not mortal injury determine the winner. Two, using a dagger is cheating." Then he grinned. "And three, most people who spend a lot of time fencing don't think of things like that."

She grinned back, shaking her head in mock dismay. "Some people have no imagina—"

"Stop it!"

Jumping at the sudden, high-pitched shriek, both James and Beauty whipped their heads around to see a busty, very annoyed-looking redhead striding out of the forest toward them. When their eyes met hers, she glared at them both before throwing out an accusatory finger at him. *"You* are supposed to be inside brooding, paralyzed by angst and suffering and whatever else you need to think about to look appropriately horrible and tragic. *I* am supposed to be *terrified* of you, huddled in a corner instead of waiting for a break in your *inane* conversation so I can show you how beautiful I am!"

Dropping his sword—he was scarier without it—he bared his teeth at the stranger and gave her a growl that promised violence. With this one, he wouldn't even have to feel guilty about it . . .

The woman, though, had already shifted her attention to Beauty. "And *you* are not attractive enough to be here at all, but if you're going to try to break the curse you shouldn't be *flirting* with the creature! You should be cowering somewhere, clearly horrified by him but willing to tough it out in order to save him from his own awfulness!"

Disgusted with the lack of terror he was getting, James flexed his claws and started forward. He was sure that being thrown against something would be enough to capture the stupid girl's attention . . .

He jerked to a halt, however, when he felt Beauty move past him. She headed towards the woman with her sword raised and a determined expression on her face, and when she was about a step away from her target pulled the sword back in clear preparation for an overhead swing. The gesture finally managed to puncture the woman's bubble of self-involvement, and her eyes widened in sudden alarm as she took a few stumbling steps backward and promptly fell on her butt.

"First question," Beauty said darkly, her sword still raised and her voice ringing with clear fury. "Who are you?"

The woman took long enough in her attempt to stammer something—apparently, no one had grace under pressure anymore—that Beauty finally turned to look back over her shoulder at James. "Do you know?"

He couldn't respond for a second, too busy staring at the scene in rapt fascination. When he realized that she was starting to glare at *him,* he shook his head and focused on her question. "An overly ambitious assistant editor put my name in an edition of a nauseatingly popular cursed nobility guidebook. Even though the company was punished severely there are still copies floating around. I tend to get about three or four of these little idiots a week looking to save me from my horrific curse."

The woman's expression immediately became indignant, her arrogance temporarily overcoming her need for self-preservation. "How *dare* you call—"

Beauty's attention immediately shifted back to the woman, gesturing a little with the sword and making "adorably menacing" the only appropriate descriptive term for the situation. "Sword, remember? This might not be sharp, but it's heavy enough that I'm sure I'll be able to make you bleed anyway."

Okay, so maybe he was the only one who would be tempted to add the "adorable" part. Not, of course, that he would ever admit that to her.

The redhead's eyes widened, her attention firmly back on Beauty. "You can't do that! It's not my fault you don't know how to—"

The rest of the genius insight cut off in a huff of pain, caused by Beauty's well-placed kick to the woman's midsection. "Leave

Beast alone, and tell any of your idiot fairytale-chasing friends to do the same." James felt a moment of disorientation at hearing his old nickname, but Beauty was too busy threatening the idiot to notice. "Believe me, the only reason I'm not killing you right now is that I like this shirt and I don't want to get blood on it."

"Actually, Waverly's really good at getting blood out of clothing," James added helpfully, baring his teeth at the woman in a gesture that no one would mistake for a grin. He flexed his claws again as the woman's attention swung back to him, finally getting that frisson of fear he'd been looking for. "He's had a *lot* of practice."

The woman kept looking back and forth at both of them, eyes getting bigger. "You're both insane."

Beauty smiled, her expression just as dangerous as James's. "Maybe, but will you live long enough to be sure?" She lifted her sword as James started advancing, and soon enough the woman gave one last shriek and scrambled on her hands and knees into the woods. Once she was safely gone, Beauty turned back to James with a disgusted noise. "Okay, that's clearly why you were so annoyed with me when I first showed up." She sighed. "I just hope I never looked like that as I was being dragged into these situations by my father."

He hesitated, wanting to say something supportive but not sure how much would be safe. She'd let him see a glimpse of her scars, but that didn't mean she wanted them analyzed. He certainly didn't want to talk about his. "I can't imagine you did," he said finally, voice careful. "Though I do think you'll have a much more interesting reputation after this."

She smiled apologetically at him. "Sorry I didn't let you do the terrorizing. She just made me *so* . . ." Beauty lifted her hands helplessly. "I snapped."

"Don't apologize." As he couldn't very well admit it was the best thing he'd ever seen, he just grinned at her. "I did wonder, though—Beast?"

Her eyes widened, as if she hadn't realized what she'd called him. Then she looked embarrassed again. "I like thinking of you like that," she admitted finally. "You just looked so happy when you talked about defeating people and taking their money. I didn't know it would bother you. I promise I won't use it again."

The sensible thing to do would be to accept her response, and leave the past safely where it belonged. Instead, he took a deep breath. "You can if you want to." It had felt surprisingly right, hearing her use the nickname from his old life. Like she could still see the man he'd once been.

Beauty just smiled. "Beast it is."

CHAPTER 7

The Perils of Proximity

66 "Two weeks?" On the other side of the magic mirror, Grace's eyebrows lifted. "Isn't that a little longer than they usually send you out on one of these jobs?"

Sitting at the big table in the middle of James's library, Beauty told herself she wasn't lying as she smiled down at her sister's image. Avoiding was a different thing from lying. "You know how it is with temp work. They just drop you someplace and don't let you go until they've gotten everything they can out of you." She shrugged, trying hard not to think about charging after the moronic redhead like she was some sort of knight in shining armor. Or, more importantly, trying hard not to think about how protective she'd felt. She'd just gotten so caught up in being with him . . .

Beauty shook her head, telling herself not to be an idiot. She'd only known James a few days. It wasn't like she was about to pick out china patterns with him. Not that she even wanted to.

Besides, Waverly probably handled all the china selection. "I just wanted to let you know where I'll be and give you the code for the mirror here."

"Thank you, and please keep that up. I know you think it's silly, but when I don't hear from you for a while I start having nightmares about Father snapping and trying to sell you to the Elves." Worry flickered in Grace's eyes, the same concern that had been there for as long as Beauty could remember. Even before their mother had disappeared for parts unknown, Grace had always been the one to take care of her little sister. "So, are there certain times I should be careful not to call you? I know you're borrowing a mirror, and I don't want to get you in trouble with your employer."

Beauty shook her head, fingertips absently tracing the edge of the mirror's newly dusted frame. "I might not always be here, but I'll be the only one using the mirror." James had lent her his old mirror, the one he'd used for business deals. The expression on his face when he'd handed it over had made her chest ache more than was really recommended for a platonic relationship, but it had also made clear that the matter wasn't open for discussion. "He hasn't used it in a while."

Grace's brow furrowed, her attention briefly caught by the smudge of colored chalk dust in the corner of her mirror. Hers had been issued by the school—when you didn't discriminate against supernatural creatures in your student body, some parent/teacher conferences were impossible to hold in person—and for a second Beauty hoped that she'd answered all her sister's questions. When Grace looked up again, however, her brow was still furrowed. "I tried to figure out what was bothering me about this, and I finally realized you're just not saying enough. You usually tell me all the random little details about your assignments because you know how much I like it, and I tell you more about my students than I'm sure you ever wanted to know. What's different about this case?"

Beauty sighed, trying to think of something to say that didn't involve sword fighting, the potential gossip she'd started, James's smile, or the fact she was already dreading going home in twelve days. Honestly, she'd be happy with anything that didn't start her talking about James, which pretty much reduced her to inane comments about the weather. "You think too much. I just felt I should mention that."

"An overly precocious chimera child said the same thing just last week as I was sending her to detention." Grace's voice was perfectly pleasant, but Beauty knew better than to question the steel in her eyes. "And you should know that avoiding the topic won't make me stop asking."

Unfortunately, she did know. Beauty hesitated, torn between wanting to ask for advice and not wanting to worry her sister. Grace had stuck with her through every magical ball, faked sleep, convenient abandonment, and cursed noble, finally taking the teaching job she wanted so badly only after being absolutely convinced that Beauty had also found a relatively sane and happy life.

Threatening strangers with a sword, unfortunately, didn't really fall into that category. "I'm helping a butler with some work he hasn't had time to deal with. If you *want* to spend your precious break time hearing all the intricate details of getting hundred-year-old bloodstains out of five-hundred-year-old tapestries, I would be happy to tell you all about it."

Grace's eyes narrowed. "And now you're about five minutes away from lying to me outright. Are you in trouble somehow, and you don't want to tell me because you think it will keep me from worrying? Because I assure you—"

"Grace!" Beauty held up her hands in a cease-and-desist gesture, wincing and dropping her voice when she realized how loud she'd just been. "I'm not in trouble, I promise."

Her sister didn't look convinced. "Then why are you being so deliberately vague about this?"

Beauty glanced at the doorway, listening for potential eavesdroppers, then looked over at a nice large armchair and briefly considered using it to block the door. Sure, that'd keep James or Waverly from accidentally wandering in, but she should probably hold on to what little dignity she had left.

There was an impatient noise from the other side of the mirror. "Beauty . . ."

She leaned forward again, elbows on the table and forehead propped in her hands. "It's complicated," she whispered.

Grace stopped whatever argument she'd been about to make, looking intrigued. "So it's suddenly gone from cleaning tapestries to 'complicated'?"

This time, it was Beauty's turn to narrow her eyes. "Don't gloat. I'm dealing with enough as it is."

Grace's expression gentled. "I can tell, sweetheart. Talk to me."

The simple response gave Beauty nothing to argue about, which made it much harder not to do something stupid, like tell her sister everything. "Before anything actually happened with Brian, could you see signs I was about to get myself in trouble?" She sighed, rubbing her eyes with the heels of her hands and trying hard not to feel like a complete idiot. "Giggle? Stare at him adoringly? Anything else embarrassingly obvious?" *Like chasing other women off his property, for example?*

Not that she was going to admit that part out loud.

Grace's brow furrowed for a moment, then her eyes went wide. "You think you're falling in love with somebody? Is it this butler you're helping?"

This was why she hadn't wanted to say anything. "It's not for me. A serving girl I worked with on my last job had eyes for the prince, and we started talking about dating nobility." Now she was lying, but she needed to know how much trouble she might get herself into. Waverly didn't know her as well as Grace, but he was perceptive enough to see just as much as her sister did. And if James figured out how much she'd started caring about him in such an embarrassingly small amount of time . . . "I don't really have the most impartial view of that whole time period, and there's no one else I feel comfortable enough to ask."

Grace hesitated, then blew out a long breath. "Honestly, you and Brian caught me completely by surprise. I knew that he seemed nice, and that he spent rather more time in the kitchens than most earls, but I thought he'd just gotten caught up in the 'lost princess' scheme Father was trying to pull. You, I think, mostly seemed surprised that he was paying attention to you." She paused, expression clouding briefly. "It wasn't until he asked you to go out driving with him that I started to see stars in your eyes."

Beauty blew out a long breath. "I don't know if that's comforting or not."

"Then I'll also remind you that he was a lying bit of gryphon dung who deserved your stabbing him in the hand with that serving fork." Grace's voice was firm now. "You need to be careful, but there's no reason to think this butler guy is anything like Brian."

"I kn—" Suddenly realizing a key detail she'd missed, Beauty's eyes widened. "Wait. I didn't mean—" She snapped her mouth closed when her brain caught up to it, sure that any explanation would only make things worse. Besides, it would probably be safer to have her sister asking questions about Waverly, since they would be perfectly safe to answer. She wasn't hiding any feelings about him, and the thought of passionately kissing him was absurd enough to be almost funny.

Of course, it also led right to the mental image of kissing James, at which point her cheeks flushed not with embarrassment but with something else entirely . . .

Grace sighed. "I take it back."

Successfully yanked back to reality, Beauty blinked and looked down at her sister. "What?"

"I'm not sure I'm ready to know whatever's going through your mind right now." There was an amused resignation in Grace's voice, the worry in her eyes carefully banked for the moment. "If you can promise me you're not in trouble, and promise you'll talk to me if it gets to be too much for you to handle on your own, then I'll leave you to fantasize about this butler of yours in peace."

"I promise." Beauty rubbed a hand across her mouth to repress a sudden and completely inappropriate chuckle. "Now, tell me about this chimera kid who's giving you trouble."

LATER THAT AFTERNOON, Beauty had an entirely different debate on her hands. She and James were in the backyard again, but this time they had extremely large lawn clippers instead of swords. Around them sat a collection of flowers that had apparently spent the last month patiently waiting in an outbuilding, probably because they were too scared of Waverly to disappoint him by dying. There had also been an unspoken but very firm implication on Waverly's part that taking care of both the flowers and the wildly overgrown bushes was the only way either of them would get more than toast for dinner.

"This isn't some plot you and Waverly have cooked up to try and get me to garden, is it?" James asked darkly, eying the flowers as if they were going to reach up and bite him. "Because if that's the case, I can save you several hours of pain and suffering by telling you it's not going to work."

She glared at him, folding her arms across her chest. "Were you not listening when Waverly ordered us out here to work on what appears to be your immensely long backlist of chores? If I were going to try and talk you into a hobby, I certainly wouldn't pick one where I'd have to do as much work as you do."

He raised an eyebrow at her. "And here I thought you were out here just to oversee things."

Beauty opened her mouth, ready to snap at him again, but stopped when she saw the glint of amusement in his eyes. It deflated the frustration, and she firmed her jaw to hold back the smile that threatened. "I should," she said with mock sternness. "It's not like you don't deserve it."

"Actually, I'm starting to think this might be your fault." He grinned, fangs flashing as he abandoned even the pretense of an argument. "Waverly didn't breathe a word about these mystical chores he insists I had until you showed up."

She shook her head, remembering all the times Grace had made her help organize the rented rooms they'd stayed in so they wouldn't leave a mess for the inn staff. "No parent wants to waste an opportunity for free slave labor," she sighed, eyeing the witches' nails bushes and trying to figure out how hard it'd be to cut through them. "Besides, he probably felt there was no point in asking while you were focusing all your energy on brooding."

He just looked at her, and she tensed a little as she suddenly realized she might have overstepped the tentative progress they'd made. Then she saw the humor in his eyes. "So it *is* your fault."

Beauty caught herself before the chuckle slipped out, wondering if melting this quickly was a sign of just how much trouble she was in. "Okay, maybe a little." She leaned forward to pick up the small trowel, deciding it would be easier to talk Beast into chopping at the bushes than planting the fragile little fairy bonnets and Snow Queen's Tears. "For all you know, though, he was gearing up for it anyway and you would have been stuck doing it alone if I weren't here."

James considered this, then inclined his head in acknowledgement. "True, but if that were the case and you'd talked him out of it I'd find some way to make it worth your while." He paused, probably for dramatic effect. "I'd also have to acknowledge your genius, which you could then remind me of endlessly any time I annoyed you."

She made a derisive noise. "You do know he was about five minutes away from making you edge the flowerbeds with the rubble from your broken statues, right? If I hadn't pushed you out the door when I did, you would have been in for hours of careful sorting and placing that would have driven you insane even more quickly than I do."

"He doesn't actually want broken chunks of ugly statues as his flower bed edging—the aesthetic sin of it would give him a muscle spasm every time he thought about it." The grin reappeared. "Of course, he's also more than capable of making me do it anyway just to prove a point." He bowed slightly. "So thank you."

She grinned, caught up in the playfulness enough that the words slipped out of her mouth before she knew she was even thinking them. "You could give me an extra day here to make up for it."

James blinked, startled, and Beauty's eyes widened as she realized what she'd just said. "For the competition, I mean," she said quickly, hand tightening on the trowel as her eyes escaped to any place where he wasn't. Picking up one of the potted flowers, she headed over to one of the flowerbeds that seemed a little less full than the others.

There was only silence from James, and when she finally braved another look up at him he was watching her intently. When their eyes met, his expression immediately smoothed out into something she couldn't quite read. "Do you really think one extra day is going to be enough to magically find a hobby for me?"

Beauty took a deep breath, sitting down on the ground in front of the flowerbed. His question had the same tense edge to it as their earlier almost-fights, and if she stuck to her excuse they could go right back to that for the rest of the day. It would be easier, certainly, and probably more professional.

She couldn't think of anything more awful.

Leaning forward, Beauty kept her eyes on the dirt as she started digging. "No, but it would mean another day before I had to leave," she said quietly, staring at the hole as if it was the most interesting thing in the world.

James was silent again, enough so that the random sounds from the woods were louder than they should have been. Eventually, he slowly walked towards the clippers and picked them up. Beauty kept her eyes on the flowerbed, pretending to measure the depth of the hole and telling herself that silence certainly wasn't the worst way this could have ended.

"Not there."

Beauty's head jerked up at the sound of James's voice. When

their eyes met this time, he put on his best haughty expression. "The color balance is all wrong, and I'm pretty sure the purple flowers a foot over are carnivorous after the sun goes down."

She just stared at him for a minute, then felt the corners of her mouth curve upward. "Then where should it go, oh wise one?"

He made a show of carefully scanning the backyard, then pointed a claw at the flowerbed closest to the witches' nails. And, she couldn't help but note, closest to where James would be standing. "There. The light's better, and there's nothing that will kill the poor thing while we sleep."

Her chest warmed, and it was taking real effort not to start grinning like an idiot. "Aren't you the one who didn't want to 'putter around' in the garden, Beast?"

He lifted a hand, fur glinting in the sunlight as his arm moved. "Lack of interest doesn't mean lack of skill."

This time, Beauty couldn't stop the laugh that bubbled up. "I must say, you've been hiding your secret gardening genius extremely well."

James swept an overly dramatic bow, barely missing injuring himself with the clippers. Not, of course, that she would ever get him to admit that. "I try."

She leaned forward a little, brushing a lock of hair out of her eyes as she abandoned all efforts to hide her smile. "Then prove it, Father Nature." She scanned the backyard, pointing to a small bush near the back door. "Clip that into a bunny rabbit for me."

He gave her his best mock horrified expression. "Absolutely not. You should be ashamed of yourself for asking for something so girly."

"But I am a girl. We have to be girly at least once a month or they revoke our union cards."

"Fine. You can be girly tomorrow." James folded his arms across his chest. "Today, pick something worthy of m—*ow.*" His arms instantly unfolded, and Beauty swallowed a completely inappropriate chuckle as she realized he must have just jabbed himself with the clippers. At the small sound she made, James looked up and narrowed his eyes at her. "You didn't see that."

She held up her hands. "Of course not." Pushing herself to her feet, she headed toward him. "Are you bleeding, or is it only your pride that's injured?"

"My pride's tougher than I am," he growled, prodding the injured area gently just in case. Beauty's fingers twitched, wanting to be the one touching him, and she made herself stop right where she was and fold her arms across her chest. Anyone who could watch her threaten someone with a sword and not get upset wasn't going to end up being like Brian, but that didn't mean it wouldn't be just as easy to get herself in trouble by following him around like a lovesick puppy. They could actually become friends, which made it that much more important not to do anything stupid.

Instead, she held out a hand. "If you want, I'll clip and you can protect yourself over there with the safe little flowers."

He glowered at her. "With those puny little arms of yours? I don't think so." He pointed back to the flowerbed. "Sit back over there and figure out how you're going to use the extra day I'm giving you to magically outthink me."

Beauty's chest tightened with a sudden, embarrassing rush of happiness. Friends, she reminded herself fiercely. "So says the man who prunes himself rather than the decorative hedge."

James was clearly readying his next volley when the back door opened, with Waverly stepping out just far enough to narrow his eyes at both of them. "If I don't start seeing some actual gardening being accomplished by at least one of you, *this* man wants to make it perfectly clear the pair of you will be forced to chew grass tonight while I enjoy my chicken cacciatore alone."

Reprimand delivered, he went back inside. As soon as the door closed, both Beauty and Beast burst out laughing.

CHAPTER 8

Love Poems and Death Threats

James had never been particularly interested in trollish love poems.

Initially, that had made it perfect for the experiment—if he accidentally tore a page or gouged a hole in the middle of a stanza, the universe wasn't going to collapse around him. But he'd made it through the first thirty pages completely without incident, and now that the initial thrill of reading again had worn off he was bored enough to be counting the books on the library shelves behind Beauty.

Of course, he could also just look at Beauty. She was deep in the middle of one of the Dwarvish mystery novels he'd really liked when he was younger, and he could just about tell where she was in the book by the way her mouth and eyes changed as she read. She had what had to be the most expressive face he'd ever seen, whether she was enjoying a story or threatening someone with heavy weaponry, and over the past few days he'd gotten far too much enjoyment out of simply watching it change. She held nothing back, even when she clearly wanted to, and every time her face lit up he was reminded that initially he had seriously underestimated how attractive she was . . .

James shut the thought down when she glanced up at him,

amused. "You can get a different book, you know. There's no rule saying you have to end with the one you started."

He lifted up the bottom edge of the book so she could see the pages. "So I pass?"

Her expression softened. "I was never the one testing you, Beast." She picked a book up from her lap, setting it on the table and sliding it over to him. "Not that you can't go pick your own, but I thought you might appreciate this one. The only reason I'm letting it go is that I finished it about three a.m. this morning, and you were kind enough to shelve the entire series together."

He carefully pulled the book closer, a little surprised at the way his throat tightened at the sight of the very familiar cover. "How do you know I'll like it?" he asked, using only the pads of his fingers to open the book to its first page. There had been several years where these particular books hadn't been shelved at all, instead staying in an enormous stack next to the head of his bed. "For all you know, they were a gift from my grandmother that was ignored from the minute they were purchased."

"One, you have better taste than that. Two, I'm pretty sure 'well-loved' is the most polite description for some of these volumes, and as far as I can tell, no one else in your family did much reading at all." She reached over, tapping the page of his book lightly. "And remember, with the more interesting books you might get a little distracted and not always remember where your claws are. Even if you poke a hole in a page or something, though, it's not a big deal."

James grinned. "Yes, Mother."

She grinned back. "I'm horrified you would compare me to your moth—" She stopped, brow furrowing in confusion as a thought hit her. "Wait. If they weren't readers, why in the world did they have a library like this? I would think you'd been the one to build it from the ground up, but if that had been the case I'm pretty sure the trollish poetry wouldn't have gotten in the door."

He smiled slightly. "The nobility all had libraries, so we needed to have one, too. My parents tended to buy the books with the most attractive covers, while my grandparents seemed to do it based on what their business associates were reading."

Beauty's expression lost some of its light for a moment. "At least your parents decided to just look like the nobility," she sighed, her mind clearly having gone someplace unpleasant without him. Given what little he'd heard about her father, James suspected he knew exactly where it was.

He watched her for a moment, remembering the minor panic attack she'd had when she thought she'd inadvertently tripped over one of his childhood scars. It was a feeling he suddenly understood far better than he'd ever wanted to.

"You know," he said casually, not sure if he was trying to fluster her or make her smile again. "You could technically argue that you just won our little competition." He kept his eyes on his book, but he could sense it when her head lifted. "Reading is clearly a hobby, and I'm not a good enough liar to pretend I'm not going to start doing it again on a regular basis. You were, in fact, right."

There was complete and total silence from her half of the table, and a moment later he looked up to find her staring at him wide-eyed and extremely flustered. "That's . . . I . . . ." She stopped, shaking her head. "No. This doesn't count."

He smiled slowly. Apparently, he'd been going for flustered. "I don't see how it doesn't."

Beauty narrowed her eyes at him, clearly annoyed that he wasn't helping her out. "Because it . . . ." She waved a hand at him, as if exasperated he didn't know this already. "I didn't actually do anything. I just pointed out something you would have figured out eventually."

James's chest tightened with a sudden, completely inappropriate rush of pleasure. He wouldn't have let her leave this fast—even if she'd agreed that she'd won, he could have made up at least a dozen loopholes to get her to finish out her two weeks—but hearing her actually say she wanted to stay was a different thing entirely. If she agreed, they could stretch out those two weeks to make them last months, or even longer . . .

James slammed down hard on the thought, disgusted with himself for already thinking about keeping her. Juliana had gotten sick of him quickly enough. No matter how enthusiastic Beauty was now, eventually something would inevitably come up that would make her leave again . . .

"Beast?"

Beauty's voice broke the silence, the hesitant edge to it so fundamentally wrong that the words came out of his mouth before he'd even thought about them. "Even if you did claim victory, do you really think I wouldn't have asked you for a rematch?"

Her eyes widened again, but after a second her entire body seemed to relax. "You could have told me that before I refused to accept the win," she said finally, eyes lit with amusement and something softer that he refused to try and interpret. Still, it was more than enough to make him feel guilty for putting her in the same thought as Juliana. No matter what happened, Beauty wouldn't curse him. She'd just chase after him with a sword until he could either talk her down or find somewhere large enough to hide.

Of course, the fact that she'd never curse him didn't mean she couldn't break his heart even *more* effectively . . .

He deliberately shook the thought away and made himself grin at her, pushing the thought to the dark recesses in the back of his mind. "Business rule number one: Never lay all your cards on the table at once."

She smiled back at him, a flash of sunshine, and James realized he was in even more trouble than he'd thought. "Remind me never to play Knights and Demons with either you or Waverly." She sat back again, eyes taking in all the books that surrounded them both. "You know, it's going to be hard for me to get any sleep when I know I could spend all my time in here rea—"

The sound of the library door slamming shut cut off the rest of what she'd been about to say, and they both looked over just in time to see the edge of the rug ruffle in a gust of wind that seemed to disappear beneath the edge of the door. A moment later, he heard

Beauty clear her throat behind him. "That was one of Waverly's winds, wasn't it?"

James nodded, eyeing the door as he tried to figure out Waverly's precise message. He had to have sent them—the elementals never wandered through the house on their own, clearly convinced Waverly would figure out a way to kill them if they ever harmed the furniture—but he couldn't imagine the circumstances under which he would. It was clearly a "Stay where you are" gesture, but since the curse about the only thing James needed to be physically protected from was a full-sized dragon in the middle of a psychological breakdown. If Waverly were the one in trouble, he was too smart to think that James would stay away, and if he had simply wanted privacy he wouldn't have called their attention to him in the first place.

Which left only one person Waverly might try to protect.

"Something's wrong, isn't it?" Beauty sounded concerned, and her expression had that same protective edge as when she'd gone after the woman in the backyard. "I didn't think Waverly was physically capable of getting spooked, but I've been in enough traumatic situations by this point to know a 'danger' signal when I see one."

"I'm not sure what it is," James admitted, keeping his suspicions silent as he pushed himself to his feet. "But unless you hear one of us screaming in the next fifteen minutes, you need to stay where you are."

Naturally, she'd stood before he'd even finished the sentence. "If you really think I'm just going to hide back here while—"

"Beauty." He met her eyes, making sure to keep his voice gentle. If he trusted anyone's protective instincts, it was Waverly's. "Please."

That stopped her more effectively than any amount of arguing would have, and after a brief internal debate she sat back down. "Fine." She pointed a warning finger at him. "But if there's anything you think I might have even the *slightest* chance of helping out with . . ."

"I'll let you know." He smiled a little as he slipped out of the library. No, she was definitely nothing like Juliana. "If we do end up needing you, feel free to grab the fireplace tools in the study across the hall. If I remember correctly, at least one of them should be sharp enough to make someone bleed."

HE HEARD THE arguing before he'd made it to the front foyer. That in itself was an odd thing, since he'd known Waverly to verbally demolish someone in less than a minute when he felt he had better things to do with his time.

Staying in the shadows, James positioned himself so that he could see both Waverly and the man on the front steps without being seen himself. He hadn't been surprised to discover the uninvited guest was Beauty's father, slightly fatter and grayer than in James's memories and nearly red with impotent rage. "I could have the constables here within moments!"

"First, unless the local law enforcement has suddenly increased their budget for transportation spells, we are at least twenty minutes from the nearest town," Waverly snapped, technically not raising his voice. There was an edge to it, however, that usually suggested he was planning a long, slow death for whomever he was speaking to. "Second, you are the one trespassing on *my* property, which means I am entirely within my rights to call those very same constables to collect *you.*"

"*Rights?*" Noble sputtered, looking as if he wanted to take a swing at Waverly. Beast, feeling rather vindictive at the moment, almost hoped he would try. "You have my daughter! I'm the only one with rights here!"

Ah. That explained a lot.

"As I said before, you have been misinformed." Waverly's voice was like ice. "There is no Beauty Tremain at this residence, and I had in fact never heard of the woman before you came to my door and made a fool of yourself. I will say, however, that she has my deepest sympathies for being in any way related to you."

James tensed, preparing for a pounce before he even realized he was doing it. From what little he remembered of Noble, he would take Waverly's physically kicking him out as a sign of encouragement. He could come back at any time, either with reinforcements or at the right moment to catch Beauty undefended. Of course, if that did happen, he had no doubt she would be more than a match for her father.

But she shouldn't have to be.

Tremain's eyes narrowed. "You think I'm too stupid to know you're lying to me? Her co-workers lied to me, Grace lied to me, but you give enough gold to enough carriage drivers and you'll find out anything you need to know." Suddenly, a certain blunt cunning lit his eyes, followed by a fury that made him look almost formidable for a moment. "She's trying to cut me out of it, isn't she? She's not good enough to catch a noble's attention, but she's found your boss and thinks she can fix his curse and get herself a nice little setup without me." He stepped back slightly, looking up as if she were watching him from one of the windows. "How *dare* she try to leave me out in the cold! She'd be *nothing* without me!"

Clearly, the time for mitigating damage was past. Waverly made a gesture beyond the edge of the doorway, summoning the elementals. "If you do not leave this instant, rest assured that I will take great joy in forcing you to."

If it had been anyone else, James might have been grimly amused at the ridiculousness of the situation. But Beauty had been living with this waste of oxygen for years. Worse still, she'd never had anyone like Waverly come along and save her.

As he felt the elementals rush past his ankles, James decided that a prompt disposal wouldn't be nearly enough of a suitable retribution. Instead, he gave the full-throated roar designed specifically to make any listeners quake in their boots. Noble gave a gratifying leap at the sound, making a small squeaking noise that might have been a shriek, and Waverly made another brief gesture that stopped the elementals in their tracks. Then, after a heartbeat of consideration, he opened the door to a sufficient width and stepped just far enough sideways to be out of the way.

Noble had only barely begun to collect himself when James started running. Beauty's father had just enough time to widen his eyes before James leapt, slamming the other half of the double doors outward as he grabbed Noble by the front of his brocade vest and took the shorter man with him down the stairs. They rolled together a small distance—he wanted to terrify the man, not break his back—ending up with Noble pinned flat to the ground. James, looming over him, bared his teeth and leaned close enough for the other man to get the full effect of all the sharp points. "I'm hungry," he growled, giving him a very deliberate sniff. Luckily, Noble had apparently forgone the cologne this morning. "What part of you should I start eating first?"

The other man made a small whimpering noise, yet more proof that he wasn't nearly as intelligent as his daughter. "You . . . you can't . . . I don't . . ." His eyes got wider and wider as he continued trying and failing to find a sentence he was capable of completing.

James shifted his grip just enough that the tips of his claws lightly dug into Noble's chest. It might not be enough to draw blood, but there would be enough bruising for him to remember the moment by. "I can, I do, and I will." He increased the pressure just a little as the other man squirmed, trying to get away. "And if you don't leave this *instant,* I will rip your legs out of their sockets and save the rest of you for a late-night snack."

"Not without—"

The words broke off in a shriek of pain as James twisted his grip slightly, making a small but definite rip in the brocade. There would certainly be blood now. "*Leave.*"

Tremain was hyperventilating now, but James needed him to get to the point where he was wetting himself. "Please . . . don't . . . hurt . . . me . . . I can . . . find you . . . someone better . . ."

James roared less than an inch from Noble's face. "Forget you even know your daughter's *name*," he growled, making the other man tremble. He knew he was admitting that Beauty was in the house, but Noble was clearly not willing to be persuaded otherwise. "And if you even *think* about coming anywhere near this house or near Beauty again, I will tear you into pieces so small that the pixies will be able to use you as hors d'oeuvres."

He pulled himself up into a crouch as Noble scrambled backwards, struggling to his feet before heading off down the roadway at a dead run. James watched him go, waiting for the man to either try to double around or make some sort of face-saving threat when he was at a sufficient distance. Noble did neither, however, simply disappearing from view as fast as his chubby legs could carry him.

Once he had disappeared completely, James heard the slow, measured sound of footsteps coming up behind him. "As satisfying as that was to witness," Waverly said with a sigh, "I suspect that Mr. Tremain will insist on continuing to be a problem."

James nodded, knowing he was right. "Any chance we could have him killed?"

"Unfortunately, not without Beauty's express permission." He patted James on the shoulder, then carefully dusted a few imaginary specks off the edge of his cuffs. "No matter how reprehensible certain family members can be, death rarely eases the emotional side effects as completely as one might hope."

"Grace would feel too guilty."

Both James and Waverly went still for a heartbeat at the sound of Beauty's quiet voice, then Waverly waited a moment longer for him to straighten so they could both turn at the same time. She was standing at the top of the steps, arms folded across her chest like she was hugging herself. "I'm sorry," she said when their eyes met, voice thick with emotion. "You shouldn't have had to do that."

"I promise you, we enjoyed it." James took a step towards her, fighting the urge to do something stupid like hug her himself. He'd never been good at being comforting. "Though I can't help but notice you didn't stay in the library like I asked."

"I moved somewhere where I could hear what was going on, and I recognized my father's voice. I stayed where he couldn't see me." She turned to Waverly. "Will you at least accept my apology? I hadn't thought he would do something like this, but I was probably legally obligated to warn you about him when you hired me."

Waverly smiled slightly. "Oh, there's no need. James got his exercise for the day, and I don't have to remove broken statues from the front lawn." He glanced over at James. "I believe I would consider that progress."

"Ha, ha," James said dryly, meeting Beauty's eyes again. She still looked embarrassed and guilty—not to mention confused, but that part made no sense—and his expression gentled. "Come on. You chased off my enemy with a *sword*. The least I could do was return the favor."

They just looked at each other for a long moment, so many emotions swirling in her eyes he couldn't even begin to read them. Then she blew out a long breath. "Thank you," she said softly.

James grinned as he and Waverly headed back inside. "Any time."

CHAPTER 9

Short and Furry Knights

Beauty wanted to hug James so hard it would've made it difficult for him to breathe. Actually doing it, however, would've just made her more embarrassed than she already was.

She should have realized that her father could find her here. There were whole, blissful stretches of time when he'd give his daughters up as completely useless, but then his latest scheme would go bad and he'd take another crack at his failed meal tickets. She could never run away quite fast enough to avoid the wreckage he trailed behind him, because he'd always manage to find her again and make more.

But James had known about her father, at least enough that he and Waverly had probably seen him coming from miles away. They would have been fully within their rights to toss her out on her ear for bringing a plague like that upon their house, and either not let her back in at all or wait until she'd beaten him unconscious with his own ego. But James had done it himself, almost like he had wanted to be the knight in shining armor she'd pretended to be with that girl.

Worse, he didn't even seem to notice that he'd done anything significant at *all* . . .

"Beauty?"

She blinked, jerking herself out of her thoughts to stare at

James's mildly worried expression over the corner of the breakfast table. His brow was lowered as their eyes met for a brief moment, then he reached over the table to get the butter he had apparently been asking for. "That looked suspiciously like brooding," he commented quietly, settling back down into his seat. "Everything okay over there?"

"Fine." Beauty let out a long breath, stabbing another forkful of pancakes and chewing them with the deliberateness of someone making up for the last three bites she'd missed. They were significantly less warm than they had been, and she refused to speculate on how long she'd been sitting there staring at the inside of her own head.

She was losing her mind, just like she had with Brian. Not that it was in any way James's fault—Brian had been a manipulative bastard, and all James had done was be her big, infuriating hero . . .

"Are you usually this terrible a liar, or did you just not get enough sleep last night?"

The question was surprisingly mild, but as Beauty looked up to meet James's eyes there was more than a little warning in them. He was comfortable with bad moods, but clearly lying was going to start an argument.

She sighed, setting her fork down. "I just don't understand why you don't seem annoyed that you got verbally assaulted by my father yesterday. *I* don't deserve to have to speak to the man, and I'm at least related to him by blood."

He scowled at her. "I don't understand why you won't let this go. All your father did was yell at me, and all I did was make him wish he'd never been born. If he dares to show his face here again I'll figure out something even worse to do to him."

"Or you could just send me home." She didn't want to go, but the shame filling up her throat made it seem like the only possible solution. Besides, it was better to volunteer before her father showed up again and Beast asked her to go. "That way, you won't hav—"

The rest of the sentence was cut off by the sheer intensity of the glare he was shooting her. "You said you didn't want to leave early," he said flatly, a sudden anger in his voice that she hadn't heard since their first argument.

Looking into his eyes, she felt the impulse to apologize even though she still wasn't sure she was wrong. "I don't," she said finally.

James's expression gentled. "Look, I'm not an idiot. I used to deal with people like him all the time in the financial world. I know he's coming back." He flashed a grin with more than a touch of evil in it. "Waverly and I will be ready for him."

She wanted to let herself just believe him. But why should now turn out any differently than the entire rest of her life? "Just . . . don't go too crazy, okay?" she said, forcing her voice to sound easy as she picked up her fork again. "I'll have to go home eventually, and if he's too furious by that point he'll be miserable for me to deal with on my own."

James didn't respond, and when she met his eyes again he had an expression on his face that suggested he was thinking too hard. "Your boss would let you stay here if it was a safety issue, right?" he asked after a moment, his tone suggesting that this wasn't up for argument. "If it gets to that point we'll have him arrested, but I can't let you go out there undefended with that useless piece of garbage looking for a target."

When she just stared at him, stunned, he made a disgusted noise. "Seriously, Beauty. How is this any different than you chasing Miss 'Happily-Ever-After' off my property with a sword? You save me, I then get to save you. Basic math."

She swallowed, chest squeezing tight. "I didn't save you, Beast. I just chased off an extremely large pest."

He narrowed his eyes at her, his expression utterly serious. "Are you really trying to take my rescue away from me?"

That froze her, scattering the dozen completely useless dismissals her brain had piled up. Then she swallowed, left only with the honesty she'd been trying so hard to avoid. "I'm not used to being saved," she said quietly.

Surprise registered on his face, then understanding. "Neither am I." The corners of his mouth curved upward a little. "That doesn't mean I'm not going to call you over when the next woman shows up, just so I can watch you chase her away with some sort of appropriately sharp implement."

He sounded like he meant it, and Beauty fought off the sudden and completely ridiculous urge to run outside and hunt up another woman to chase off for him. The moment the thought hit she could feel the blush start, and she immediately ducked her head and tried to think about nothing more embarrassing than pancakes.

Her brain, however, wasn't willing to let go of the thought quite so easily. "Does it have to be a sharp implement?" she heard herself say, lifting her eyes so that she could see him smile again. "Because I've also had pretty good luck with frying pans."

James's sudden laugh was almost startling, a full, deep rumbling sound that made her throat catch and her arms tingle like miniature bursts of lightning were going off under her skin. Beauty made herself breathe, taking slow deep breaths, and behind her she heard the door into the kitchen swing open.

James blinked, almost as if he'd surprised himself just as much as he had Beauty and Waverly, but then he shook his head and returned to his pancakes. "I'm not sure Waverly would let go of any of his frying pans, but we can ask him if he'll let you carry around some of the busts from upstairs."

Beauty raised an eyebrow, fighting the urge to rub at the spot over her heart. "That's sweet, but I think you're overestimating my upper body strength a little here."

"Not to mention the lack of statuary unattractive enough to fall outside the circle of my protection." Waverly's voice was as briskly efficient as always as he approached the table, and it took Beauty a moment to realize he must have been standing at the doorway ever since it opened. "Though I would be happy to sacrifice the bust of your mother's first pet poodle to the most terrible of fates, the rest of them are sufficiently inoffensive to the eye that they will remain exactly where they are currently."

She watched Waverly hesitate a moment before collecting the not-quite emptied syrup container for a refill. "Her poodle, seriously?"

"It was originally a gravestone, but the spot where Mother insisted the dog be buried was a little too close to Grandmother's zombie spell." James winced slightly at the memory. "Poor thing kept trying to chew its own leg bones."

"Though it did smell better than your grandmother," Waverly added, just before he swept back into the kitchen.

Beauty shuddered and swallowed a laugh at the same time. "I don't know if I should give you my undying sympathy or wish I had been there so I could have seen it with you."

"From what little I've heard, you have plenty of stories of your own." The comment was just a little more deliberate than the rest of the conversation had been, a gentle prod that Beauty had been tempted to use more than once herself. "Though any story with your father in it probably qualifies as horror, you're well-adjusted enough that there had to have been at least a few good moments."

Beauty grinned at him, temporarily side-stepping the question. "I think that's the first time anyone's called me well-adjusted."

He grinned back. "Of course, you have to remember the people I'm using as a comparison."

Her grin widened for a moment, then her expression sobered. It had been kind of him to ask for the best parts of her childhood, and she'd heard enough about James's past that he definitely deserved to hear about some of hers. "My sister managed to provide me with a lot of good moments. Grace is older than me, and when Father was ignoring us she filled in the school I was missing and gave me a chance to play. She's sort of doing the same thing now, teaching art and literature at an all-inclusive school a few miles away from me." Her smile snuck back. "I can't say they're more trouble than I was, but at least she didn't have to worry about me biting anyone's head off."

"Not through lack of trying, I'm sure."

"Flatterer." She sighed. "When Father found some new way we could get him to the top of whatever social ladder he'd managed to dig up, we did what we could to watch each other's backs and get through it."

His brow lowered. "She didn't protect you?"

Beauty shook her head, not wanting him to underestimate her sister. "She did everything she possibly could, but Grace was always in just as much trouble as I was." Embarrassment coiled low and heavy in her stomach as she defied every voice in her head that told her to stop talking immediately. She'd spent years trying her hardest to keep the mess of her life as secret as possible, but nothing she could say would be worse than seeing yesterday's disaster live. "Father broke whatever rules he ran across to chase the mythical happily-ever-after he always dreamed of, and most of the time it was all we could do to not get arrested as accessories while we beat off overly-friendly enchanted princes with a stick."

James's jaw tightened, and there was the faintest flash of fang as his lip pulled back. "Now I'm sorry I didn't kill him."

It was probably inappropriate that the comment made her smile again. "I told you, Beast—Grace would feel too guilty. She'd happily move us both to the outer reaches of Beyond if she thought it would be enough to keep Father from tracking us down, but she actually kept this berserker she was dating a few years ago from just chopping off Father's head when he wanted to." Beauty sighed, remembering the conversation they'd had after that. It was the closest they'd ever gotten to a fight. "She doesn't like him any more than I do, but she feels that it would be wrong to put a hit out on the only parent we have who is still willing to acknowledge our existence."

James still looked like he wanted to punch something, or at least send a few more statues flying off the roof. "I was hoping for her sake that your mother died a conveniently early death in childbirth."

She preferred the temper to the sympathy, and it somehow made it a little easier to keep going. "No such luck. She left early enough that I only have vague memories of a very short, frail woman obsessively fanning herself, but the fact that she left him for the tax collector is a really convenient insult to throw at Father when he's being annoying." She paused, brow furrowing as she caught herself. "But you said good stories."

James shrugged, his own expression easing a little. "Hey, I told you zombie stories. Good is relative."

"Still, I should try." She thought a moment, digging through the stories that she and Grace had told only each other. "When I was seventeen, Father left us for the weekend with a family of giants in the hopes that we find their gold and help him break in. Instead, we found out that the giants' son and the magic harp were in love and helped them run off together. The dad was really nearsighted, so I helped them sneak out the back while Grace stood very still with a big fake harp attached to her back."

He grinned. "Did they let you stay after that?"

"Absolutely. Grace can look innocent better than anyone alive, and she just told them I'd come down with something and couldn't talk to them until we were both sure my expression wouldn't give anything away."

James laughed again, making her heart skip and sending the shivers skimming along her arms just like they had last time. It wasn't at all fair that the man had such a dangerous laugh. "I think you two actually had a more interesting childhood than I did. I'd like to both offer my deepest sympathies *and* wish I'd been there to see it."

Beauty felt a lump in her throat. "You think we would have been friends?"

His eyes were deep for a moment. "Yeah," he said softly. "I think we would have been really good friends."

She hesitated, then took another risk. "Were you and Juliana friends?"

Any good humor immediately left James's face, and for a few

heartbeats there was nothing but complete silence. Then he took a deep breath. "No. It never occurred to me that I should want to be friends with the woman I was going to marry. My parents barely spoke, and though I'm sure Waverly's found plenty of feminine company over the years I'm quite certain none of them have even seen the house. Your wife did her thing, you did yours, and you both interacted with whatever kids came along on your own time. That's the system I knew."

Beauty hadn't seen enough even semi-functional relationships to comment one way or the other about that particular perspective of marriage. She knew that Grace held out more hope, but Grace was more hopeful about a lot of things. "So how did you and Juliana find each other?"

"I worked with her father a little while. He had turned a golden goose hatchery into a lending bank, but he was one of those people who needed someone looking over his shoulder all the time. I helped him get it stabilized for a percentage of the profits. One day, we had a dinner meeting over at his house and Juliana was just . . . there." He paused, as if he couldn't quite find the right words. "She was . . ."

Beauty tensed, knowing she had to keep listening but not particularly wanting to. She remembered the perfect, delicate vision from the painting, and braced herself for a poetic enough description of the woman's magnificence that *she* would have to send a statue off the upper floor.

James stopped, shaking his head. "She was just so serene. I'd never met a calmer, more even-tempered person in my entire life." He gestured vaguely back towards the kitchen. "Waverly fakes it, but he's actually one of the most dangerous people I know. Juliana, though . . . it was almost impossible to be angry at someone who was so calm." He paused again, brow furrowing. "It was almost impossible to be anything, really. She just . . . evened me out."

Beauty swallowed. Somehow, that was almost worse than sheer physical magnificence. "And you were drawn to that."

He lifted a hand. "I hadn't ever experienced anything like it before. It . . ." He stopped again, shaking his head more firmly this time. "We were engaged. Now we're not, and I look like I skulk through the woods chewing on unfortunate bunny rabbits. End of story."

No, it wasn't. And if she ever met this Juliana in person, Beauty decided instantly, she was going to do a lot more than just threaten her with something painful. "Do you really think Juliana was the one who cursed you?" she asked quietly.

James's jaw tightened, and for a moment she thought the conversation really was over. She stayed silent as he looked down at his plate, then back up at her. "The timing is too convenient for me not to think she had something to do with it," he said finally, half-growling. Then something almost fragile flashed across his eyes. "But I still don't understand how. She didn't get mad at anyone." He opened his mouth, taking a breath to speak, then stopped and closed it again.

Beauty, however, already had a pretty good idea of what he'd been about to say. *She must have really hated me.* "Actually, you got off better than you think," Beauty said deliberately, voice encouragingly light. If she couldn't push Juliana off a very tall cliff, the least she could do was make up for the fact that she'd dragged the woman into the conversation by immediately getting her out of it. "The agency has a standing monthly assignment to polish a baron who got turned into a silver tea set."

James's brow furrowed. "An entire set?"

Beauty nodded. "As far as we can tell, different parts of him were transformed into different pieces of the set. We know he's still in there because the pieces will sort of hum occasionally."

His eyebrows lifted. "So if a piece got stolen before he was transformed back . . ."

"His estate set up two very large body guards to make sure that doesn't happen." She paused for effect. "And all of the employees are very careful not to touch the sugar bowl."

After a heartbeat, he grinned. "Too bad his estate didn't set up a regular appointment to take care of that."

Beauty grinned back. "The estate's being managed by the baron's younger brother. If he lets something happen to the baron their mother will string him up by his thumbs, but that doesn't mean he wants the man to enjoy himself."

James shook his head, still looking amused. "Cruel, cruel man."

Beauty watched him, feeling something inside her chest ease as he relaxed. "Any time you want me to beat someone up for you, just let me know." She knew her voice was softer than it should be, but all her restraint was being used up not reaching across the table and hugging the man. "They won't know what hit them."

James's eyes held their own softness as his grin returned. "But I would."

CHAPTER 10

Cuddles and Lies

Technically, they were still looking for a hobby for James. Yesterday they'd attempted cooking, which had resulted in a cake that had somehow managed to be both blackened and undercooked at the same time. The only reason they'd gotten Waverly to agree to the experiment at all was the memory of their attempt at knife throwing the day before.

It felt like an unspoken agreement between them. If they pretended she was still here because of the bet, neither of them had to think about why they didn't want it to end.

"CLOSE YOUR EYES."

Beauty gave him a suspicious look. "You're not going to suddenly disappear on me, are you, Beast? Because while that could count as a practical lesson to see if I'd learned anything, the fact I'd have to kill you the moment I found you again would completely ruin the rest of my afternoon."

James grinned. They were in the woods at the moment, trying to teach Beauty enough basic forest sense that she'd notice the next falling tree branch before it tried to kill her. So far the lessons had consisted mostly of good-natured arguing, on topics ranging from what direction north actually was to whether or not unicorns would give useful advice if you bribed them sufficiently.

It was the most fun he'd had since . . . well, yesterday.

"Of course not." He gently laid his hands on her shoulders, silent proof he wasn't about to go anywhere. "There's no point if you're expecting it."

Beauty's eyes narrowed, but after a moment she made an exasperated noise and closed them like he'd asked. "So what am I listening for, oh wise one? Will the leaves suddenly start whispering, 'No, you fool, you're going the wrong way'?"

"Even if they did, you shouldn't listen to them. Tree nymphs who live anywhere near civilization are generally pretty bitter." He squeezed her shoulders, careful to keep his claws from digging in at all. "This won't work all the time, but what I want you to do is listen for the wind."

"What, does it—" Whatever comeback she'd been about to make was cut off as her ears caught something, and James watched her expression change as she focused on the tell-tale sound he himself could hear in the distance. After a moment, she opened her eyes. "There's a whistle." She hesitated a moment, then pointed behind her and to her left. "Coming from that direction."

James nodded, pleased that she'd picked up on it so fast. "That's the house. There's a space just behind the far left tower where my great-uncle used to keep his harpy menagerie. The family shut it down after the harpies decided to band together and break out by eating him, but there's still enough wire left behind to cause some interesting side effects."

This time, it was Beauty's turn to grin. "Does it ever worry you that you're probably the most norm—"

"Help me!" The cry was delicate, feminine, and vibrating with despair. "Oh, please, won't some big, strong man help me?"

Beauty closed her eyes with a groan. "Do you think it would be inappropriate to suggest that the woman hire a playwright or a bard before we chase her off? Someone desperately needs to write her some better dialogue."

"Depends on how generous you're feeling." James knew he should be sympathetic—Beauty had just chased the last girl off the roof the day before. That girl had been the sign of a sudden uptick in popularity that normally would have required him to call out the lawyers again. If he did that, though, he'd miss out on the opportunity to experience the sheer pleasure of watching Beauty scare them all to death. The woman had a definite protective streak about her. "Or even better, you could charge her for the advice. First client for your very own consulting firm."

Beauty sighed, but he could see the corners of her mouth starting to sneak upward. "Even if I could figure out how to work with these women without getting frustrated enough to kill them, Manny would never forgive me." Shaking her head a little, she started scanning the ground around them. "So what do you think, branch or rock?"

He picked up a branch that looked to be about the right size, testing the weight briefly before handing it over to her. "You like it better when you get to swing something at them."

Her smile widened. "Yes, I do."

WHEN THEY'D LOCATED that day's pest, however, it was clear she'd already gotten up close and personal with the local tree population. Someone stumbling on the clearing who didn't know any better would see a rather delicate-looking brunette pinned underneath a conveniently medium-sized tree, tear tracks of distress marking her pink cheeks and anxiousness in her eyes. Worrying about saving the poor damsel, the theoretical person probably wouldn't notice how dried out the broken end of the branch looked, or the rather large rock beneath one end of the branch that was mostly covered by the tall grass.

The woman turned her head a little as soon as she heard the

sound of people moving towards her. She couldn't see them, though, since they'd made sure to approach from the blind spot directly behind her head. "Oh, kind sir, thank—"

The words cut off suddenly as Beauty stepped close, thoughtfully tapping the tip of her very large branch on the ground a few inches from the woman's cheek. "Want to try that again?" Beauty asked dryly, looking directly down into her eyes. "Maybe use a line that will leave your dignity slightly less bruised in the morning?"

"Oh, I'm so sorry." Surprisingly, the woman sounded apologetic, and even Beauty was caught off guard as the other woman immediately slid out of the space beneath the branch and moved into a sitting position. "I got tired of the serving girl routine, so I thought I'd try something new. But I had no idea I was working someone else's territory."

James couldn't see Beauty's face from where he was standing—a problem he was about to fix immediately—but he could practically feel her glare. The heat of it was actually singeing the air a little. "It's my temper you should be worried about, not my territory. Besides, do you have any idea how far—" She stopped abruptly, jaw tightening as she caught herself from finishing the sentence.

The woman, though, seemed to know exactly what she'd been about to say. "I know it's not close to the road, but I know there's someone with a castle a few miles from here and I was hoping I could catch him out hunting . . ."

"And you didn't think to do a little *research* fir—" She stopped herself again, shaking her head fiercely. "No. Will you stop trying to give me flashbacks and just go away? You're on private property, you can't have Beast, and you are seriously getting on my nerves. You have about thirty seconds before I start gesturing violently at you."

The woman narrowed her eyes in sheer feminine indignation. "I *said* I was sorry," she huffed, pushing herself to her feet. "You'd think someone who had found her man would be at least a *little* more sympathetic to someone who's still looking." She glanced over at James, and he realized that she had apparently been aware of him the whole time. "I mean, it's not like I'm making snippy comments about the fact you haven't gotten around to breaking the curse yet. I knew a girl whose second cousin spent several perfectly happy years with a talking frog. What a couple does in the bedroom should be their business, not any nosy neighbor's."

He saw Beauty's expression melt into pure shock a split second before his own brain processed what the woman was saying and stuttered to a halt. With his higher-level thinking no longer able to contribute, the instincts that had kept him alive through any number of attempted hostile takeovers decided to take charge. "Very true," he rumbled, letting just a little bit of a growl out in his voice as he moved to stand beside Beauty and put a deliberate arm around her shoulders. Beauty almost jumped at the contact, and he could feel her suddenly turn to stare at him with an expression he flatly refused to let himself analyze. "And we hate to be rude, but we're very protective of our time together."

The woman's face instantly softened, and she gave a happy little sigh as she flattened her hand against her chest. "Oh, how *romantic*. She might not have broken your curse yet, but if any of the reports I heard about you were true I can see the power of love has already worked wonders." She smiled, brushing off the few bits of grass left clinging to her skirt. "With all the rumors floating around, I honestly didn't know what to expect."

He felt Beauty flinch beside him, but she made sure her voice was calm before she risked speaking again. "You know how it is with rumors."

The woman waved her hand dismissively. "They're just jealous. There are some people who don't think you should give a cursed person the time of day if they're not nobility of some kind, and others who think you must have cheated to not get kicked out like all of the other women." She grinned suddenly, more than a touch of evil in the expression. "Though there are a few ladies who will love you *forever* for scaring Scarlett like you did."

"Fantastic," Beauty said weakly.

Clearly, it was time to wrap this conversation up. "The castle is an abandoned summer home, I'm afraid, but I do know that Baron Rothington takes regular evening rides near Odette Lake," Beast offered. "Last time I checked, he was between wives."

The woman curtsied. "Thank you kindly, good sir." She turned to Beauty. "Congratulations. It's always nice when one of us snags such a clear winner."

Luckily, the woman disappeared before Beauty could draw enough breath to correct her.

OF COURSE, THAT didn't stop the argument that occupied them the entire way home. James had known it was coming—he probably deserved it, though he he'd never admit it—but it hadn't given him much of an advantage so far.

"I can't believe you thought that was a good idea," she huffed, stalking ahead of him despite the fact that her shorter legs should have made it hard for her to even keep up. At least they were going the right way this time. "I didn't realize the rumors would run this wild, which is bad enough, but you pretty much held up a sign back there saying 'Yes, they're all true. Please make up new and even more extravagant stories about us to occupy your time.'"

If he'd really wanted to quiet the rumors, James agreed his strategy would have been a terrible one. In reality, though, he felt pretty satisfied by how the encounter had turned out, which meant he'd clearly stopped listening to his own advice that he think of Beauty as just a friend.

Not, of course, that he was going to mention this to Beauty. "Denying rumors is what makes them worse, not agreeing with them," he shot back, refusing to give in to the urge to hurry enough to catch up with her. "Now she knows the actual truth, which means she won't feel the need to add to whatever stories are going around."

Beauty made a frustrated noise, stopping suddenly and whirling around. "She doesn't know the truth! You fed her a line about us cuddling up in some big, furry happily-ever-after, and now that she's seen you at your most charming she won't believe anything else!"

"What do I care?" He knew he had cornered her, and that he'd be annoyed if she'd done the same thing to him. But that didn't mean he had to like how easily she was able to dismiss that "big, furry happily-ever-after." "Maybe this means my pest problem will disappear!"

She glared at him for another moment. "I thought you enjoyed having me chase them off for you."

Now she'd backed *him* into a corner, with truth or cheating as his only escape options. Clearly, now wasn't the time for truth. "Is there someone at home who you're afraid will hear the rumor? A boyfriend who's such a big part of your life you haven't bothered to even mention him before now?"

She flexed her fingers as if she were seriously considering throttling him. "You . . . you . . ." Apparently finding no words violent enough to finish the sentence, she whirled around again and disappeared through the trees just ahead of them. James, growling some of the more colorful Djinn curses Waverly had taught him under his breath, pushed through the trees after her.

And, a few steps later, nearly ran into her back.

He caught himself just in time, jerking to a halt just behind the now frozen Beauty. She was staring at a slightly taller woman with her arms folded across her chest, the expression on her face remarkably similar to the one Waverly got whenever James was making his life difficult.

It took another second to realize that the woman had Beauty's eyes, and a certain set to the jaw he was already becoming familiar with.

By this point, Beauty had managed to recover the power of speech. "Grace! What are you doing here? Did something happen?" She stepped forward. "Please tell me we didn't push Father off the edge enough to make him come after you."

Grace's eyebrows lifted at that last sentence, as if it was news to her, then her eyes narrowed. "Well, I guess that at least sort of explains it. And if you ever answered your mirror, or called me again, I wouldn't have had to come up here and interrupt your shouting match with . . ." She glanced up at James, clearly hunting for the most polite term to use. ". . . your friend here."

Beauty sighed, scrubbing a hand across her face as she turned to look back at him herself. There was a distinct guilty tinge to her expression, and the sudden stab of sympathy eased the frustration in him somewhat. "Grace, this is Beast. Beast, Grace."

Grace made a small, shocked sound as she glared at her sister. "Beauty!"

Beauty held up her hands in an "It's okay" gesture. "It's a nickname, Grace, and I promise he gave me special permission to use it. He used to be in finance, and they called him 'The Beast' because he enjoyed terrifying people with how talented he was." She glanced over at him again, eyes narrowing. "Not that I can see much sign of that genius *now* . . ."

"It wasn't as if your wide-eyed staring was a better response," he shot back, meeting her glare with one of his own. "If you'd actually said something instead of just standing there like an enchanted statue, I might not have—"

A short, sharp, and extremely loud whistle cut off the argument, and both he and Beauty turned to find Grace attempting to split her glare equally between them. After a few back and forth looks, however, her eyes widened suddenly and snapped back over to her sister. Beauty just stared at her for a second, completely confused, then her own eyes widened in what could only be described as complete panic. "Grace, no." She took another step forward. "It's not . . ."

Completely ignoring her sister, Grace narrowed her eyes and looked over at James again. "You're not a butler, are you," she said flatly, the words clearly not a question.

"No," he said carefully, glancing over at Beauty to see if she could give him some clue about what was going on. Instead, she deliberately didn't look at either of them, staring up at the sky as if desperately looking for a dragon to eat her and save her from the situation.

Grace, clearly having none of it, whacked her sister on the arm to get her attention. "You lied to me."

Beauty finally met her sister's eyes, the accusation having had almost more of an effect than the hit. "I did not." She hesitated, voice less vehement than it had been. "I merely didn't correct you when you came to a conclusion that wasn't true."

Grace made a disgusted sound, and this time James's eyes narrowed as he glared at Beauty. "You told her I was the *butler?*"

"Of course not! I just . . ."

His jaw tightened. The guilt was back in her eyes. "Didn't bother telling her I was here at all?"

"I . . . it's . . ." Her voice failed her, then she squeezed her eyes shut and pressed the heels of her hands against her eyes. "Grace," she said slowly, each word spoken with the extreme care people use when they're trying not to snap completely. "Not that I'm not happy to see you, but why are you here? I thought you had classes all week."

Grace sighed, suddenly looking tired as she rubbed a hand across her forehead. "I got a substitute. I thought you might want backup." She glanced over at James again, expression softening for just a moment. "I didn't know you already had some."

Beauty dropped her hands, revealing cheeks that had turned bright red. *"Grace,"* she said sharply, deliberately not looking at James. Then she blinked, as if just now processing everything else her sister had said. "What would I need backup for?"

Grace's voice was grim. "Father's trying to have you declared incapacitated by enchantment. It's a long shot, and no one's listening yet because it's one of those cases that takes a legal loophole and stretches it big enough a giant could step through it. But I talked to a legal professor I know, and technically . . ." She stopped, caught on the next word.

James, however, knew exactly what she'd been about to say. "If she spends too much time in isolation with someone who's cursed, you could argue there's enough secondhand magic exposure to potentially be an issue."

Beauty swore in Dwarvish, about the only words she'd managed to pick up in the language so far. "Of all the stupid, cheating . . . He doesn't really think that's going to work, does he? I mean, a five-minute mirror conversation with the judge will be more than enough to prove I'm still exactly like I was two weeks ago."

"No, it won't," James cut in with a growl. He'd faced this more than once after he'd been cursed, and locking Waverly down as his legal heir was the only thing that had kept there from being more trouble. Also, Waverly had been feeling extremely protective at the time. "You could still be under enchantment, or the entire conversation could be an illusion. If he convinces a judge to take the case, only an in-person appearance, interview, and magical scan are considered sufficient rebuttal."

Beauty stared at them both as if that was the stupidest thing she'd ever heard. "But why is he even trying this? If he's got a brain in his head he knows I've made sure Grace gets what little I have if something happens to me. What benefit does he get out of this?"

Grace, if anything, looked even more upset than Beauty. "If the last twenty years of our lives is any indication, he's using this to distract us so he can come up with something worse."

James's jaw tightened as he gestured everyone back toward the house. "We need to talk to Waverly."

INTERLUDE

Battle Plans

Waverly would never be caught dead doing something so painfully obvious as listening at a doorway. If nothing else, the information gained through such a method had the tendency to become useless if someone saw you acquiring it.

Fortunately, he'd discovered through experimentation that the elementals could retain and later repeat conversations in their immediate vicinity, a convenient trick that apparently had something to do with the elementals' existing on the same frequency as sound waves. Whatever the reason, they had proven extremely useful on any number of occasions over the years, and ever since Beauty's father had made his appearance Waverly had had them on alert for any unexpected visitors who set foot on the property.

He hadn't expected the sister to arrive so suddenly, a sensible-sounding woman whose annoyed mutter held both love and more than a little of her sister's fire. The tone of the mutter had implied something far more serious than a casual visit, and he listened to just enough of the resulting conversation to get the shape of Noble Tremain's attempt at a countermeasure.

Though he would have liked to deal with the matter himself—he wondered if Grace would feel as guilty if the man simply disappeared without a trace—he was already mentally drafting instructions for their attorney by the time he heard the three of them come inside. Even if her relationship with James didn't work out as Waverly intended, Beauty had already ingratiated herself so deeply into their daily lives that there was no question of their resources being at her disposal.

He had no doubt James would agree, though the younger man would likely phrase it in a way that involved considerably more shouting. As, of course, he was doing now. "Waverly, we have a guest." James's roar as he strode in was loud enough Waverly could have heard it clearly on the roof, let alone the kitchen. "And we should have definitely killed Noble."

"I'm starting to agree with you." Beauty sounded like she was only a step behind James. Her voice was somewhat quieter but carrying an edge that suggested she was looking for something to hit. It astonished Waverly sometimes, how similar they had proven to be. "This is nuts, even by Father's standards. What does he get out of this? Even if I lose, all that will happen is Grace gets my books and a bunch of old furniture."

"Distraction," Waverly answered her, heading into the main foyer to intercept the trio. Behind James, he could see the back and shoulder of Beauty's sister as she turned to shut the door behind them. "But if he actually attempts any of this foolishness, I assure you that we have a lawyer who would be more than happy to earn his retainer by tormenting your father."

"You sound as if you want to be that lawyer." Grace had moved around James to join the conversation, the thread of humor in her voice giving it a warmth and richness that immediately caught his attention.

"Your father would inspire violence in even the gentlest of men," Waverly retorted smoothly, shifting his attention to meet Grace's eyes. "And though I've been call—"

There was a jolt as their gazes connected, a faint shock of rightness that left his brain unable to hold on to whatever else he'd been about to say. Her face was lovely, softness and strength in exactly the right proportions, but it was her whiskey-colored eyes that left him truly enthralled. There was such a depth to them, suggesting secrets it would take an entire lifetime to explore . . .

Waverly blinked, stunned at the direction his thoughts had taken.

He forced his attention back into the moment, where Grace was staring at him with an astonished look that could be interpreted as anything from shock at his rudeness to worry for his mental health. James and Beauty didn't meet his eyes, their expressions suggesting they'd suddenly thought of several questions they were kind enough not to give voice to.

The only thing left to do was take a steadying breath and reclaim his dignity as quickly as possible. "Unfortunately, we can't make a move immediately." His voice was brisk, and he gave Grace a quick nod before turning his attention to Beauty. "If we attempt counter-measures before your father locates a suitably sympathetic judge, it could be seen as an implicit acknowledgement on our parts that his claim has enough merit to concern us."

Beauty's brow furrowed as she tried to find some actual logic amid the legal reasoning, then she gave her head a quick shake and turned to her sister. "Please tell me we can kill Father now. Seriously, we'd be doing the universe a favor."

Waverly saw Grace's eyebrows lower, and a steely look crept into her eyes that suggested a woman ready to charge into battle. It was magnificent, and not something he should be dwelling on at the moment. "I told you no."

Beauty made an exasperated noise. "When this many people have offered to do it for us out of sheer sympathy, there's no reason to still feel guilty about it."

"It's not that I would feel guilty." Grace held her sister's gaze, voice gentler than before. "But letting someone kill your parent drags you into the kind of story I don't want either of us anywhere near."

James opened his mouth to say something, then stopped and turned to Beauty. "I hate to say it, but she probably has a point."

"She does indeed," Waverly seconded quietly, acknowledging the wisdom of the sentiment even as it occurred to him that Grace had suffered each and every one of the indignities Beauty had. More, perhaps, because there were likely at least a few years where Grace had been sent out on her own.

Perhaps he could have a . . . *talk* with Noble. Murder wasn't the *only* option available when one wished to make a point.

"Fine," Beauty sighed, shoulders dropping in acknowledgement. "So we can't kill him, and we can't sic a lawyer on him until someone actually decides to listen to him. Is there anything we can do right now to keep Father from rampaging around the countryside?"

James considered this for a moment, then curled a lip back as a thought hit him. "I'm sure there are any number of people who would love to hear that Noble Tremain is back in town. People with entire fleets of lawyers, just waiting to express their displeasure with the man."

Beauty caught James's eye, then grinned. "I even have names and addresses of several of those people."

"I have a few favors I can call in as well," Waverly added, catching himself as his gaze began to wander over to Grace again. It was ridiculous—the woman was at least a decade younger than he was, likely more so, and had come here solely on an errand of mercy for her clearly beloved younger sister. He had no idea whether or not she was already spoken for—though if she wasn't, the men in her life were clearly idiots—and the complications that would result from even broaching the question were enormous. Relationships with the opposite sex needed to be dealt with in a mature, intelligent manner. As that was clearly not possible with Grace Tremain, his only option was to remain silent until sanity once again presented itself.

"What contact information Beauty doesn't have, I can give you." The relief in Grace's voice was profound, lightening it enough to let some of that entrancing humor come back. "I can either leave it with you before I go, or send it by mirror if Beauty can pull herself away from arguing with her new friend long enough to actually talk to her sister occasionally."

Waverly refused to acknowledge the kick of panic in his chest at the thought of her disappearing. His ability to never panic had carried him through pirate attacks, inconveniently-timed wars, and one particularly tense discussion with a horde of well-armed dwarves. He was not about to start now.

The part of him not focused on arguing, however, had other priorities than being right. "It would be safer for you to stay here as well," he heard himself say, aware of the three pairs of eyes that immediately swung around to stare at him again. "Your father is too likely to consider you a suitable target for retaliation, and it will be easier to protect you if you remain nearby."

There was a moment of perfect silence. "I . . . I certainly don't want to impose . . ." Grace began, sounding confused but thankfully not opposed to the idea.

"It's not imposing if they ask you," Beauty chimed in, voice brightly encouraging enough to embarrass a lesser man. "Besides, you know he's right about Father. After your favorite student set him on fire I'm pretty sure he wouldn't be stupid enough to do anything at your school, but do you really want to apologize to your landlord again?"

"Waverly's an excellent cook, if that helps," James added, trying much harder to look nonchalant and yet still failing miserably. "You'll never want to lea—" The sentence ended abruptly, and Waverly felt an immense rush of gratitude as he caught sight of Beauty's elbow returning to position. There was another moment of silence, and Waverly found that he had temporarily stopped breathing as he met Grace's eyes again. When she gave him a small, hopeful smile, it warmed him in a way that should have been physically impossible.

"Okay." Grace let out a breath, as if she couldn't quite believe what she was saying. "I'd love to."

CHAPTER 11

Vacation Time

From the other side of the mirror, Manny's eyes narrowed. "I know your life stinks, kid, but you can't suddenly cut out in the middle of an assignment for vacation time."

Beauty scrubbed a tired hand across her face, deeply regretting the attack of conscience that had caused her to make the call in the first place. Manny would have probably been thrilled to let her stay out here for months racking up James and Waverly's bill, but with Grace temporarily moving in the situation had mutated so far beyond what could legitimately be defined as work that it was ridiculous.

And there was so much she didn't want to have to include in a report . . . "It wouldn't be in the middle of an assignment. I talked to the butler, and he said he'd be happy to send in the job completion report before I officially started my time off." She leaned forward slightly. "With the legal mess Father's trying to make, you know it would be better for the agency if I lie low for a while. He's perfectly capable of trying to interfere with a job I've been sent out on if he thinks it will help whatever larger scheme he's cooking up." Now Manny looked almost offended. "Then I'll eat him and solve all our problems. You know the agency would side with you on this one, kid."

"I do." And was touched by it, though right now she didn't have much time to really appreciate the feeling. "But it'll be easier for both of us if Father doesn't force you into doing something that could get you in trouble later."

He tapped his claws on the desk, clearly not happy. "I could send Steve up there with you, if you wanted. I've sent two people out on the same project before, and he's more than happy to knock your dad around again."

"That's sweet, but I've surrounded myself with enough easy-to-swing weapons that I should be okay." Semi-true, and far less likely to make her blush than admitting that she already had bodyguards. James had apparently decided his real hobby was going to be saving her and Grace from their father, and Waverly seemed to be right behind him.

Honestly, she still couldn't quite believe it was happening. But she'd finally gotten smart enough to stop trying to argue with them about it.

Manny's brow lowered, clearly trying to find a way to offer help she would accept. "What about Grace? I know she's tough, but even you've gotta admit she's just not as vicious as you are. Want me to send somebody to keep an eye on her?"

Beauty blinked, more than a little startled by the offer. He really was worried about her. "She's fine, too. Waverly—" That was as far as she got before her brain processed what she'd been about to say, slapping her hard enough that she immediately cut off the rest of the sentence. As sweet as it had been to watch Waverly stare at her sister, she was definitely not ready to start pouring out the entire saga to her boss.

Manny, however, had clearly heard more than enough. "The butler?" His eyes widened slightly, than narrowed again in interest. "What does your sister have to do with the butler?"

"Nothing, I promise." Beauty held up her hands in a placating gesture, willing to do just about anything not to set off a Manny lecture. "She just came over to tell me what Father was up to. She and Waverly talked."

Manny just stared at her a minute, a completely unreadable expression on his face. "Talked?"

Beauty hesitated, faintly aware of an alarm bell going off in the back of her head. This was not the way she'd expected the conversation to go. "She's good with people."

He mulled this over, then flashed a grin that seemed to show each and every one of his teeth. For once, there wasn't any mistaking it for predatory intent—it was too full of sudden, almost surprised pleasure. "Interesting."

Somewhere in the back of Beauty's brain, pieces clicked into place. This time, it was her turn to narrow her eyes. "Why is that interesting?"

Manny's expression instantly snapped into wary defensiveness. "It's one of those random comments people make in key points of a conversation. I know the old man screwed you up, but you seemed pretty on top of your basic social skills."

Beauty waved the evasion away. "You looked happier than you did last time the agency's monthly profit report came in, so don't try to feed me the 'random comment' line. The fact that Grace and Waverly hit it off was the best news you'd heard all day, and you don't know my sister well enough to care that much about who she's talking to. So you must know Waverly." Her voice seemed to get sharper with every word she spoke, and she couldn't stop her hands from trying to clench at the table. "You set me up, Manny."

She'd told him all about her father and everything else two weeks after she'd first been hired, leaving out some of the most mortifying bits but still giving him more than enough information to have blackmail on her for life. Beauty had fully expected the confession to get her fired—even evil sorceresses would consider Noble too cruel a curse to voluntarily subject anyone to—but Manny had just shrugged and said that employees who had led interesting lives tended to be better at crisis management than others.

And then he'd lied to her, and dropped her in the middle of the one fairy tale she couldn't quite make herself walk away from. He was just as bad as her father.

As if he knew exactly what she was thinking, Manny held up a warning claw. "I didn't 'set you up,' kid, so stop with the accusations. And don't think I don't know you just compared me to your old man in your head. Do it again, and I'll set you up on permanent assignment with the agoraphobe so fast your head will snap."

Hearing the genuine anger in his voice, she made herself take a deep breath. "Manny, please. Just tell me everything."

He sighed, a thin stream of smoke escaping from his nostrils. "Waverly called in looking for someone to shake that kid of his out of his curse funk. I told him I'd see what I could do, but you were the only one stubborn and annoying enough to even be a possibility. He had no idea who'd be coming." He scowled briefly. "Though if I knew he'd slip up badly enough to think you were one of those thick-brained princesses, I would have at least warned the idiot."

She swallowed, lifting cramped hands from the table to wipe at her suddenly damp eyes. "I'm not sure if sending me was the smartest thing to do, Manny."

"Until I hear about someone dying over there, I'm sticking by it." His claws started tapping again. "You really want to burn through all your vacation and sick days for this?"

"No, but I'd like to keep getting paid as long as possible and the situation is pretty desperate right now." Hopefully her father would get scared off or lose interest by the end of the week, and if not, Grace had tossed out the last minute idea of faking a job offer from someplace extremely far away. Whatever was happening between her and James . . . she had no idea where in the world it was even going, let alone how long it would last.

For that matter, she wasn't sure James knew any better than she did. His words echoed through her mind. *We're very protective of our time together.*

For just a second there in the woods, it had sounded completely true . . .

"We'll work something out." Manny's voice was mild, but he was watching her with an evaluating expression that was almost worrying. "Until then, keep your head down. You're good at handling nasty surprises, but I didn't expect your dad to toss you such a big one."

Something in the way he said that made her suspicious. Her brow lowered. "Meaning you were expecting a nasty surprise from someone else?"

He hesitated, then shook his head. "No. I don't know enough about the situation to be sure I'm not giving you bad intel." Catching her expression, he tried to look supportive. "I do know it's not more than you can handle."

Beauty sighed. "Of course, even an inaccurate warning might help me handle whatever's coming a little more effectively."

"Or it'll start you looking in the wrong direction. I don't want to be responsible for your getting ambushed."

Her eyes narrowed. "If I die, I'm blaming you anyway."

"Like I said, don't worry. You're one of the scariest employees I've got." He grinned, meaning the words as a compliment. "I'm looking forward to seeing this James kid in person. I know you well enough to know it's not Noble who's rattled you this bad."

Beauty dropped her forehead into her hand. "Has anyone told you you're a bit of a sadist, Manny?"

"Only a bit?" His grin widened as he moved to break the connection. "Must be losing my touch."

Almost the exact moment the mirror went dark, Beauty heard the library door open and close behind her. She panicked for a second, thinking it might be James, then told herself she was being an idiot. She knew exactly who it was, and she'd gone and practically asked for it by letting herself get cornered someplace relatively private.

Beauty moved the mirror aside, closing her eyes as she dropped her head down onto her folded arms. There was no way she was going to avoid this conversation, so she might as well get it over with. "Thank you for waiting until the call stopped to yell at me."

Grace sighed, sounding just as long-suffering as Beauty had. "I'm not going to yell at you." She heard her sister move around to the other side of the table, taking a seat in one of the smaller chairs, and Beauty opened her eyes. Grace looked absolutely frazzled, and tired enough that she might fall asleep sitting up, but if you looked close you could also see a faint flush on her cheeks and a little bit of a sparkle in her eyes.

Beauty grinned. "Waverly's quite the conversationalist, isn't he?"

Grace couldn't stop the instant rush of pink that spread across her cheeks, and even though she got a nice warning glare started she couldn't quite get her blush to disappear completely. "No. You do *not* get to tease me after I saw that little dance you and James are doing. You're already calling him by an affectionate nickname!"

"That someone else came up with," Beauty tried to argue. "It's not that big a deal." Grace shot her a disbelieving look, and Beauty gave up. "Okay, it is. But it sort of slipped out one day after he'd told me about it. I just . . ."

Smiling, Grace held up a hand to stop her. "You don't have to explain it to me. By this point, I think I know you well enough to work it out on my own."

The fact that Grace was probably right mildly terrified Beauty. "For the sake of my sanity, please don't mention any of this to Waverly. The man's already dangerous enough without the extra ammunition."

Grace flashed her own grin. "I don't know. It depends on how persuasive he is."

That was enough to make Beauty lift her head, returning her sister's grin. "You *do* like him."

She opened her mouth as if thinking about making a protest, then closed it and waved a hand helplessly. "How can I not? He's intelligent, attractive, funny, thoughtful—" Seeing the sparkle in Beauty's eyes, she cut the list off immediately and lifted a warning finger. "But that is completely irrelevant until you tell me what in the world is going on. I've met the people you've done assignments for once or twice, and while they have always been perfectly pleasant to me, I've never had a single one offer to let me move in."

With a groan, Beauty dropped her chin back down onto her arms. "I had nothing to do with that part. Waverly wants to keep you around."

Grace leaned forward so she could look her sister in the eye. "And James, apparently, wants to keep *you* around enough that both men seem quite willing to marshal armies for you. However you think Waverly feels about me, he and James were clearly ready to destroy Father long before I showed up. They care about you."

Beauty stared hard at the tabletop, tracing patterns on the surface with her fingertip. "So they've adopted me," she said flippantly. "Apparently, Beast wasn't allowed to have a pet as a child."

She felt a sharp whack on her arm, and when Beauty met her sister's eyes again. Grace was glaring. "If I want to argue with a mouthy twelve-year-old, I'll go back to work and get paid for it. If you aren't attracted to the large furry man who seems to be trying extremely hard to keep you here, you need to tell me now so we can sneak out of the house without either of them knowing."

There was an exasperated seriousness in her sister's voice that suggested she was fully prepared to do just that, and that it was nowhere near the weirdest thing they'd had to do together over the course of their lives. Beauty couldn't quite stop the slightly desperate-sounding chuckle that bubbled up. "I want to kill him half the time, and the other half the time I'm annoyed that I don't want to anymore."

Grace gave her an amused look. "I do hope you're talking about James now."

"Yes." The laugh was easier this time. "Don't worry. I'm not thinking about stealing your man."

Ignoring the tease, Grace squeezed her sister's arm. "That's why you didn't tell me anything about James, isn't it?" Her voice was gentle. "You were afraid if you talked about him at all, I'd hear something you didn't want me to."

"What would I have said?" Beauty dropped her head onto her folded arms. "Hi, Grace, I've found my Beast Charming. I've known him less than a week, but I'm pretty sure I want to move in forever?"

There was a long, significant silence. "I suppose that was an option," Grace said finally, sounding like she was torn between surprise and a barely held-back laugh. "If I didn't know any better, I'd say that sounded suspiciously like the tru—" This time it was Beauty who held up a warning finger, and Grace kindly swallowed the rest of the sentence. Then she bent down enough to look her sister in the eye. "It's okay to like him, you know. I haven't spent much time with him, but I can't help but cheer on a guy who's both loyal and stubborn enough to keep you interested."

Something clenched in Beauty's chest, and she pushed herself up into a sitting position as the realization of what she'd really been worried about finally crystallized. "Grace, we don't even know if *he's* interested."

Her sister rolled her eyes. "Were you not paying attention during the entire conversation we just had?"

Beauty sighed, leaning back in the chair. Sometimes, it occurred to her that she thought way too much. "Sure, Beast wants to keep me around, but I'm also the first person he's talked to in about a year that wasn't either screaming in terror or trying to marry him. For all we know, he'd be just as happy with an old, married ogress as long as she was willing to argue with him."

The worst of it was, she knew exactly what that was like. The people at the temp agency had been the first she'd gotten to know without worrying about her father conning them or forcing her to move away in the middle of the night, and it had been like suddenly discovering an entire branch of the family no one had ever told her about. No, even better—she liked Manny and Steve far better than she liked most of the people she was related to.

And James liked her . . . probably the same way she liked Manny and Steve. He wouldn't care about rumors, and being attached to someone who was at least a friend was certainly safer than any other option that had come up.

It made sense.

"Even if you're right—and I'm not saying you are, because I've known the man less than an hour and don't have a lot to argue with—why are you accepting defeat just because he's not kneeling on the ground at your feet?" There was genuine worry mixed in with Grace's frustration, and not for the first time Beauty sympathized with her future nieces and nephews. Her sister had the sneakiest way of yelling at people that Beauty had ever seen. "You're cute, you're smart, and you're more interesting than any woman he's probably ever met. Who knows what will happen if you actually, oh, I don't know, let him know that you're interested in him?"

In most ways Grace was a sensible, clear-headed woman, except for the persistently delusional belief that her little sister was a wonderful person full of good qualities that someone else would finally recognize one day.

For just a second, Beauty let herself picture it. Actually explaining how she felt wouldn't work—even if she could trust herself to make sense, she'd die of embarrassment before she could get the words out. She'd have to figure out a way to just catch him by surprise and kiss him. Maybe she could sneak a chair over when he wasn't looking . . .

Beauty jerked herself out of the image, staring at her sister's all-too-knowing smile and fully aware that her cheeks were as pink as Grace's had been earlier. Her only option, clearly, was to desperately lunge for the last line of defense she thought had any chance of holding. "If I let Beast know I'm interested, you have to do the same thing with Waverly." If both of them suddenly lost their minds, at least she'd have the comfort of knowing they were about to do something stupid together.

Grace's eyes widened, but the fact that she looked flustered again was a good sign. "I've just barely met the man!"

"Which should make it easier, since it will be at least slightly less mortifying if he tells you no." Beauty leaned forward again, gaze still locked with her sister's. "And by all means, take as much time as you need to get to know him better—if you decide he's not as wonderful as he seems at first, you'll be much less interested in having them both stick around for the next forty or fifty years."

Beauty and Grace stared at each other for a long moment, exchanging looks that held an equal measure of challenge and sympathy. Then Grace sighed, dropping her own head so that it rested on her folded arms. "What do you think Father would say if he could see us right now?"

Beauty echoed her sister's move. "That we're the bane of his existence, and his entire life would have been different if he'd just had better looking, more likeable daughters."

Grace closed her eyes. "You should probably worry about the fact that you can quote him that closely."

Beauty sighed. "I do."

CHAPTER 12

How to Win an Argument

James nearly made the mirror calls himself.

Beauty was using his to talk to her boss, but he and Waverly had made calls on one another's mirrors when the situation had required it. Since the older man was currently downstairs in rapt conversation with Beauty's sister, James suspected that he wouldn't mind anything that would give him the excuse to stay there a little while longer.

Besides, it would give James the chance to do something. He had most of the same contacts Waverly did, at least in the area, and he enjoyed the thought of hurting Beauty's arrogant lump of lard father even when he was out of immediate punching range. He lifted his hand to Waverly's office door, ready to push it open. You didn't threaten what belonged to James Hightower, and if you did, he'd make absolutely certain you regretted ever being born . . .

His thoughts trailed off as he stared at his hand, resting on the office door. His huge, furry hand, tipped with claws.

What was he thinking?

James stepped away from the door as if it had burned him, staring down at his hands. He'd hidden himself in the house for almost a year, skulking through the woods like an animal. Now, suddenly, he was ready to call up old associates as if nothing had ever happened.

He'd felt almost . . . normal.

Behind him, he heard the sound of someone clearing his throat with exquisite care. "James?"

He jerked around to stare at Waverly, who had carefully schooled his own expression to hide even the slightest trace of emotion. He realized he was breathing hard, as if he'd just run, and he forced his body to slow back down into something approaching normal. "I . . ." No matter how dangerous it was, or how stupid, the only thing that would come out was the truth. "I'd planned on making some calls."

Not even Waverly could keep his eyes from widening a fraction, and the two men looked at each other for a brief, endless moment of silence. Then Waverly made a small invitational gesture in the direction of his office door. "You're welcome to still do so," he said quietly.

"No." But the denial wasn't quite as immediate as it should have been, and for a second he actually found himself thinking about why he'd said no. He realized he didn't care whether his former business associates would be afraid of him—they had been before the teeth and claws, and it had only ever worked to his advantage—but he couldn't stand the chance of seeing pity. His biggest failure was written all over his face.

To Beauty, however, it never seemed to matter. There was no pity in her eyes, or fear, or even calculation at how he could best be used to further her own ends. Sure, she'd looked like she wanted to kill him more than once, but either he'd enjoyed getting her that mad at him or was too furious at her to care. And when she laughed, it made him ridiculously pleased with the universe as a whole.

Even though he still looked exactly the same, she made him feel like he'd never been cursed at all. No wonder he wanted to keep her.

The realization staggered him enough that he nearly missed

when Waverly started talking again. "If you were intending to follow through with your plan to alert parties who might be interested in Noble's whereabouts, many of the relevant mirror codes remain the same as when you dialed them last." Waverly's expression had eased, and there was a deep understanding in his eyes. "Those few that have changed are in the bottom right-hand drawer of my desk."

James shook his head. "I'll let you do it." He hesitated, knowing he owed Waverly more than that. "I'm . . . not as ready as I thought I was."

Waverly just looked at him for another minute, then nodded. "Fair enough," he said quietly. "I'll do it later this evening, when I send Beauty's employer the job completion report."

James let out a long breath, grateful for the chance to focus on practical matters. "But she's staying, right?"

The corners of Waverly's mouth quirked upward. "Yes. I believe both she and her sister intend to stay for at least the immediate future, though at some point I believe I will have to make arrangements for Grace to resume her teaching duties."

Grace hadn't been afraid of him either, or horrified, even though Beauty hadn't told her that he'd even existed. And when her sister *had* found out, Beauty hadn't tried to explain him away at all. "How far away is the school?" James asked, wanting to make it clear he'd be happy if both women stayed on indefinitely. Having family here would make Beauty less interested in leaving, and anyone capable of putting that entranced look on Waverly's face was worth expending any number of resources for. "If it's too far to commute by carriage, we can see if that wyvern service is still in business."

There was another flash of surprise in Waverly's eyes, startled out of him quickly enough he hadn't even made an attempt to hide it. Seeing it, James grinned. "Don't tell me that's not what you were thinking. I'm actually wondering how you managed to peel yourself away from Grace's side long enough to come up here at all."

Waverly lifted an eyebrow, his expression a little too deliberately dry to not be hiding other emotions. "She needed to speak to her sister, presumably in a private enough setting where neither they nor we would be caused mortal embarrassment."

He refused to let himself wonder what they were talking about. Whatever it was, it didn't matter as long as Beauty didn't go anywhere. "Intelligent, good-looking, and discreet." James's grin widened. "No wonder she's hooked you so quickly."

A muscle in Waverly's jaw twitched, though James knew that if he pointed it out the older man would insist he'd only imagined it. The challenging light that leapt into his eyes a moment later, however, was much harder to dispute. "Perhaps I'm simply being duly influenced by the romance I've seen blooming around me these last few days."

James narrowed his eyes at the older man. "It's not a romance."

Waverly's expression was serene. "And I was simply being hospitable to Grace."

Stalemate. A wise man would probably have backed down and let them both pretend they didn't want more than friendship from the Tremain sisters, but that would only leave the situation to spring back up at him when he least expected it. "Fine," he growled. "But don't tell Beauty."

Waverly sighed. "And what other explanation are you planning to give her for your tendency to panic every time she says anything that might be construed as an attempt to leave?"

The fact that he might possibly have had a point only made James more stubborn. "We're helping her and Grace with their father. It's easier for us to protect them here than wherever it is they live."

"A valid excuse that will last for another few weeks, perhaps, but I will be horrified at all four of us if we haven't managed to sufficiently neutralize her father by then. What will your explanation be then?"

James growled, knowing he didn't have a good answer. "I'll think of something."

Waverly raised an eyebrow. "That she'll believe?"

He wasn't about to answer that one. "So what's your suggestion? Let her leave when she realizes it's a relief not to argue with me all the time, handle it like a mature, rational person, and then never see her again?"

The corner of Waverly's mouth quirked upward again. "Unless I've misinterpreted her dramatically, I believe Beauty would be disappointed if she *didn't* get to argue frequently with someone."

James narrowed his eyes. "That doesn't mean she'd come back, Waverly."

Waverly's expression gentled. "I'm not saying you shouldn't try to keep her from leaving, James," he said quietly. "I'm simply saying that the simplest way to do that is to be honest with her about the real reason you want her to stay."

James pictured himself walking up to Beauty. *Your laugh makes me happy.* No, that definitely wasn't going to work. "So does that mean you're going to follow your own brilliant advice when Grace wonders why her sister's former boss invited her to spend the week?"

Waverly froze for a split second, as if realizing that James's admission had cut off his own options for protest. Then his expression eased into something like resigned acceptance, and he took a deep breath. "Yes. Eventually." He paused. "As soon as I figure out a sufficiently reasonable way to explain the situation."

James scowled at him. "Which we won't need to do until their father's been taken care of."

"Fine. But if Beauty decides you're attempting to hold her prisoner in the interim, I'm leaving you to deal with the consequences."

"If she honestly thought I was holding her prisoner, she'd just hit me with something and head for the nearest exit."

Waverly considered this, then tilted his head in acknowledgement. "True. But perhaps a bouquet of flowers would ease the burden on any easily removable wall ornaments."

James tried to hold the glare, but he couldn't stop his chest from clenching as the truth of what Waverly was saying sank in. She made him feel like a person again, but what if he didn't have enough to give her in return? "What if she leaves me anyway?"

"Anything's possible." Waverly's expression was gentle as he patted James's shoulder. "But she certainly hasn't been trying very hard."

JAMES CAUGHT GRACE as she was leaving the library, and the excited and mildly worried look on her face made him wonder all over again what she and Beauty had talked about. Then she looked both directions down the hallway, as if searching for someone, and he suddenly realized whom she had *really* been thinking about.

"Waverly's in the kitchen getting started on dinner," James said quietly, stepping out into the light to make sure he wasn't accidentally lurking. "I'm sure he'd be happy to have some company."

Grace blinked, a blush spreading across her cheeks. Well, it was good to know that Waverly affected her just as much as she seemed to affect Waverly. "I wouldn't want to bother him."

"Believe me, you won't be bothering him." James smiled, wanting to put her at ease. He knew how—even in the business world, you had to use the carrot occasionally—but he wanted Grace to feel at ease simply because she deserved it. Anyone did who knew how to take care of family the way she did. "He usually cooks alone, but that's only because I have a nasty tendency to burn water when left to my own devices."

Grace smiled back. "Oddly enough, Beauty has the same problem."

James nodded with amused solemnity. "There's a cake deep in the compost pile out back that is the sad proof of both of our failings."

Grace laughed. "If you're looking for Beauty, she's still in the library." She hesitated, then stepped forward to lightly touch James on the arm. "Thank you for helping her with Father," she said softly. "Neither of us is really used to having backup."

She turned and headed down the hallway toward Waverly, and James watched her go for a moment before slipping into the library.

Beauty was still sitting at the central table with the mirror pushed to the side, her chin resting on her folded arms. When James closed the door behind him, she lifted her head and turned around. "Grace, I told you I'll be down in a minute. Go flirt with Waverly until I . . ." The words cut off when she met James's eyes, and her expression went blank for a split second before shooting him that grin he'd gotten far too fond of. "I take it you're giving them a little alone time, too?"

He grinned back. "Great minds think alike." He headed toward the only chair in the library big enough to let him sit properly—his grandmother had had size issues to rival those of most men—and sat down. Beauty, his mind helpfully pointed out, had chosen the seat right next to it. "So . . . meeting your sister was interesting."

Embarrassment flashed across Beauty's face, and she leaned back slightly as she scrubbed a hand across her face. "Sorry about that," she said tiredly, dropping her hand back down on the table. "And I'm sorry I didn't tell her about you. I swear, the only reason I didn't is because I didn't know how to explain you. She's a worrier, and when I can't finish too many sentences in a row it gives her the impression that I'm in over my head."

James shifted his hand over so that it was closer to hers, almost but not quite touching. "So I rob you of the power of speech," he teased, keeping his voice light even as he explained to himself what a simple thing it would be to reach over and take her hand. Then his mind drifted to a time he'd once closed a deal with the elves, whose interpersonal protocol was so cutthroat you could get yourself killed by touching your ear at the wrong moment. Moving his hand six inches further to the right would be nothing in comparison . . .

Beauty flushed, distracting him from what was turning out to be a ridiculously long pep talk, but she recovered enough to give him an amused look. "Okay, I'll admit it. Exasperation tends to do that to me." There was laughter in her voice as she said it, making his chest warm, and before he had the chance to think about it or stop himself he lifted a hand to brush an errant lock of hair away from her face.

She went absolutely still as the pads of his fingers touched her skin, and for a terrible second he was afraid he'd made a mistake. But it was a breathless stillness, not a shocked or horrified one. The kind of stillness a predator used when he was being careful not to scare someone off.

His own lungs were having a little trouble working as their eyes locked, and though he didn't dare try and interpret anything he saw in hers he let his fingers finish their long, slow path across Beauty's forehead. "So," he asked softly, laying his hand back on the table. "Did everything go okay with your boss?" She looked confused for a moment, as if she'd forgotten what they had been talking about. James's chest warmed at the thought that he could distract her, too. "The mirror call?"

Understanding dawned in Beauty's eyes, immediately followed by amused resignation. "I'm officially on vacation as soon as Waverly turns in the right forms." Her expression softened as she hesitantly laid her hand on top of James's, her fingers gently stroking the shorter fur along his knuckles. "Since I'm now your houseguest, that probably means it's your turn to keep me entertained."

A witty comeback would have been easier if she weren't touching him and making little sparks of magic shoot through her fingertips and all the way up his arm. "Just don't go anywhere, and I'll keep you entertained as long as you want."

She smiled, then the humor vanishing to be replaced by something much more fragile. "You know, Beast, we could still be friends even if I left. You don't have to keep doing things for me."

Panic hit, low and fierce, and he felt his claws dig into the table-top just a little before he made himself take a deep breath and reign the emotion back in. "If you want to go, you can," James said carefully, not quite able to keep the growl out of the words. *"After* we've taken care of your father."

Beauty made a small, helpless sound. "I'm not saying I want to go, but has it ever occurred to you that you're going to want to get on with your life at some point? A permanent houseguest tends to put a damper on your options."

The words didn't make sense, but that might have been because most of his brain was focused on not shouting at her. No matter what Waverly thought, or James hoped, Beauty clearly didn't see herself as one of those options. "How many choices do you really think are out there for a monster?"

Beauty's eyes narrowed as her grip on his hand tightened. "Stop calling yourself that! Sure, you don't look very human anymore, but neither do half of Grace's students and some of my favorite co-workers. And believe me, stacked up against the average short, pale, skinny-shouldered guy out there you would take home the prize every time."

It was something a friend would say if he or she were being nice, and from anyone else it wouldn't leave a raw, scraped feeling inside his chest. He didn't want Beauty to just be nice to him. "Yet somehow," he growled, "looking at me makes you think of buying your co-worker *pants.*"

Her brow furrowed, clearly having no idea what he was talking about. When memory hit a moment later, frustration chased the brief moment of embarrassment right off her face. "What else was I supposed to say? 'I'm sorry I wasn't paying attention to the argument, but the sight of your gorgeous chest muscles moving under all that silky fur temporarily robbed me of the ability to form a coherent thought?' If you would put on a shirt occasionally it wouldn't have come up!"

This time, it was James's turn to be stunned. "Really?"

"No, I'm making up *extremely* embarrassing lies just for my own amusement." Letting go of his hand, she leaned back in her own chair with a huff, her face flaming. "And while we're at it, you were never as scary as you thought you were. Even when I wanted to kill you, I never wanted to be more than shouting distance away from your extremely annoying self. Compared to you, the rest of the world is boring."

Slowly, James felt himself start to smile. "At the risk of repeating myself . . . really?"

Beauty closed her eyes before she could see his expression. "Yes. Really." Slowly, she tilted her head back so that it rested against the side of the chair. "And now if you don't mind, I'd like a little privacy to kill myself before the embarrassment finishes me off first." She paused, expression still stoic. "And if you see Grace, tell her she gives terrible advice."

James just looked at her for a long moment, grinning like an idiot. Then he scooted his chair out and around, going through the logistics in his head as he swung Beauty's chair around so that it faced his. Picking her up might get him hit, but looming over Beauty would leave her completely without options . . .

She still didn't open her eyes, but her voice was suddenly more fragile than it had been. "Don't you dare be nice to me right now."

James's grin widened. "Wasn't planning on it." Then he leaned over the distance between them to capture her mouth in a quick, toe-tingling kiss. It wasn't as deep as he would have liked—he'd never kissed with fangs before—but the rush of heat hit him like a punch as Beauty's hands lifted to clutch at the fur on his chest.

When he pulled away, she was staring at him wide-eyed. Happily noting that she hadn't let go of him yet, he leaned forward again so that his lips were against her ear. "You make the rest of the world seem boring, too," he whispered, then gently took her hands in his and laid them back on her lap. "And your eyes make me want to write really bad poetry."

She swallowed as he straightened. "Well," she said finally, voice unsteady. "Maybe the embarrassment won't kill me after all."

He grinned again, dropping another kiss on the top of Beauty's head before heading out the door. Clearly, he had some work to do. "That's good to hear."

CHAPTER 13

Best-Case Scenario

By this point in her life, Beauty had gotten pretty good at preparing for disaster. Growing up with her father had left her expecting every situation she was in to dissolve into a complete mess. By the time she'd hit adulthood she automatically predicted the worst and focused her energy on trying to survive it. Other people's disasters had come as a refreshing surprise, which made her good at her job but had left her out of practice dealing with her own crises.

Of course, it could also have been the fact that her Beast refused to turn into a disaster. A thousand things could have gone wrong since she'd gotten here, and she'd tensed up waiting for the crash every time. Only it never came, not even when her father had shown up and shared his special talent for wrecking his daughters' lives. Waiting for James to decide she wasn't worth the trouble was killing her, and the fact that she'd almost started to believe it wasn't going to happen had scared her to death. Telling him everything had almost been a relief—there were worse ways for things to collapse than a painfully awkward conversation.

Then he'd kissed her and whispered ridiculously romantic

nonsense in her ear, and suddenly the world was a completely different place than it had been Beauty's entire life.

And she didn't have the slightest idea what she was doing.

EVEN AFTER JAMES was out of sight Beauty stared at the doorway, eyes wide and breathing like she'd just chased a centaur. He'd sauntered as he walked away, curse him, but since her lips were still tingling she didn't really have any room to argue.

She closed her eyes, hands twitching to do something stupid like reach up and touch her mouth. James had kissed her, and right now the only thing she knew for certain was that she very much wanted him to kiss her again.

Which wasn't going to happen if she just kept sitting there like an idiot.

Slowly, she stood up, her expression turning speculative. Her father's "training" once again proved spectacularly unhelpful—he'd never really told her what to do after the first kiss, though she couldn't say whether that was because he didn't know or because he never thought she'd get that far. She'd had an assignment once in which she made sure a frog who kept pretending to be cursed went to his court-appointed therapy session, though his advice hadn't been useful, either—he tended to get first kisses and then restraining orders. Of course, she could just grab James and kiss him again—she was pretty sure he'd appreciate the sentiment, even if her technique needed work. But she'd missed her chance when he was leaning over her chair within easy reach, and if she chased after him she'd probably have to find another chair to stand on. Though it would be fun convincing him to stand still . . .

Beauty grinned, hurrying into the hallway as she tried to listen for where James had gone. There were enough chairs, tables and desks scattered throughout the house that she could improvise pretty much anywhere, though if she saw any sign of Waverly's little wind helpers she was definitely going to suggest a change of location.

She stopped, realizing that the faint sounds of conversation coming from the kitchen now had three voices instead of two. Apparently, James had decided that what he needed right now was as many witnesses as possible.

That *sneak*.

Frustrated and more amused than she probably should have been, Beauty took a deep breath and squared her shoulders. With her best troublemaking smile firmly in place, she strode breezily into the kitchen. "No matter what he tells you," she said lightly, "Don't let Beast touch anything you're baking. We don't want to burn the building down."

Waverly and Grace immediately turned to look at her, amusement and a great deal of speculation in their eyes. James, on the other hand, swallowed a chuckle as he deliberately avoided meeting her gaze. Beauty just widened her smile at all of them, shooting James a glare she knew he'd feel even if he couldn't see.

After a moment, Waverly smiled slightly. "Believe me, I learned long ago not to let James anywhere near baked goods." He lifted an eyebrow that somehow managed to be directed at both her and James, and it was Grace's turn to swallow the chuckle. "And neither of you hide your baking disasters as well as you think you do."

James turned back to face everyone, his expression all innocence. "Who says we were hiding it? We were just trying to clean up after ourselves."

"Of course he was," Beauty said dryly, folding her arms across her chest. "Because Beast would never do *anything* for the sole purpose of driving someone insane, would he?"

James finally met her eyes, a question in there somewhere beneath the humor, and she was pretty sure he could see the amusement in her own eyes as she glared back at him. Grace, long used to being the voice of reason, stepped between them and handed her sister a plate of ham. "Beauty, could you take this to the table, please?"

"I'll get that," James cut in, swooping in and grabbing the plate before Beauty could touch it. She briefly considered trying to snatch it back out of his hands, wanting to protest on principle, but then he made sure to brush deliberately close as he went by. He also paused just long enough to lean over and press a kiss against her hair. "You can kill me later," he murmured, just before he disappeared out the door to the dining room.

The rush of affection she felt, buoyed by that same disorienting happiness, managed to pretty much collapse any of Beauty's remaining frustration. Knowing everything she felt was probably all over her face, she took a deep breath and turned to face the two very interested people who were now looking at her with undisguised questions in their eyes.

Beauty was well aware they were both going to have to be told at some point. She also knew both of them were good enough to have the truth out of her in about five seconds with minimal effort. Which meant that James, who knew this as well as she did, was probably hiding again.

Feeling the growl slip out, she pushed open the door and went after him. Waverly and Grace were both perfectly capable of eavesdropping, and at least then she wouldn't have to repeat herself.

He was waiting for her, hands up in the classic "cease and desist" gesture. "When I said you could kill me later, I actually meant after I got the chance to explain myself," he said quickly, watching her with a wariness that suggested he expected her to pick up a particularly pointy fork at any moment. "Also, let me remind you Waverly will get extremely annoyed if you get blood on the tablecloth."

Beauty wanted to laugh, but she tamped it down firmly and narrowed her eyes at him. If she let herself be charmed this easily, there was no chance she'd get a straight answer out of the man. "Once I told him your latest plan to drive me insane, I'm sure he'd forgive me. Who in their right mind kisses a girl senseless, then goes and hides out with *relatives* before she can form a coherent thought?" She threw her hands up in the air, not entirely sure whether she wanted to kiss him or hit him. Both, probably. "Because if this is part of some long, convoluted plan you have in mind, let me tell you right now at least one of us won't survive it."

She felt self-doubt nip at her, just like it always did, but it wasn't enough to make her think he was actually regretting the kiss. If nothing else, he'd have been brooding rather than trying not to laugh.

He moved closer, catching her hands in his before she could even consider doing something sensible like hitting him. "I didn't want to be there if you decided the kiss was a terrible idea," he said carefully, still looking at her with that searching expression. Suddenly, Beauty realized potential violence wasn't what he'd been worried about. "I figured if we had an audience, I could tell by your expression whether or not you were planning on breaking my heart. It wouldn't make things any easier, but then at least I wouldn't have to hear it out loud."

Beauty just stared at him for a second, then blinked slowly. "That actually makes sense," she said after a moment, a little stunned someone other than Grace understood her enough to think all that through. Then she grinned. "So, what is my expression telling you now?"

He grinned back, still holding onto her hands. "It's hard to tell. You're a little too far away for me to really study all the nuances."

She nodded, closing the little bit of distance left between them. Though grabbing a chair would probably be considered presumptuous, she was pretty sure they would manage. "Is this close enough?"

His eyes lit as his mouth curved upward into a slow, wonderful smile. "Almost," he murmured, leaning towards her.

He had to take a step back to get the angle for the kiss exactly right, but the moment their lips touched she felt the same spark of lightning she had back in the library. She slid her hands out from his so she could hold onto his shoulders, wanting to hold on as long as she could, but after a moment of precarious balancing he broke the kiss with an almost growl. "I need to start carrying around a chair," he muttered.

Not quite able to stop the laugh, she hooked a nearby chair with her leg and dragged it towards them. Without further ado he picked her up and set her on the seat, then immediately resumed the kiss that had been so rudely interrupted. Without the height difference to worry about her arms wrapped all the way around his neck, eliminating the last little bit of distance between them, and Beauty closed her eyes and let herself get lost in the unfamiliar rush of sheer happiness that flooded through her. Sure, you had to stay just aware enough to dodge the fangs, but the risk was definitely worth it . . .

They broke the kiss at the sound of discreet knocking behind them, turning around to see Waverly and Grace standing in the doorway into the kitchen. Waverly's hand was still lifted, knuckle resting against the side of the door, and the corners of his mouth were quirked upward. "As pleased as we are to see the two of you behaving sensibly for once, I'm afraid dinner is cooling even as we speak."

"If you'd like, Waverly and I can have a quiet meal in the kitchen while the two of you finish up," Grace added, smiling widely. "We might have started already and just left you to it, but . . ."

Waverly shot an amused look of warning, and there was a teasing light in Grace's eyes as she swallowed the rest of the sentence. Then he cleared his throat, moving to stand in front of her as he added his own ending. "But it seemed impolite to deny you both at least the option of participating in the meal."

Grace leaned forward over the shoulder. "Also, he was worried about the ham you'd already taken out." Her voice had a conspiratorial edge. "He didn't want to leave it out there all alone in the cold."

Waverly glanced over at her again, but there was an amused light in his eyes as he cleared his throat again. "The glaze is very delicate."

Beauty, who had shifted around in James's arms to get a better look at the show, looked over at James. "Should we be embarrassed, or see if we can tease Waverly enough to actually make him blush?

Waverly made a polite, disbelieving noise. "My dear, I do not blush. And what you should feel is astonishment that neither of you were intelligent enough to do this a week ago. Anyone with eyes or even an occasionally functioning brain could see you had feelings for each other. Simply admitting that would have saved us all a considerable amount of grief."

James grinned over at Beauty. "We can't tease him now. I'm too weighed down with guilt over the fact that we're apparently both blind idiots."

Beauty just looked at him for a moment in surprise, then laughed. "If I'd known kissing you would make you this easygoing, I would have done it days ago."

"See?" James pressed a kiss against her cheek as he helped her off the chair. Even when her feet were securely on the floor, however, he didn't let go of her. "Blind idiots."

"That's okay," Grace said easily, sliding out from behind Waverly and walking the basket of rolls she'd been holding over to the table. "Both of you have been managing pretty well so far."

Beauty grinned up at James. "We have, haven't we?" Squeezing his hands, she slid out of his arms to go help bring the food to the table. "Seeing how well it's worked with Beast, you might want to try kissing Waverly." As she passed by Waverly, she nudged him with her hip. "He could probably do with being a little more easygoing."

She couldn't see her sister blush, but James's sudden laugh from the dining room was just as enjoyable. Waverly turned back to the kitchen to pick up the potatoes, refusing to say a word but shooting her a remarkably effective death glare as he went by, and Beauty laughed again as she picked up the vegetables and followed him out into the dining room.

Over Waverly's shoulder, James met her eyes. "For the record, it turns out Waverly was wrong about never blushing." He grinned when Waverly shot him a death glare that matched the one he'd given her. She didn't really believe Waverly had blushed—probably only Grace could make him do that, if it was even physically possible—but she wasn't about to argue with James over a little thing like reality. "And your sister can hit surprisingly hard."

"She can, can't she?" Beauty set the vegetables on the table, then jumped up on the chair so she could be the right height to press a kiss against his cheek. "It's kind of terrifying."

"If you want to see how terrifying I can be, try dating my little sister," Grace said sweetly, giving them both her "Queen Teacher" glare as Waverly finished some minute adjustments to the table and pulled out a seat for her.

Beauty hopped down from the chair, giving Grace a "What are you doing?" look that she hoped was more discreet but just as effective as saying either "When was the last time I dated anyone?" or "I'm begging you not to mention Brian" out loud. James, however, just smiled a predatory smile and pulled out a chair the rest of the way for Beauty. "Luckily, I'm feeling particularly brave at the moment."

Grace tried to hold the glare for another while, then lifted a hand to hold back the chuckle. "I'm sorry." She turned to Waverly as he sat down next to her. "That was a good response."

Waverly sighed dramatically. "Thankfully, I have years of practice at torturing the poor boy." He gave them both a long, pointed look. "And if James and Beauty aren't wise enough to exercise some restraint in certain areas, I'm afraid I'll be forced to decimate them verbally."

Knowing exactly what he meant, Beauty and James glanced at each other before holding up their hands in acquiescence. "Okay, okay, we're sorry." Beauty said.

"We promise to restrain ourselves from repeatedly pointing out how perfect the two of you would be for each other," James added.

"Oh, I'm sure we'll all be busy enough watching the two of you try to sort everything out," Waverly said dryly.

Grace smiled as she looked at James. "You can keep up with her and give very good responses to pop quizzes, but you should know that I really will kill you if you hurt my sister. I may look nice, but after years with Beauty I have a few tricks up my sleeve."

Beauty was saved from having to make any kind of response to this when a gust of wind suddenly rushed past her legs. She ducked her head underneath the table as she watched it complete the circle of everyone's legs. When it hit Grace, her eyes widened and she glanced at Waverly. "I take it that's not a draft?"

"They're lesser air elementals," he explained, instantly sharing more information about them than Beauty had been able to get out of him since she'd gotten here. "The djinn keep them as pets, and they're more discreet and informative than the chime spell most people have on their mirrors." He turned to Beauty. "Unless James has been using his mirror again, I believe you have a call."

Beauty froze a moment, surprised, and James looked over at her with concern in his eyes. Touched, she gave his arm a squeeze as she stood up. "Just make sure to save me some," she murmured, then headed upstairs to her room.

The mirror was tucked away on a high shelf, placed there to keep it safe from the normal wear-and-tear of her daily life. The chair was still in place from the last time she'd put it away—seriously, she needed to figure out a way to put a resize enchantment on one and just carry it around with her—and she hopped onto it and gently brought the mirror back down. The mist swirled, which meant the wind was right about a call coming in. She headed out the door, not wanting whoever it was to have to stare at the clutter of her borrowed bedroom.

After only a few steps, though, Beauty hesitated. With Grace here, Manny was the only person she knew who had the number, and they'd pretty much covered anything they might have needed to conceivably talk about a few hours ago. If he was getting twitchy about the form already, he would have contacted Waverly directly.

She hoped her father hadn't somehow gotten the sequence for this mirror . . .

Taking a deep breath, she pushed the "accept" icon on the glass near the mirror's edge. The mist began to thin out just enough for Beauty to make out the vague, indistinct features of someone who might have been a woman, then the mirror suddenly snapped back into its normal reflective state.

Beauty stared at the clear glass, pretty sure she'd just been hung up on. It could have been a wrong number, but it also might've been the first sign of the trouble Manny had mentioned. There had been something weird about the disconnected call, as if the person on the other side had stayed on just long enough to see all he or she needed to . . .

No. She shook her head against the thought, refusing to let herself start thinking up worst-case scenarios again. It was probably nothing.

And even if she was wrong, there wasn't much she could do about it now.

Deliberately pushing the worry aside, Beauty returned the mirror to its spot on the shelf and headed back down to the dining room. Her dinner was getting cold, and she was missing out on some good conversation.

CHAPTER 14

Gargoyles, Flirting, and Lawyers, Oh, My

If happy little songbirds showed up, he'd have had to chase them away on principle.

The thought made James grin as he sat perched on the roof the following morning, dangerously tempted to think poetic things about the sunrise. It felt a little odd to be up here when he wasn't brooding—though that was best done at night—but at the moment it would take real effort to even be annoyed.

In fact, part of the reason he'd come up here was to hide in case he decided to do something ridiculous, like break into song. Beauty might be astonishingly willing to kiss him on a regular basis, but even the bravest souls fled in terror when he tried to hit a high note.

Apparently, the poets hadn't lied when it came to this whole romance thing. Oddly enough, that thought almost managed to be sobering. He'd thought he was in love with Juliana, but one (okay, five) kisses from Beauty and he felt cheerful enough to frighten himself. If this euphoria collapsed, how hard would he hit bottom?

Worse, he wasn't sure what the next step should be. Juliana had essentially moved herself into the position of his significant other, and before that, dating had fallen somewhere below polishing the silverware on his list of life priorities. How were you supposed to properly court someone when you weren't comfortable leaving the house? Could you consider what they'd already been doing as proper dates, or would he have to figure out how to up his game?

And, if his curse was really as unbreakable as he'd always thought, what came next? She seemed fine with how he looked, but he had no idea how much Waverly had told her about the curse. What if she—

"If you're planning on dropping another statue after everything that happened yesterday, I should warn you I'm going to be kind of offended. I will also, of course, have to make you sorry."

James's grin returned at the sound of Beauty's voice, and he leaned forward enough to see her head poking out of the window just beneath him. "No statues, I promise. Though if you ever want to experience tossing one off the roof yourself, just say the word and I'll sneak both you and the trollish goddess of cleaning products up here whenever you want."

Beauty considered this, then her brow furrowed. "I didn't know there was a trollish goddess of cleaning products."

"There isn't, except in the imagination of one of my great-great-uncles. He was obsessed with soap, and he wanted to create a worthy deity for it."

She just looked at him for a moment. "I can never tell whether you're serious or not." She leaned a little further out of the window, eyeing the roof with a certain amount of speculation. "Could you really get me up there without both of us falling to our deaths?"

James considered a few possible options he might use to get her safely up on the roof with him. Then he slid off the edge of the roof, making her shriek and reach for him before he grabbed the edge and swung in through the window just like he usually did.

When he got his feet on the ground, Beauty whacked him on the arm. "Do you flirt with death like that every time you get off the roof?" she asked exasperatedly, narrowing her eyes at him. "Because if you do, I'm pretty sure I didn't want to know that."

"I've been sneaking up and down from the roof since I was

eight," he reassured her, oddly charmed by the thought of her worrying about him. "I was ten the last time I came anywhere close to falling, and even then the worst that happened was I spent three hours hanging from a gargoyle."

He hadn't mentioned the trial and error it had taken to figure out how to get back up and down from the roof after the curse. James didn't want to even think about that, not when he had Beauty to focus on instead.

She narrowed her eyes at him, but he could see her mouth twitch. "Funny."

He put on his best innocent expression. "I'm completely serious. When night hit, the gargoyle thankfully woke up and helped me get inside. He retired up in the mountains when I was sixteen, but every now and then I'll still send a dead pigeon his way as a thank you."

Beauty fought it for a few more seconds, but then she shook her head as the laugh won out. It warmed him better than the sunlight. "Next you'll be telling me that you plan on carrying me up to the roof the same way that poor, long-suffering gargoyle carried you down." His only response was to grin at her, and after a few seconds the laughter faded as she stared at him with wide eyes. "Seriously?"

"Why not? Piggyback's the easiest and safest way to get both of us up there, at least without wings or major injury for one of us." He leaned his shoulder against the windowsill, enjoying how flustered she looked. "You just wrap your arms around my neck, and I'll take care of everything else."

She blushed just a little, which pleased him immensely, then rallied and narrowed her eyes at him again. "You can't—" The words cut off as she caught sight of something outside the window. Brow furrowing, she moved to get a better look at the backyard spread out beneath them.

For a moment, James just watched her, waiting for any sign of worry or confusion. "Has your father suddenly made another appearance?"

"No, Waverly and Grace have." She smiled, waving him closer so he could get the same view she had. "I can't make out what they're saying, but she just slid her arm through his and is about thirty seconds away from leaning her head on his shoulder."

James moved to stand next to Beauty, not needing to lean forward like she did to see Waverly and Grace taking what appeared to be a tour of the back yard. If he concentrated a little harder, he could hear Waverly pointing out the names of the various plants and sharing stories from James's teenage years that in his opinion were being wildly embellished. They made Grace laugh, however, and since that was clearly the intent James decided he could condone the behavior.

Beauty wedged herself in a little bit closer, her attention suddenly on him instead of on the scene below. "You can hear them, can't you?" she asked, the tone in her voice suggesting she wouldn't believe him if he tried to deny it. "Come on, Beast. You've got to tell me what they're saying."

James shifted an arm so it was around Beauty instead of just behind her. "Waverly apparently thinks that sharing embarrassing stories about me is the quickest way to Grace's heart, and no, I'm not telling you any details."

She grinned up at him. "Then you can't use any embarrassing stories you overhear Grace telling Waverly about me. It's not as much fun if we're not evenly armed."

"If your sister were actually telling him any, that might be something for me to worry about," James grumbled. "She's too busy enjoying what a terror I apparently was in order to provide any useful commentary."

"*Apparently?*" Beauty echoed with a disbelieving laugh, then patted his hand consolingly. "Don't feel bad. I'm sure I was just as frustrating as you were, but compared to my father, even battle orcs look sweet and easy to get along with."

James listened to the conversation for another moment, then shook his head. "Why isn't he following his own advice? I know for a fact that he's hoping to move Grace in on a permanent basis, but the closest he's come to even hinting in that direction is asking about her commute." He sighed. "Grace doesn't happen to be a mind reader, does she? Because that would be really helpful right about now."

Beauty looked up at him in amused disbelief. "You do remember it took a while for either of us to make a move, don't you? Grace has only been here for a day."

"Yeah, but he's supposed to be smarter than I am." Deciding he was getting too impatient with subtlety, he gave in and wrapped his arm around Beauty's waist. "Besides, he's not seven feet tall and furry."

"Actually, I think that would probably be harder on Waverly," Beauty said easily. "You clearly enjoy walking around without a shirt on, but I don't think Waverly would know what to do if he didn't have his suits."

James didn't say anything, trying to fight off the thought that now would be the perfect time to bring up the sticky fact that the curse seemed unbreakable. It might even work out well—she'd already kissed him looking like this, and hadn't even brought up what he'd looked like before the curse since they'd been in the attic together.

And if she did have a problem with it, at least he'd find out what it was before he fell for her any harder . . .

He only took a small step back, but it was enough to make Beauty turn around and look at him with a question in her eyes. Before the newly besotted parts of his brain could muzzle him back into silence, James took a deep breath. "So . . . how much has Waverly told you about the curse?"

She just stared at him a moment, as if she couldn't quite understand the question, then squeezed her eyes shut. "I'd forgotten about that part," she said softly.

This time, it was his turn to stare at her. Somehow, that was the last response he'd expected. "You're trying to tell me you'd forgotten I'm seven feet tall and furry?"

Well, *he'd* forgotten, hadn't he? Not for very long, but . . .

Beauty opened her eyes to shoot him a disgusted look. "Of course I remember you're huge and furry. Even an old, blind beggar woman would know how tall you were the first time you got mad and started *looming.*" She stopped, shoulders sagging as her eyes slid away from his. "But I did forget about your malicious ex-girlfriend, and just because you have a tendency to chase off every woman who gets within fifty feet of your house doesn't necessarily mean you don't have a secret fantasy of someone swooping in and breaking the curse for you."

She sat back against the windowsill. "And you've only been cursed a year. For the record, that kind of turnaround time only happens when the cursee's parents work it out with the evil sorceress in advance. They tell everyone the curse can only be broken by True Love's Kiss, but in reality it's set to unravel at a 'Gee, you're really hot' kiss." She sighed, closing her eyes again. "Not that you wanted to know that."

James closed the small amount of distance between them, leaning forward to place a gentle kiss on top of Beauty's head. "What I was going to say is that my curse is such a mess of badly stitched-together parts that we're not even sure it *can* be broken," he said softly, wrapping his arms back around her as something inside his chest eased. "I was prepared to apologize, and if you needed it, maybe even sound ridiculously optimistic."

She didn't say anything for a moment, but she also didn't pull away from him. "This isn't you trying to be nice, is it?"

"You must really like me if you're delusional enough to think I'm capable of being nice," he said easily, and she slid her arms around his middle as if that had been the reassurance she'd needed. "And you should be proud, by the way. It's seriously starting to look like your sister is better at flirting than Waverly."

Beauty snuggled in closer rather than turning around to look. "She put her head on his shoulder, didn't she?"

"She did indeed." Waverly and Grace had abandoned the pretense of walking and were sitting together on the bench, with Grace doing most of the talking at the moment. He couldn't quite tell at this angle, but if Waverly didn't have his cheek resting against Grace's hair then the man was far less intelligent than James had always given him credit for. "And Waverly definitely seems appreciative of the gesture."

That was enough to make Beauty turn around, still staying in the circle of his arms. "Which means they're making progress, even if it's not quite as fast as their adoring but impatient audience would like." She smiled down at her sister and Waverly. "You know this means you have to let Waverly help you beat up my father the next time he comes around, don't you?"

"That might not be a bad idea, actually. Waverly can get pretty creative when he has enough inspiration." The reminder of Noble Tremain sent a little flame of anger flaring back up inside him. "Waverly made the calls last night, which means that your father should start facing all kinds of interesting and potentially fatal harassment over the next few days."

Instead of the pleased and at least mildly bloodthirsty response he'd been expecting, Beauty sighed. "That's great."

"That didn't sound like it was great." He held her a little closer. "Having an attack of conscience?"

"Yes, but about you and Waverly." She looked up at him, a touch of embarrassment in her expression. "As great as it is to have you rushing to our defense, I feel like I'm cheating by letting the two of you do all of the work. I know you have the resources and entertaining vindictive streaks, but I should at least be helping."

He saw her point. It was never as much fun watching someone else defeat your enemies for you. "Want Waverly and I to hold him down while you hit him a few times?"

That made her smile again. "While that's sweet, it wouldn't exactly have the impact I'm looking for."

"True." It had been too long since he'd done some serious scheming, but he could feel the mental muscles stretching as he ran through possible scenarios. "What about suing him first? He may have gotten the idea before you did, but until he finds a lawyer to listen to him there's still a chance you can get yours in front of the courts first."

Her brow furrowed. "I thought Waverly said doing anything legally might make it look like we think Father's case actually has some merit."

"Your lawsuit won't have anything to do with the one he's trying to shop around for, but if your case is already on the books by the time your father finds someone desperate enough to take him on . . ."

"It should take care of whatever shred of credibility he might have left." She turned back around, clearly intrigued by the thought. "But what can I sue him for that we could get a lawyer to bother pursuing? As much as I'd like to, I can't take him to court for being a terrible father—people hand their children over to licensed wicked stepparents all the time. They hope it'll put them in the right place to be found by a handsome prince or wish-granting fairy, and as much as I hate it, Father could just argue he'd wanted the same thing."

Just like that, the idea clicked. "True, but he isn't licensed." James's eyes narrowed. "Your father never actually consulted a Fairy Godmother or a licensed wicked stepparent when he was coming up with one of his schemes, did he?"

"Definitely not. He thinks he's smarter than they are." She breathed out a laugh. "You really think I could sue him for being a bad father without the appropriate paperwork?"

"It's worth a shot." Beast glanced down at Waverly, who he knew had their lawyer's mirror code memorized. From the way he was gazing adoringly at Grace, however, now definitely wasn't the time to ask. "I don't want to interrupt them, though."

Beauty looked back around just in time to see Waverly kiss Grace's hand. "No, we'd better not." Her expression softened. "It can wait."

The bravery that had abandoned him the last time he'd considered making a mirror call returned at the look in her eyes. "It doesn't have to."

BEAUTY SET THE mirror down on the library table in front of James, then touched his arm. "You don't have to do this if you don't feel ready," she said quietly, her tone making it clear she could see all the nerves he was trying so hard not to show.

He let out a long breath, then squared his shoulders and reminded himself he used to do this all the time. "I'll be fine. I once told Oscar I wanted to devote my life to kraken wrestling, and his only reaction was to ask whether or not my will was up to date." He lifted his hand to punch the code in, fingers hesitating over the keys. "My face . . . might hit him a little harder than that."

He met her eyes, and he swallowed at the concern he could see radiating out of them. After a moment, though, she gave him a deliberately skeptical look. "A kraken? Really?"

Recognizing that she was trying to distract him from worrying about Oscar's reaction James let it ease the tightness in his chest a little. "I generally don't plan things out in advance when I'm trying to be annoying. It was all I could come up with."

Then, before he could think about it anymore, he punched in the code for his and Waverly's lawyer.

The mist had barely had time to form before it started clearing again, revealing a small, pathologically neat man with wire spectacles and an unflappable expression. When he caught sight of James, however, his face took on a subtle frozen quality. "If you obtained this mirror code by eating one of my clients, I will remind you that lawyer-client privilege holds until I see some proof of his or her death."

It was, surprisingly, the one response he hadn't expected, and it had the added benefit of making him angry rather than hurting his feelings. He leaned forward with a growl, ready to say something that would undoubtedly have caused its own legal trouble, when Beauty leaned in close enough to be seen in the mirror. "Well, it's obvious this idiot doesn't want to take your case, James," she said clearly, deliberately not looking at Oscar. "I'm sure Manny can refer us to someone who knows how to answer the mirror when such a long-standing client gives him a call."

Touched and extremely impressed, James squeezed Beauty's hand as Oscar was actually struck silent for a few moments. Eventually, however, he cleared his throat. "Mr. Hightower, I presume?"

"Oh, I don't think you should presume just yet," James said, voice dark. "But yes, I'm James Hightower."

The lawyer hesitated again. "My . . . apologies, sir. I was informed of the curse when the legal measures you had set up were first activated, but . . ." He stopped, removing his glasses. "I hadn't spoken to you in some time. I was . . . unprepared."

For Oscar, this was practically groveling. Not sure if he found that comforting or even more annoying, James stood and let Beauty take the seat instead. "We need to sue someone for operating as a Fairy Godmother or wicked stepparent without the proper licensing—find the specific charge that will get him in the worst trouble. Beauty Tremain will be the plaintiff."

"Tremain . . ." Grateful to have moved on to another topic of conversation, Oscar immediately focused. "Would this be a daughter of Noble Tremain, the odious man who has been making the rounds of the legal community as of late?"

Beauty nodded. "If you can help us, this should stop him from harassing everyone."

"What an encouraging thought." There was a predatory gleam in Oscar's eyes. "Now, if you can provide evidence he attempted to place you or another young woman at private balls without the appropriate authorization, we should specifically cite Fairy Godmothers, Inc. in the lawsuit. That company can be absolutely ruthless when it comes to copyright infringement . . ."

CHAPTER 15

Timing Is Everything

Beauty had never been prouder of anyone than she was watching James make that mirror call. Despite the lawyer's idiotic opening—she still didn't understand why everyone immediately assumed the tall, furry guy ate people when high-quality steak was an option—it had even gone fairly well. By the end, Oscar had even seemed pleased by the thought that James might get back in the game enough to make his caseload more interesting.

All in all, it was the kind of accomplishment that deserved even more recognition than the enthusiastic kiss she'd planted on him at the end of the call. James, however, was having none of it.

"Beast, I still don't understand why you won't tell Waverly how impressive you just were," Beauty said in frustration, resting her hands on her hips and tapping her foot. "Are you worried he'll think the lawsuit was a mistake? Because your logic made total sense, and even if he thinks it's a bad idea he'll be so proud of you he probably wouldn't care if you really did try to wrestle a kraken."

"I'm not worried about what he'll think of the lawsuit," James growled, his own arms folded. "Even if it's not what he would have done, it's as smart as anything else we're doing."

"Then you have even less reason not to tell him!" She threw her hands up in the air, half-hoping that Waverly and Grace would hear them arguing from outside and solve the problem for her by coming in and overhearing the conversation. "When you do something brave, you're supposed to make sure you get credit for it!"

Suddenly, he grinned. "I thought you did a pretty good job taking care of that for me."

Beauty fought back her own smile, narrowing her eyes at him in an attempt to keep her expression serious. "Yes, but it would take absolutely no effort for you to get not only an 'I'm so proud of you' kiss from me, but *also* a fatherly pat on the back from Waverly."

James sighed. "He won't pat me on the back. He'll want to hug me, but restrain himself to one of those looks he gives that are almost as good as a hug." His voice got a little rough on the last few words, and he had to clear his throat. "Grace looks like a hugger."

"She is, but I'll try to hold her back if the situation comes up." Beauty dropped her arms and walked over to him, feeling herself melt even though she was still exasperated. "If you're not looking for recognition, then do it to make your life easier." She laid her hands on his arms, looking up at him. "The less Waverly worries about you, the less likely he is to try scheming you into mental health."

"You're enough to make him worry less about me, especially since I saw sense and started kissing you on a regular basis," he said wryly, unfolding his arms to brush the hair away from Beauty's face. "And I'm hoping Grace will distract him enough that he won't have time to worry about me at all."

"From everything I've seen, Waverly's really good at multitasking." Throat tightening with a rush of tenderness, Beauty laid her head against James's chest. She'd have to work up a good argument with him soon just to make sure they still remembered how to do it properly, but not about this. "So what's really the matter?" she asked softly.

He sighed again as he wrapped his arms around her back, hands resting so lightly she couldn't even feel the tips of his claws. "Once he found out my name, Oscar had to treat me a certain way no matter what I looked like. If a slime demon paid him enough, he'd have offered him coffee and would have complimented him on dripping less than usual."

"That doesn't mean other people couldn't get used to you if you gave them a little while." She listened to his heartbeat. "Manny still gets stares sometimes from people who've never met him before, but once he says something sarcastic about showing them what a roast feels like they always get their manners back."

James was silent for a moment. "I don't mind them being afraid of me," he said finally, as if weighing the words to test how serious he really was. "The more worried your competition is that you'll bite their heads off, the less likely they are to notice the money you've just made off their bad investment."

She moved her head so her chin was resting against his chest. "I hear a 'but' coming on."

He looked down at her, and Beauty swallowed as she recognized the fear in his eyes. "They all knew me before, Beauty. They saw Juliana and me together at social events, and knew she disappeared the same time I was cursed. They know any business rival that had cursed me would have had a plan to swoop in and claim some of my assets or at least taken credit for it. And they'll realize that, if I had any idea *who* cursed me, I should have manipulated them into changing me back." He closed his eyes briefly. "Or at the very least have bitten their heads off."

"You don't want them to see you as a failure, because if they do you're afraid they'll forget everything else you were." Beauty's voice was quiet, remembering years of strange ballrooms and crowds of the kind of people even magic couldn't have made her fit in with. "It's better to be terrifying than to not be anything at all."

When she felt him go still, she squeezed him tight. "It's okay, Beast. I won't say anything to Waverly."

He didn't say anything for a little while, then leaned down and pressed a kiss against the top of her head. "Thank you," he said softly, his voice rough.

She smiled. "Of course, when Waverly *does* find out he'll be mad you didn't tell him yourself. I'm much too short to protect you from his wrath."

His chuckle was a rumble against her skin. "I'll try to make sure it doesn't get to that point."

BY THE NEXT morning, it was clear James had no plans to tell Waverly himself. He was making such a concerted effort at being charming, however, that Beauty still couldn't bring herself to say anything.

Besides, he kept plying her with books.

"I'm sure we could find a set of shelves around here someplace," he said that afternoon, thoughtfully eyeing the tall, haphazardly stacked towers of books filling up the space between the foot of her bed and the wall. A few of them were Dwarvish phrase books, part of James's continued efforts to try and teach her the language, but most of the others had just magically appeared any time she'd expressed an interest in a particular author or genre. "I doubt they'd be in any of the rooms—my parents' usual houseguests weren't what you'd call big readers. But there has to be a set or two upstairs in the attic somewhere."

"Are you inviting me on another attic adventure?" she asked with a grin, handing James the stack of books she'd just finished. It was considerably shorter than the stack James had just carried in for her—the only thing she liked more than reading was talking to James and Grace. "Because if you are, I think we should pack a lunch and see if we can make it all the way to the wall this time."

James made a *tsk* noise. "So ambitious." He took the books, tucking them under his arm as he grinned back at her. "Though if we point out that our little adventure would give him more alone time with Grace, he might give us a three-course meal just to make sure we stay up there longer."

Beauty laughed as they left the room together, his free hand resting warm against her back. "Maybe we can use the time to find out if any of your relatives had some decent fashion sense. If there isn't, I'm going to have to go back to my apartment and get at least a few more clothes to cycle through. I love this blouse but if I see it too many more mornings in a row I'm going to set it on fire."

When she felt James go silent next to her, she slid her own hand around his back. "We've got it pretty well established by this point that I'm definitely coming back, right?" She asked, slanting a look up at him. "In fact, we could go together if you wanted. I'd love to take you on a hilariously sarcastic little tour of what my sister politely insists on calling the 'less financially fortunate' side of town."

James took a deep breath. "Actually, I was just thinking about the fact y—"

He immediately cut off the rest of the sentence when they stepped into the living room, which was enough to give Beauty a pretty good idea of what he'd been about to say. Grace was on the couch, sketching a still life that featured a candelabra and a large, extremely cutesy-looking teapot. Waverly was doing paperwork next to her, trying hard not to stare adoringly.

Beauty looked up at James again, hoping her eyebrows were expressive enough to get the question across without having to drag him back out the room to ask it. James looked contemplative, as if he really could tell what she was thinking, then he tilted his head to the side in what seemed like a gesture of conditional agreement. Taking it as a positive sign, she came up behind her sister and leaned her arms against the back of the couch. "So, Beast and I came to a decision. Unless one of his ancestors has better taste than I've seen so far, I have to go back into town soon for more clothes. Do you want me to pick you up some while I'm out, or would you rather come with me and shake your head despairingly over the state of my wardrobe?"

Startled, Grace looked over her shoulder at Beauty. Even though she hadn't planned on staying when she'd arrived, her sister tended to keep an overnight bag in the carriage in case of emergencies—after years of being left stranded in the woods or in strange cities, it was a habit they'd both picked up. Apparently, the bag's contents had been enough that the distraction of having both Waverly and Beauty so close had made her forget it wouldn't last forever.

Clearly realizing all this, Grace's cheeks colored faintly as she turned back toward her sketchpad and set down her charcoal. "I'll come with you. I normally would have already started on next week's lesson plans by now, and with the end of term coming up I'll be so busy grading final projects I'll have even less time to do them." She glanced over at Waverly, mouth opening as if she wanted to say something. When nothing came out, she closed it and looked back at Beauty. "I know we were worried about Father doing something, but if we haven't heard from him by now there's a chance he's just given up. Maybe I should . . ."

Waverly cleared his throat. "I don't believe we can assume that silence means he's given up," he said, almost but not quite meeting Grace's eyes. James, who had undoubtedly noticed the same thing, gave him a discreet poke in the back that was completely ignored. "If you're concerned about your lesson plans, you're welcome to bring everything you need here to work on them. We have plenty of room, and from what you've told me about your school the commute should be no greater from here than the cottage you rent."

Grace lifted a hand without being quite sure what she wanted to do with it. "It was wonderfully sweet of you to open your home to me, but I can't expect you to take on another houseguest just because we're having family problems. A week should be plenty of time to settle the situation with Father, at least on my end, and if there's still trouble I could always come back for a visit next weekend . . ."

Recognizing their shared tendency to babble when nervous, Beauty decided to see if she'd have better luck than James and poked Grace in the back. Her sister immediately stopped, shooting Beauty a look that was half pleading, half relieved. "And, as that was a much longer answer than you'd asked for, I'll immediately stop talking," she finished, picking her charcoal back up just to find something to do with her hands.

Beauty looked over at James, remembering all the times when she'd offered to go home, and he gave her an amused eye roll that suggested he was remembering the same thing. He stepped forward, looking like he was ready to poke Waverly again, but the older man had already shifted around to face Grace. "I feel compelled to correct you on one point," he said softly, taking one of Grace's hands in his. "It was selfishness that made me ask you to stay, not sweetness. Even then, I knew I wanted to spend as much time in your company as I possibly could."

Beauty reached over to pull James away again, but he'd already taken the step back on his own. Instead, she grabbed his hand, and they held onto each other as they both tried to be quiet enough not to interrupt the moment.

Grace smiled at Waverly, eyes alight as she leaned towards him a little. "Are you sure?"

"I am absolutely certain," Waverly murmured. He leaned towards Grace as well, and Beauty held her breath. He was almost there . . .

The sound of someone pounding on the front door snapped everyone out of the moment. After a few good hits it cut off abruptly, only to be followed by a single, rather loud thud.

For a few blessed seconds, Beauty had no idea what had just happened. That was all the time it took for memory to slap the realization into her, winding her muscles tight with the stress of what she knew was coming.

Thankfully, James said the words so that she didn't have to. "I guess this means your father hasn't given up."

Grace stood up, looking worried. "What I want to know is why he stopped so suddenly." She turned to Waverly. "You didn't put an attack spell of some kind on the door, did you?"

Waverly didn't respond at first, cocking his head as if listening for something. When his attention refocused, he looked intrigued enough to unsettle anyone who knew him really well. "It seems as though elementals are either capable of a minor degree of independent thought, or are sensitive to even unconscious commands on my part." He paused, pondering the possibility obviously enough to suggest he was attempting to ease the sudden tension. "Either way, it's probably best I wasn't aware of this before now."

James shot him a stern look that was equally obvious as he squeezed Beauty's hand. "Waverly, you are *not* allowed to start raiding temples or stealing enchanted treasures from evil sorceresses."

Waverly, whose grip on Grace's hand was just as secure, raised an eyebrow at him as they all headed toward the front door. "You mean without you, of course."

He grinned. "Oh, and the girls should come too."

Beauty smiled weakly and took a deep breath as Waverly and James pushed open the front doors, revealing Noble Tremain, pinned to a patch of ground several feet away from the front steps. Above him, a small, very angry cyclone kept him firmly in place.

Waverly held a hand flat in front of him, slowing the wind down until it only seemed mildly annoyed, and Noble staggered to his feet radiating poorly restrained fury. "At least you didn't set your *creature* on me this time," he gritted out, jerking his head in James's direction even as he attempted to glare daggers at Beauty. "Though if you think your doorman is any more intimidating now that I've found out he's a one-trick hedge wizard, you're just as wrong as you ever were."

Beauty took a deep breath, deliberately forcing her muscles to relax. James, all the more supportive for his silence, squeezed her hand and made the process just a little bit easier. "Should I be flattered you're so sure all this is my fault?" Beauty asked, voice mocking. "I thought you were shopping that lawsuit around because the magic had turned me into a puppet."

Noble gave her a disgusted look. "Don't play dumb with me, you ungrateful brat. We both know you're not actually attractive or charming enough to have gotten any of this legitimately, which means you must be smarter than I always thought you were. And you've stopped playing stupid at just the right moment to cut me out of my fair share of the take."

Any hurt Beauty might have felt at the familiar assessment was eased by the fire in Grace's eyes and by James's slowly building growl, the tone of it suggesting there was going to be another death threat within a few minutes. "What about me?" Grace asked suddenly, hand still holding Waverly's as she moved forward to stand next to Beauty. "Aren't I in on the plan, too?"

Fury lit their father's eyes, mixed with a level of betrayal that felt almost offensive. "You, I'm not speaking to. I know this can't be your fault—you don't hate me enough to have hidden the necessary level of intelligence from me all these yea—"

The wind suddenly slapped Noble again, knocking him sideways and cutting off the rest of the sentence. That would have only been the beginning, Beauty was certain, but out of the corner of her eye she could see Grace look over at Waverly and very deliberately squeeze his hand.

James, for his part, leaned close to Beauty's ear. "Can I kill him now?"

Even though she was sure Grace would still say no, Beauty gave it some serious thought. By the time Noble staggered back to his feet again, however, she shook her head. "We need to know why he's here," she whispered, then turned back to her father. "Please tell me you didn't risk death just to insult us one last time," she called out, shifting a little closer to Grace so they presented a unified front. "If you're here to tell us you're skipping town, though, we might even be willing to pack you a lunch."

"Of course," Waverly said smoothly. "A witch was kind enough to teach me several rather interesting poisons made out of common kitchen supplies."

Noble ignored this, glaring at Beauty with a sudden focus that was somehow more intimidating than anything he'd managed up to this point. "Don't bother being coy. Stirring up the hounds was a relatively intelligent return salvo, but suing me for not having some ridiculous Fairy Godmother license struck at the heart of everything I've spent my entire life trying to achieve."

Waverly raised an eyebrow and shot a look at James, who stared determinedly ahead. Grace looked confused, and Beauty realized the moment she'd warned Beast about had just happened. Right now, though, there were bigger things to worry about. There was something in Noble's eyes that almost seemed like respect, along with more awareness of Beauty than he'd previously managed to convey in her entire life. She didn't know if she found it funny or painfully sad that the plot he'd been so impressed by hadn't even been her idea.

Noble took a step forward, stopping before he could slam into the wall of wind suddenly blocking his way. "All of my future ambitions, gone in one fell swoop. You don't even have to win for the damage to be permanent, unlike my attempt on you." Surprising everyone, he bowed. "Congratulations. It was a masterstroke."

Beauty and James's eyes met as worry began to twist in her stomach. Weeks of ranting and insults, and now this? It made no sense.

It meant trouble.

Noble straightened. "Both you and your sister failed me utterly as daughters devoted to their father, but I had no idea you'd become such a worthy adversary."

Then, without another word, he turned and walked down the driveway. When he had disappeared from sight, Waverly looked at both Beauty and James with an expression that was too bland to be at all safe. "Tell me about this masterstroke of yours."

INTERLUDE

Sweet Simplicity

Beauty opened her mouth, clearly ready to defend her sweetheart from whatever she imagined was building behind Waverly's eyes, then closed it again at a silent gesture from James. He then took a deep breath—for courage, perhaps—and quickly outlined the discussion with Oscar and the suit that had resulted.

When James was finished, he met Waverly's eyes. "I should have told you," he said quietly. "I'm sorry."

Waverly was silent for a moment, almost surprised at how hurt he felt. "It was a perfectly legitimate tactical move," he said finally, letting none of the emotion out in his voice. His gaze slid away from James. "It was done more quickly than I might have chosen to act in your place, but that doesn't mean it wasn't an intelligent choice."

James hesitated, then rested a hand on Waverly's shoulder. "I still should have told you."

Waverly inhaled, telling himself that should be enough. Somehow, though, the ache hadn't lessened, and he had no desire for any of it to spill out in the midst of company. "If you will excuse me." He slid his hand out from Grace's firm and steady hold, making absolutely certain not to meet anyone's eyes. "I believe I will get an early start on dinner."

He slipped inside, his steps measured and even until the kitchen door closed behind him. When he got to the counter he stopped, closing his eyes briefly and taking a few slow, deep breaths. Then he selected one of the carrots on the counter and began to methodically and thoroughly chop it, focusing entirely on preparing the most complex, time-consuming stew he could think of.

"Do you want to talk about it?"

Waverly's hand stilled at the sound of Grace's voice behind him. "I'm fine," he said after a moment. Though he appreciated the concern, he preferred to will the emotion back into silence than explore it to any degree.

When he heard nothing behind him, he sighed and set down the knife. "You have enough family drama to navigate through without having ours added to it," he said, turning around to look at her. "I assure you, I will be fine."

Grace simply watched him, her expression making it clear that he had been utterly unconvincing. "You said 'will be' that time." There was nothing he could say to that, and her expression softened. "I have never seen Beauty look that guilty about anything, and she once accidentally turned a neighbor of ours bright blue for almost a week. If anything, James looked worse than she did, and you immediately went off and hid." She took a step forward. "I'm not saying I understand what happened, but I know it was bad. Please talk to me."

Even then, Waverly hesitated. He'd left home when he was eleven years old, and had spent the thirty years that followed learning to handle anything and everything on his own. He very much wanted Grace to stay, but surely she didn't need to be here for this part.

She took another step towards him. "I hadn't quite turned six when my mother got pregnant with Beauty, and I remember feeling so bad for my future brother or sister because she was going to end up with the same parents I had. The first night she started crying, I was the one who woke up and soothed her back to sleep. I wasn't old enough to do much, but I told myself that at least she'd have me."

There was a world of understanding in her eyes, something much more solid and realer than simple compassion. Giving in, Waverly exhaled as he leaned back against the counter. "I was only supposed to be passing through this area, divesting the locals of—" He stopped suddenly, realizing there were portions of the story he should have thought to edit in advance. It was mildly horrifying how utterly out of practice he was at this . . .

Grace smiled at him with genuine amusement. "By the time I was fifteen, I had taught myself how to pick locks just by watching my father break into strangers' castles. When Beauty was old enough, I taught her." She crossed the rest of the distance between them, and patted him on the arm. "Don't worry about shocking me."

That surprised a chuckle out of him, and he felt the knot in his chest start to ease for the first time since he'd seen the guilt in James's eyes. "I'd been trading fairy gold to wealthy individuals in exchange for more . . . practical funds." His hand lifted to cover Grace's, keeping it in place. "I had knocked on the door to this house, simply intending to make another transaction, when a young man answered with the most profoundly solemn expression I had ever seen on a child. He gave me a long, searching look, then offered me all of the money in his father's private safe if I would help him run away from home."

Grace leaned close, and Waverly closed his eyes as he rested his forehead against hers. "I had more experience teaching ogres to dance than I'd had raising a child. I told myself I would only stay a few years—just enough to make sure James survived his parents' attempts at instruction—then move on to greener pastures."

"You were an idiot," Grace said softly.

Despite the tightness in his throat, the corners of Waverly's mouth quirked up briefly as he nodded. Then he opened his eyes, lifting his head on an inhaled breath that held more in it than he was comfortable with. "I would give all the gold I've ever earned or taken to see James reclaim the life that he abandoned after the curse hit, and he can't even bring himself to tell me he's spoken to our lawyer for the first time in almost a year." His hand tightened on Grace's. "Had your father not stopped by unexpectedly, I'm not certain he would have told me at all."

And that, Waverly suspected, was the worst part of all of this. Did James not have any idea how much of his day, even now, was spent worrying about him? He still hadn't devoted the time or attention needed to properly hunt down Juliana because he hadn't wanted to leave James alone in the months after the curse had taken effect. He had understood James's unwillingness to talk then, but if he clearly had no interest in sharing something *good* . . .

Grace rested her free hand against his other arm. "You're telling me that this is the first time James has ever done something stupid?" she said softly.

That stopped him. "As pleasant as the idea sounds, I can't attribute everything that upsets me to stupidity on his part," he said after a moment.

"Personally, I find it makes my life easier." She pressed a kiss against his cheek. "Of course, I'd never actually tell Beauty this, which is another thing that makes my life easier."

The knot loosened a little further, and he felt his mouth ease upward into a genuine smile. "I promise to keep your secret."

"Good." She smiled back at him, moving her hand upward to rest it against his cheek. "James loves you, Waverly. I've only been here a few days and I can already see that. And if someone who genuinely loves you hurts you somehow, it's usually because they did something dumb and they feel terrible about it afterward."

He leaned in to her hand a little, wondering if what had really hit him when he'd first seen her days before had been that he'd found a kindred spirit. "You make it sound so simple."

"If I didn't keep it simple, I'd end up snapping and I'd have to go be a hermit in the woods." Her smile widened into a grin. "I'm sure Beauty wouldn't mind wearing ratty, old clothing all day, but I couldn't stand it."

He squeezed her hand, his own smile widening. "I knew you were a woman of taste and discernment."

"Which is why I know how special you are." She stepped back, pulling him along with her. "Now come and yell at James properly so we can all get on with the rest of our day."

Waverly went.

CHAPTER 16

Who's Afraid of an Office Tour?

It was so much easier when he got yelled at.

James knew he should have been the one to go after Waverly, but if "I'm sorry" hadn't worked he wasn't sure "I was an idiot" would do much better. So while Grace followed Waverly inside, James sat down hard on the front steps and tried to figure out what he needed to do to make things okay again.

After a moment, Beauty quietly walked over and sat down beside him, close enough that her arm pressed up against his. As the seconds ticked past, she still didn't say anything, and after a while James swore softly and closed his eyes. "Thank you for not saying 'I told you so.'"

"I was busy trying to figure out how to apologize for my father's terrible sense of timing." There was enough lightness in her voice that he could have taken it as a joke if he'd wanted to, and when he didn't respond he felt her rest her head against his arm. "He has to forgive you. It's his job."

James shook his head. "If Waverly has an actual job, I'm pretty sure it's along the lines of 'Master of the Universe.'"

She nudged him with her elbow. "You know what I mean."

James hesitated, trying to explain. He and Waverly had done such a good job of not talking about things for the last decade that he still wasn't used to having to put things into words. They'd both just seemed to know what the other was thinking, at least until the curse had knocked everything sideways. They had just started to get their old bond back. "I don't think I've ever hurt his feelings like this before."

Beauty gave him an incredulous look. "Seriously? Never?"

He lifted his shoulders. "We argue about all kinds of things. He blames his gray hairs on me, and when I was sixteen, he threatened to sell me to the dwarves after he caught me gambling with a bunch of djinn. But . . ." James sighed, eyes fixed on the ground in front of him so he wouldn't have to look at Beauty's face. He still had no idea how she had made him talk about all this. "I knew he was all I had, and a part of me was always afraid that if I went too far he'd leave."

She didn't say anything for what seemed like a long time. Finally, he saw her stand up out of the corner of his eye. "I feel I should warn you, Beast. I'm going to have to hug you now," she announced, as if expecting him to say no. "You can try to argue, but I'm pretty sure you have no say in the matter."

James moved into the hug as Beauty slid her arms around him, adjusting so they could both get as close as possible. They were still holding on to each other when James heard the door open behind him, and there was a bit of quick untangling as they both helped each other straighten and turn around. Grace looked happy, which was a good sign, and when her eyes met Beauty's the two sisters smiled at each other in what seemed to be complete understanding. Waverly had that penetrating expression that always suggested he was reading the mind of whomever he was looking at. James had seen the look cause a few lawyers, several clerks, and one particularly annoying town magistrate to burst into tears over the years, but right now it was an immense relief.

No one said anything as the two men looked at each other for a long, steady moment. Then a wry warmth softened Waverly's eyes. "You're an idiot," he said simply.

James nodded, fighting the urge to grin. Everything was okay again. "I agree with you completely."

Waverly, knowing that everything had been resolved between them, rubbed his hands together in anticipation. "Now that we've had the chance to become suitably refocused, I suggest we adjourn to a more comfortable location and decide whether Noble's vague but atmospheric threat should inspire any action on our part."

Both men turned to look at Beauty and Grace, who wore matching expressions of unease. "I don't know," Grace admitted, brow furrowing as she thought. "Father isn't intelligent, but he does get terrifyingly obsessed when he wants something. Up until now all he's ever really wanted was a connection to nobility, but if he's decided Beauty's a direct threat to his chances I have no idea what he'd be capable of."

"Why *is* he so obsessed with marrying the two of you off to someone 'suitable'?" Waverly asked. "I understand a yearning for money and power, but several of the most traditionally successful ways of acquiring them would have nothing to do with either of you."

"I think he wants the recognition more than the money or power," said Beauty, sounding far more tired than she had only moments before. She leaned her head against James's side, snuggling in a little closer as James tightened his arm around her. "Mother had some distant relative that was nobility, and Father was absolutely obsessed with him."

"We met him once, long after Mother had disappeared," added Grace, shaking her head a little at the memory. "I was thirteen and the man had already gone through his second divorce, but Father couldn't stop himself from hinting that one of us could become wife number three at some point."

"I think he'd given up on finding anyone willing to marry me even before we'd escaped, though." Beauty's voice was resigned, as if commenting on bad weather. "It just made him angrier at me, because he thought I was making you look bad."

Waverly took Grace's hand, holding it tight. He didn't say anything, but he gave James a look that would have taken at least a few heavily underlined paragraphs to transcribe properly. If James had had to summarize it, though, he probably would have ended up with something like, "You *are* planning on proving her father wrong about this at some point, aren't you?" It was a ludicrously pushy question, even asked silently, but Waverly tended to get protective of anyone he was fond of.

It wasn't as if he hadn't thought about it, James admitted to himself. He had no interest in letting Beauty leave him for longer than it took to finish her workday, which seemed like a far better qualification for a potential wife than anything he'd tried up to this point. On top of that, she'd already made it clear in a hundred different ways that she was about as different from Juliana as a woman could be. Their relationship might eventually involve accidental homicide—thrown plates ricocheting in surprising directions, for example—but something told him he could definitely trust her with his heart.

The problem was, Beauty would want more out of a husband than someone who hid in his manor all day and let the money come in. And while he could believe there was a life out there for a huge, hairy monster with a knack for making money, he didn't know if there was anything for a man who'd gotten tricked into being a monster. A man who had worked for every ounce of respect he'd been given, and then had fallen far enough to become the "after" picture in one of those stupid enchanted nobility guidebooks.

People didn't mind monsters, at least as long as they had their mauling insurance completely paid up. What they weren't comfortable with were failures . . .

A poke in the side jerked him back into reality, and he looked down to see Beauty watching him with a questioning expression. "So, are we all agreed?"

James froze a moment. As the furrow between Beauty's eyebrows deepened he realized that key parts of the conversation had clearly been happening without him. "I think we all know by now that I wasn't paying attention."

Beauty sighed. "Grace and I will go into town, see if we can figure out what Father's up to, and maybe warn a few key people along the way. You and Waverly will stay at the house, get more information from lawyers and your other shadowy informants, and make sure he doesn't try anything clever while we're away."

James's eyes narrowed, moving his arm away as he shifted around to face her. "There is no way I missed that much of the conversation."

Beauty's brow lowered as she took a step back. "You're seriously going to argue about this? Remember, we were just talking about this before Father showed up and decided to be creepy. It's not as if anything's changed."

"This just means we'll do a few more errands along the way," Grace chimed in, watching him as if trying to pick up Waverly's trick for reading minds. "If nothing else, we both have neighbors and co-workers we should warn. Most of them already have some idea what he's like, but there's a chance he could do something genuinely dangerous this time."

"For all we know, he might even be working with a partner." Beauty turned back to her sister with a small shiver. "I know he hates the thought of having to listen to anyone else, but that might explain why he was so out of character."

Waverly considered this. "That would complicate things significantly. Do you have any ideas of whom he might have approached to form this partnership? Even a list of options might give us a better idea of what resources he now may have access to."

James held up a hand. "So their father sounds like he's suddenly become *way* more vindictive, could be capable of *anything* now depending on whose evil sidekick he's suddenly decided to become, and we *still* think it's a good idea for them to go off on their own?" He might not be as familiar with Noble's insanity as Beauty and her sister were, but even he had heard the difference in the man. Rage-fueled bluster didn't turn into icy cunning without something dangerous happening. "Grace may be compassionate enough to not want her flesh and blood dead, but I don't think we can trust Noble to be that generous."

Now Beauty was glaring at him, hands on her hips. "As sweet as I normally find this insane protective streak of yours, I'm not about to let you lock us both in your big house just to keep us safe. We've both managed against Father for our entire lives without either your *or* Waverly's help, and I am *not* going to let him reduce me to looking through your mother's clothing because I'm just that desperate for something new to wear."

He understood stubbornness, but that didn't mean he had to like it. "We can hire people to pick up anything you and Grace need. That and crushing your enemies are what money is *for.*"

If he'd been thinking a little more clearly, his brain would have hopefully pointed out to him that both Waverly and Grace had gone completely silent. Given a little more time, he might have even worked out that this probably wasn't a good sign.

Beauty, at least, was too fired up to be paying any more attention than he was. "So you expect me to let some perfect stranger tromp through my rooms, probably breaking the very few breakable things I still own, just because you're having control issues? I don't think so! What about when Grace has to go to work at the beginning of next week? What about when *I* eventually have to go back to work?"

"We'll have the problem solved by then," he growled, moving towards her.

"Why, because we've done such a good job of it up to this point?" Beauty made an exasperated noise, throwing her hands up in the air. "My life hasn't been this ridiculously complicated since my *father* was managing it!"

That stung more than any straightforward insult could have. "You were as involved in putting the suit together as I was!"

Beauty let out a breath, her anger seeming to deflate a little bit. "That's not what I'm saying. I'm not against anything we've done so far, but my father is as much of a curse as your furriness and sharp teeth. I've fantasized about finding a magic cure somewhere that would finally make him disappear for good, but the truth is he's just going to keep bouncing back the same way he always has." She let her hands drop. "Which means I'll have to suck it up and deal with him, just like I always have."

With nothing to crash up against, James's own anger wavered. "He just threatened you, Beauty, far more convincingly than I'd thought the man was capable of." He rested his hands on her shoulders. "I'm not letting you go out there alone."

Beauty stopped for a moment, like a thought had just occurred to her. James braced himself for her to argue that, since Grace was going with her, she technically wouldn't be out there alone. When her eyes lit, however, she hit him with something else entirely. "Come with us, then." She looked up at him, clearly pleased with the idea. "It'll solve both our problems, and I can introduce you to Manny, Steve, and everyone else back at the office."

James froze, realizing he'd walked right into it so thoroughly he'd actually blocked up the path behind him. This resulted in the first moment of silence since the shouting had started, and Grace took advantage of it by turning to Waverly. "If you locked up the house for a few hours and left the winds here as bodyguards, we could all go." She squeezed his arm, sounding excited. "I'd really love to have you meet my students."

He could see Waverly's expression soften, and any hope James might have had of talking the other man out of it melted in the face of Grace's enthusiasm. "I would very much enjoy seeing you in your domain." Waverly's voice was tender as he lifted a hand to cover Grace's. "If it would be agreeable to you and your sister, we can leave tomorrow morning with little trouble."

"Wait." Panic clutched at James's chest as he listened to everyone else happily take control of the situation, wondering if this was some kind of cosmic punishment for not being brave enough to just tell Waverly about the lawyer right away. Sure, a trip into town probably wouldn't be as bad as facing his former business associates—Beauty wouldn't mind his snarling at any strangers who stared too long—but he hadn't even had time to think about it. Everything was moving too fast. "We don't even know if I'll fit in the carriage."

Waverly arched an eyebrow, expression suggesting clearly he knew James was stalling, but Beauty patted his chest in a reassuring manner. "It's okay, Beast. Grace has a big, open-air wagon that once held eighteen squirming twelve-year-olds. You should be no trouble."

Feeling his hands try to clench, James pulled his hands away from Beauty's shoulders so he wouldn't accidentally jab her. "What about her horses? They get nervous around predators."

Beauty's brow lowered. "Did I not mention the eighteen twelve-year-olds? I'm pretty sure a sorceress could work a lightning spell next to Grace's team and they wouldn't even blink."

"And even if they did, I'm sure I could persuade the elementals to propel Grace's wagon in much the same manner as they do the carriage," Waverly interjected smoothly, still holding onto Grace as they both turned around to head back inside. He looked over at Grace. "That, however, is for the morning. Right now, I suggest we head inside and enjoy some relative privacy while these two continue their burgeoning argument on the front porch."

"That sounds like an excellent idea," Grace replied, sounding amused as she shut the door behind them both. That left James alone on the porch with Beauty, who was back to glaring at him with rapidly increasing suspicion.

Once the door clicked closed, Beauty took a step back. "So you won't leave the house even for this," she said flatly, something more dangerous than annoyance putting an edge on each word. "And you won't even admit it to my face."

He opened his mouth to argue, or at least defend himself, then snapped it closed when he finally recognized the emotion simmering in her eyes. He'd managed to hurt her, too, enough that she was bracing for an even harder hit.

James closed his eyes, cursing himself for being an idiot. Had he always been this bad at dealing with people who actually mattered? If so, Juliana hadn't given him nearly enough of a warning.

Which probably should have been its own warning, come to think of it.

"How threatening can I be to your friends if they stare too long?" he growled, opening his eyes again. She just stared at him, eyes wide, and he clenched his hands. "As long as I don't go far enough to get myself arrested, I can't imagine you'd care too much about what I do to strangers. I want to know how far I can go with the people you do want protected."

Beauty was still staring at him, hands half raised as if they'd gotten lost on their way to whatever they'd meant to do. After a moment she took a deep breath, forcing her hands back to her sides. "I just bullied you into that," she said quietly. "As mad at you as I am, that's not right."

Until Beauty, he'd never met anyone as defiantly stubborn as he was. It should worry him that he found it this appealing. "When you win an argument, the gracious thing to do is to simply acknowledge your victory without making the other person admit that, technically, they were wrong." Despite the nerves still twisting around his insides, James felt the corners of his mouth curve upward. "Hopefully, the other person will then return the favor on the off chance that you ever happen to be less than correct."

He held her gaze until the muscles she'd knotted up so tightly finally started to relax. James, relieved, forced his own hands to relax and told himself he was worrying about nothing. Beauty's friends—people who didn't know him, and who conveniently had a boss with his own set of teeth and claws—were his best option for a test group. And if they did react badly, he'd have to learn to face it eventually anyway. He needed to either remember he was a fighter and start taking his life back, or let it go once and for all.

If only it didn't have to happen quite so *fast* . . .

His thoughts scattered when Beauty crossed the distance they'd put between them, wrapping her arms around his middle. "If anyone even *thinks* about making you uncomfortable, you won't have to worry about how far I'm okay with you going," she said fiercely, pressing her cheek against his chest. "I'll make them sorry they were ever born long before you got the chance to do *anything.*"

James's chest squeezed tight, his own muscles finally easing as he wrapped his arms around her. Maybe this wouldn't be so scary, after all. He smiled. "My hero."

CHAPTER 17

On the Road Again

The next morning, Beauty went over possible scenarios for the day while she got dressed. Most of her neighbors probably wouldn't be home, and old Mrs. Hubbard was so blind she would probably just compliment James on his beard unless she actually managed to find her glasses. With anyone else, she was confident they could be safely ignored or glared into submission.

Work, however, would be a little more complicated. The people she cared about most wouldn't be a problem—Manny had schemed with Waverly to set this up in the first place, and Steve would probably be thrilled to find someone he could talk to without getting a crick in his neck. They were the most important introductions, but she'd make it a point to have James meet everyone she was at all familiar with. A larger group would help James get that much more used to talking to people again, and even the most annoying of her co-workers would probably save any snarky comments for when she officially came back to work. The rest of them would be either polite or actually friendly, then later delight in teasing her about her new . . .

Okay, that might be a problem.

Beauty hesitated for a moment, wondering if she would make

things more or less awkward by talking to James about their exact relationship. Then, remembering how great they both were at picking the absolute worst interpretation of everything, Beauty hurried over to James's room in the hopes of intercepting him before he headed downstairs to breakfast.

Fortunately, he was just barely leaving his room when she got there. Unfortunately, she nearly ran into him before managing to skid to a stop. "Whoa, slow down." James steadied her with his hands on her shoulders, an amused expression on his face. "If you're suddenly trying to escape, this probably wasn't the best direction to take."

Beauty's own hands were braced against his chest, which for once was covered in what felt like high-quality fabric. Even though she'd yelled at him earlier about his constant need to walk around shirtless, she was oddly disappointed. "Since when did you start wearing shirts?" Beauty asked, mouth entirely forgetting to consult her brain first.

"About six months after the curse hit, Waverly snuck in a tailor in the hopes of having more clothing ready should I suddenly decide to rejoin society. The fit isn't the best, but given that he took most of my measurements while he was cowering in the corner, I'm actually pretty impressed. I'm wearing it now because I thought it might make me look slightly more dignified in front of your co-workers." James raised an eyebrow. "Something tells me, though, that you didn't just rush over here for a fashion consultation."

The only thing keeping her reaction from being mortally embarrassing was how pleased he looked by her disappointment. Still, she felt her cheeks redden as she dragged her thoughts back to the matter at hand. "I didn't want to ask you this in front of Waverly and Grace, but how should I introduce you?"

James's brow furrowed. "You mean whether you should call me Beast or James?" He paused, then winced. "Better go with James. Even your sister was a little horrified by the nickname, so I can't imagine—" He stopped suddenly, the furrow back again as he stared down at her. "You shouldn't stop using it."

The corners of her mouth curved upward. "Not a chance."

He grinned. "You know, you probably deserve your own nickname." He pretended to consider it. "I've always liked Florence . . ." She laughed. "See if I kiss *you* again." Then, realizing she'd let herself get distracted—clearly her subconscious didn't want her to have this conversation—Beauty took a deep breath. "What I actually meant, though, is at some point I'm going to have to say, 'This is my . . . blank.' How do you want me to end the sentence?"

His expression went instantly neutral, though whether from the awkwardness of the question or from suddenly disguised emotion, she couldn't say. "Ah."

Either way, she wished she hadn't brought it up. But would it really be easier to deal with later? "Because I'm fine with anything," she said hurriedly, hoping to get through the moment as quickly as possible. "I just wanted to make sure I cleared it with you first."

James's face was still blanker than she liked, though she convinced herself it had relaxed slightly. "Are you worried about how they'll react?"

This question she could answer safely. "Actually, I was panicking about how *you'd* react. I didn't want to say we were . . ." Dating? Involved? Boyfriend and girlfriend? ". . . *together* and have you think I was being pushy. I also didn't want to call you my 'friend' or something else safe and make you wonder if I was embarrassed or something stupid like that."

The corners of his mouth quirked up. "So you think I'm in the habit of passionately kissing women I'm not romantically involved with?"

Beauty made an exasperated noise even as she felt herself blush again. "I don't know! I've never done this before!" She leaned her forehead against his chest, grateful she hadn't tried this in front of

Waverly and Grace and relieved that James hadn't started laughing yet. "As for how my co-workers will react, the people who like me will happily tease me about my 'boyfriend' for the rest of my life. The ones who don't will either faint dead from shock at the thought of me dating anyone or ask you if you've really thought this through."

James wrapped his arms around her a little more tightly, rubbing a soothing hand up and down her back. "Somehow, watching you panic is surprisingly comforting."

She breathed out another laugh. "Thank you. I try."

WHEN THEY FINALLY made it downstairs to breakfast, however, the overly solemn expression on Waverly's face immediately flattened the buoyant relief the conversation with James had managed to inspire. She glanced over at Grace, hoping for some kind of signal, but her sister's sympathetic expression only told her that the news wasn't going to be good. Not fatal, though—there was none of that resigned dread Father had always been so good at inspiring.

Beauty's stomach tensed, willing to wait for further word before twisting itself into a knot.

James shifted so he was standing closer to her, sliding an arm around her shoulders. "Since the four of us seem to be alive and kicking, I can safely say no one we actually care about has died. So what's the bad news?"

Waverly cleared his throat. "I just received word that Juliana has been seen near the border of Somewhere, only a few days travel from our area. Though it's impossible to be certain, she appeared to be heading in this direction."

There were a few moments of complete silence, during which Beauty's insides immediately began knotting themselves up into a pretzel. She could still see Juliana's perfect painted face, the same one that had promptly disappeared just as James had been hit by a curse. It made sense to think she'd caused it to happen, but at the very least she'd abandoned her fiancé right when he'd needed her most. No matter how you looked at it, the woman certainly sounded like the trouble Manny had warned her about.

Beauty made herself look up at James. His jaw was tense enough it probably hurt, making her press in closer to him. "If Juliana comes back here, I'll just hit her with something," she said quietly, hoping desperately it was the right thing. "Then we can tie her to a chair, and the four of us can get any answers out of her you need."

"That is an excellent suggestion," Waverly seconded firmly, a predatory light coming into his eyes. He smiled slightly. "I know several interesting tricks in which the other person remains conscious and responsive the entire time."

Grace raised an amused eyebrow at him, her expression softening as she turned back to Beauty and James. "Not that we can be sure she's even coming here. From what Waverly told me, she'd have to be either desperate or a complete idiot to expect any kind of welcome."

James let out a long breath. "If she does come back, she's coming back with answers." The sheer depth of the resolve in his voice was unnerving in its own way, but he seemed to force himself to relax. He turned to Waverly and the corner of his mouth quirked upward in a wry smile. "I should have known you still had minions on the lookout."

"Of course." Taking that as a sign that the tense part of the morning had ended, Waverly shooed them all toward the table before disappearing into the kitchen. He returned with a covered tray, setting it down on the table before pulling out a chair for Grace. "Though I believe my informant would be less than pleased at being called my minion." He paused, amusement lighting his eyes. "Perhaps I should tell him, anyway."

Something in his expression made Beauty remember Manny's smile at the thought of Grace and Waverly's being interested in each other. She already knew Manny had contacts in all kinds of strange places, and though she was sure Waverly had his fingers in all kinds of pies, it comforted her to think that someone she knew was helping them out. "If it's Manny, it's probably not a good idea to tease him before he's had his coffee. He won't admit it, but he still feels guilty about the time he singed a secretary."

Both men immediately snapped their heads around to look at her. Waverly's expression was the first to change, easing into a kind of pained resignation. "How long have you known?"

"When I told Manny I needed vacation time, he asked if someone had an eye on Grace, too. When I mentioned you did, he was way more interested than he should have been."

Waverly rolled his eyes heavenward. "Fantastic." He headed back into the kitchen with a longsuffering sigh, while Grace sat down with a thoughtful expression that Beauty wasn't quite able to interpret.

James hadn't moved yet, but his eyes narrowed at Waverly as he reemerged from the kitchen. "So you *did* set us up," he said, the growl back in his voice.

Waverly set the basket of rolls on the table before moving around to take his own seat. "Not in the way you mean. Though I would love to take credit for that degree of foresight, I must admit that sending Beauty was entirely Mandrake's idea." He glanced over at Grace, his expression softening. "And now I will owe him doubly."

Beauty gave James's arm an affectionate squeeze. "I do know he's going to be impossible to work for after this." Though, thankfully, the fact that he was Waverly's friend meant the only danger from today's meeting would be embarrassing stories from James's childhood. And Beauty would be more than happy to start collecting those. "Since he turned out to be right, I don't think I can do too much complaining."

James glared at Waverly for another few seconds, then shook his head. "The two of you are as bad as old women," he grumbled.

Waverly gave him an affronted look as Grace laughed and shook her head. "Don't start making trouble for yourself, James. Call them old women long enough and they'll eventually embrace the role and start harassing you about grandchildren."

Though the fur made it hard to tell whether or not James was blushing, Beauty would have laid money on the fact that he was. Since she was sure her own cheeks were sunburn red, she sympathized completely.

THEY WERE SCHEDULED to leave right after breakfast, but realized they couldn't go until they'd dealt with the transportation question.

"Maybe Grace's horses won't have any problem with you, Beast." Beauty had thought the assurance sounded weak even as she'd said it, but she'd needed to offer up something to counteract the effect of those sealed stable doors. She'd met her sister's latest team more than once, but somehow knowing they were behind such firmly barred gates had made them seem far more intimidating than they normally were.

It didn't help that Grace and Waverly had stationed themselves several yards away, a fact that she was sure James had noted as well. Still, she had to try. "They took a gorgon student to a field trip at the local palace once, and though the kid had to wear a wig and sunglasses, they made it the whole way without any trouble."

"Unless the kid was also seven feet tall, I don't think that's going to help our current situation any." James glared at the doors as if they had offended him personally, but there was a fatalistic edge to his voice that Beauty wasn't sure she liked. "Animals tend to be less twitchy about predators shorter than they are."

"We could also simply allow the horses to spend the day right where they are." That was from Waverly, speaking loudly enough there was no chance James could pretend he hadn't heard him. "As pleased as I am to see you once again facing your challenges head-on, you know as well as I do that there's no need to prove this particular point. The elementals are perfectly capable of moving Grace's wagon as well."

James sighed, pushing up the sleeves of his shirt. "But I'll need to know eventually, and it's better I find out now than in some place where I might get some poor civilian trampled." He glanced over at Beauty. "You may want to get back there with them. I care about you a lot more than some theoretical civilian."

Beauty gave him her best stern look even as she started walking backwards. "And if *you* get yourself trampled just to prove a point, I'm going to drag you back from the edge of death just to kill you myself."

That made him grin. "Yes, ma'am." Then, taking a deep breath, he strode forward and unbarred the doors of the stable. Then he flung them open, and there was that breathless instant that always comes just before everything explodes.

This time, though, nothing exploded. All that followed the silence was more silence, and Beauty deliberately let the air out of her lungs as she made her muscles relax. James, his own shoulders less tight than they had been, gave a disgusted snort and headed deeper into the shadows of the barn.

Now they heard the panicked whinny.

Beauty hurried after him, her eyes adjusting to see the smaller of Grace's two horses dancing circles around James in the back corner of the stable. James kept trying to head for the wall, presumably just getting out of the animal's way, but every time he tried to move, the horse somehow always managed to be in just the right place to block his escape.

When James caught sight of Beauty, he tried once more to head for the door. The horse, naturally, chose that exact moment to skitter sideways in the wrong direction, and he had to flinch back or risk being slammed into by a decently sized chunk of horse. "You didn't tell me the horse was this stupid," he growled. "At this point, it's going to end up killing me completely by accident."

Beauty glanced back over her shoulder to see Waverly and Grace heading for the stable as well. Deciding that Grace would be there in time to save her if she was about to be as stupid as the horse, she headed toward James. "Stop moving for a second, Beast, or at least try to scare him in my direction. If I can get hold of his reins, maybe I can calm him down enough he'll start thinking a little more clearly."

"And let you get trampled? I don't think so." Wisely deciding that trying to argue with her wasn't going to do any good, James lunged sideways for the reins. The horse skittered back even further, considering the move an attack, but James managed to snag his claw on the very edge of the loop and stop the horse's sideways momentum. He was dragged a little, but managed to get a firmer grip with his free hand. Once he was sure he had his feet under him, he turned back to Beauty. "I'm hoping you have a next step in mind."

"Sugar cubes," Grace chimed in from behind Beauty, moving past her to head towards the struggling duo. Always making sure she stayed further away from the horse than James was, she dropped the treats into his hastily-freed hand before quickly moving back. "It doesn't always work, but if you can get through Noble Jr.'s thick skull the incentive of something sweet generally holds his attention better than anything else."

James looked skeptical, and Beauty moved close enough to her sister to whisper in her ear. "You couldn't have thought to mention this *before* the thing decided to have a nervous breakdown?"

"I wasn't sure we'd get to the point where it would even be an option," Grace whispered back. "If I'd offered them to James only to have the horses bolt at the sight of him, I would have felt terrible."

James, meanwhile, had temporarily solved the problem of holding onto everything by pinching one of the sugar cubes between his thumb and finger while grabbing the reins with both hands. He stumbled a little when the horse stopped throwing all his weight in the opposite direction, changing tactics to try and nip the sugar cube out of James's hand without actually going near him. James, catching on, moved his hand back a fraction. After a few minutes, when whatever horrible fate Noble Jr. had imagined didn't come to pass, the horse reached out and nipped it out of his hand.

Beauty let out a covert sigh of relief as James let go of the reins, flexing his free hand as Noble Jr. kept eyeing his new sugar cube supplier. "Now, if you'd like, Beast, you can either make friends with him or glare him into complete submission while we hook him up to the wagon."

"I can assist as well." Waverly's voice was even as he moved forward to join their little group. Only the ruffle of a sudden wind around her legs betrayed any tension the man might have been feeling. "It's been some time since I've used more conventional transportation, but I do believe I remember the essentials."

"Wait a minute." Grace stopped, peering around into the stable's more shadowy corners. "Where's Bob?"

Slightly more detailed exploration revealed her sister's other horse to be still placidly chewing his breakfast over in the opposite corner, where he had presumably been the entire time. James tensed, clearly ready to start another dance, but when the animal caught sight of him all it did was give a single unimpressed snort and return back to his meal.

"Well," Grace said brightly, breaking the sudden silence. "At least that solves that problem."

CHAPTER 18

The Terrors of Polite Company

James, it turned out, wasn't terribly fond of wagons. They hadn't been on the road very long before he'd started calculating the cost of outfitting the thing with cushioned seats and somehow upgrading the suspension. He'd spent even more time working out the best way to approach Grace with the offer to pay for it all without accidentally offending her.

It was easier than tensing up every time someone passed by, trying to watch them out of the corner of his eye even as he pretended they weren't there. He'd gotten a few stares so far, with only one being obvious enough to make Beauty yell at the man giving it, but others had been so focused on their own destinations they hadn't seemed to even notice him. One little boy had gawked openly, but when James had growled at him the kid immediately burst into a grin and started waving at him.

The crowds thickened as they got closer to town, which increased both the number of people gawking and the ones who were completely ignoring him. Most of the gawkers immediately snapped their gazes straight ahead when they realized they'd been caught, and there was only a little scurrying when Grace found a parking spot next to Beauty's rented rooms. James eyed everyone carefully as he helped her down, watching for any unpleasant surprises.

Beauty touched her sister's leg. "We'll be quick, I promise." When she turned to lead them inside, there was something about the way she moved her head that made James realize she was scanning the crowd just like he was.

It relaxed him in a way little else could have. "So . . . any annoyingly persistent landlords or too-loud neighbors you want me to threaten while we're here?"

She glanced over at him as they headed up the stairs, the corner of her mouth quirking upward. "Actually, I pay the landlord extra every month ever since Father showed up at three a.m. one night with a banshee who used to go drinking with him. He says he puts it toward charms meant to keep out the riffraff, which probably explains why the drum player who used to live downstairs suddenly turned into a rabbit one morning."

He raised an eyebrow as he followed Beauty down the hallway. "And you have trouble figuring out when *I'm* embroidering the facts?"

Her smile widened for a moment as she pushed open the door. "My landlord's not much of a music lov—" She stopped dead, staring at something inside, then pinched the bridge of her nose with a long-suffering sigh. "I should have known."

Beauty's rooms were about like he'd expected them to be, as disorganized as her room back at the manor, with towers of books heaped on every available flat surface. Her couch, however, was something of a surprise, given the fact that it was occupied by several small, feathery balls of sleeping gryphons and an ancient-looking woman that snored loudly enough to shake everyone involved.

He leaned close enough to Beauty that he didn't have to raise his voice. "Please tell me you're not related."

Beauty shook her head, holding her hands out toward the couch. "Behold, the only one of my neighbors who actually likes me." Her arms dropped as she turned back around. "It'll be safest for everyone if we just let her sleep, but if she wakes up, her eyesight's bad enough that she'll probably just think you forgot to shave this morning."

With that deeply enlightening explanation, she hurried back toward her bedroom. James, not at all willing to be left alone with whatever was happening on that couch, immediately followed her. "So does she have a key, or do locked doors just not bother her? Because either way, I really hope she's not someone you were planning on leaving a forwarding address with."

Still throwing clothes and books into a bag, she shot him a look that suggested he wasn't being particularly funny. "Everyone calls her Mrs. Hubbard. There are rumors that her son's a werewolf, but all I know for sure is she has a hard time remembering that people don't like hearing a 'Hello, dearie' out of the darkness at three o'clock in the morning." She found her mirror, shoving it into her bag with the rest of her things. "Even though she's currently snoring on my couch, I still wouldn't bet money that she knows I haven't been here for two weeks."

There was the faintest edge of bitterness to the words, not so much for the old woman as for the fact that those few sentences apparently constituted the closest relationship she had with any of her neighbors. Beauty had mentioned that her father had made an appearance here as well, and he knew better than anyone how effectively a curse could cut you off from the rest of the world.

No wonder she understood him so well.

James felt a fresh surge of protectiveness hit, but given the lack of immediately accessible enemies, he wasn't entirely certain what to do about it. He was still trying to figure it out when she lifted her head again, closing the bag before slinging it over her shoulder and heading towards him. "Don't tell Grace how many books I brought."

"I won't breathe a word." He reached for the bag, then hesitated as he thought better of it. "I can take that, you know. One of the fringe benefits of dating a looming beast-man is having him carry your luggage for you."

Her brow lowered for a moment as she looked up at him, checking for something in his eyes. Not seeing it, her expression relaxed and she lifted the strap off her shoulder. "You are very good at looming," she said finally, the corners of her mouth curling upward again as he took the bag.

He grinned. "I try."

She put a finger to her lips, motioning for him to be quiet as they crept back through the living room. They were close enough that Beauty had actually touched her hand to the knob.

Later, he wondered if the old woman had actually been waiting for them to get that far.

"Why, hello, dearie." There was a rustling that suggested that baby gryphons were being gently moved. "I was beginning to think you'd finally run off and joined a dwarf mine like you kept threatening to."

Beauty sighed, pivoting around on her heel. A second later, James resigned himself to his fate and joined her. "We didn't mean to wake you," she said brightly. "We were just picking up a few things."

Mrs. Hubbard chuckled. "No need to humor me, dearie. We both know perfectly well that a responsible old woman would be sleeping in her own bed." She stopped, leaning toward them and squinting her eyes. "Though I see why you're in such a hurry. Who's your friend, here?"

"James, this is Mrs. Hubbard." She touched his arm. "Mrs. Hubbard, this is James. He's the one who's been occupying my time these last few weeks. We've been seeing each other."

"Actually, I'm planning on stealing her away," James added, hooking an arm around Beauty's shoulders and pulling her close. "She's amazing enough that I'm talking her into moving in with me for good."

If she thought he was worth claiming in front of everyone she knew, the least he could do was make it clear he was just as willing to do some public claiming of his own.

He wished he'd found some way to do this before now when Beauty looked up at him, a little surprised, then smiled and leaned her head against his side. The old woman, still peering at both of them, clapped her hands and settled back against the couch. "Wonderful! I'd been worried at the distinct lack of Prince Charmings in the area." Still squinting at them both, she absently reached out to scratch underneath the nearest gryphon's beak. "You look like you could use a shave, young man, but you have excellent taste in women. I remember this one time . . ."

James raised an eyebrow at Beauty, who just shrugged and quirked her mouth in an "I tried to tell you" gesture as Mrs. Hubbard continued talking. He briefly considered whether or not buying the old woman glasses with a charm making them impossible to lose would be a community service, but he suspected she would be even more dangerous if she could see properly.

". . . and he has such nice, white fangs, too. Shows he takes good care of himself. Doesn't walk around with yellow teeth and claws like *some* people . . ."

James's eyes widened, but they were no match for Beauty's. She opened her mouth, clearly planning on investigating this sudden revelation further, but he gently but firmly started steering her back around toward the door. "We actually have someone waiting on us, so we should head out," he said quickly. "It was . . . interesting meeting you."

Beauty turned back around just long enough to give Mrs. Hubbard a small wave. "I'm not sure when I'll be back for the rest of my stuff, so as long as you keep the gryphons from pooping all over everything, you can stay as long as you want."

The old woman waved them off. "Go have fun, dearie. I'll keep an eye on everything for you." Her voice dropped to a murmur. "Such a nice young man . . ."

As they carefully closed the door behind them, James leaned closer to Beauty. "I think she likes me, but I'm still not sure whether or not that's a good thing."

She held up an open hand in a helpless gesture. "At least the worst is over. It only gets easier from here."

EASIER, OF COURSE, depended on your perspective. Next on the agenda was Grace's building, which was inconveniently located in a much more respectable part of town. Neither Beauty nor her sister actually said that out loud, of course, but if the paint and stonework hadn't been enough to tell him that there was also the ever-increasing number of people who stared at him as they drove. After a certain point, however, the people on the street rigorously began to avoid even glancing in his direction. They weren't avoiding the carriage, specifically, just managing to look anywhere but directly at his eyes.

Clearly, this is where the *polite* people lived.

"I'm sorry," Grace apologized, turning back to pat James soothingly on the leg after Waverly had helped her down. This time, he and Beauty were the ones staying in the wagon, which had seemed like a much more agreeable idea before he'd seen the neighborhood. "But private schools are obsessed with the reputations of their teachers, and they were only willing to include a housing stipend if it was in a neighborhood they approved of."

"I can tough it out," he assured her, giving Waverly a nod that meant the same thing. He tilted his head in Beauty's direction. "Besides, if there's any trouble she'll be here to protect me."

Once they'd gone inside, Beauty squeezed his hand. "Don't worry about it, Beast. The first time I came here to visit Grace, they had to issue me a special pass before I was allowed to walk the streets."

He stroked the side of her hand with his thumb, marveling at the fact that even truly unpleasant things seemed slightly less horrible when she was next to him. "Maybe we should have stopped somewhere and picked one up for me."

She shook her head in mock regret. "There's an eight-page questionnaire and a two-hour interview, and it's really hard to get all the necessary civic leaders together before noon."

"Ah." James smiled a little. "We wouldn't want to get them out of—" He stopped talking when he caught sight of a well-dressed, middle-aged man who had stopped dead on the sidewalk to stare at them. There was something . . . focused about his expression, as if he were looking at something he didn't particularly like. "We might be getting company in a moment," he muttered.

She turned around to follow his gaze, at which point the man's expression immediately transformed into the shiniest, falsest grin James had ever seen. When Beauty immediately looked away, the man stepped off the sidewalk and began to head straight for them.

Beauty's jaw tightened. "Of all the people . . ." Shaking her head a little, she squeezed James's hand again. "I'm going to apologize in advance for this, and if afterwards you want us to go inside and hide until Grace and Waverly come out, I completely understand."

She collected her expression just as the man made it to the side of their wagon, looking him in the eye before he'd even opened his mouth. "Mr. Altaire." Beauty stretched the name out until it was almost an insult. "Just what are you doing out and about this fine morning? Aren't you supposed to be at the witch's office making sure that little hex you picked up has completely cleared up?"

James's predatory instincts, which he'd picked up long before he'd inherited the fangs and claws, stretched in satisfaction at the subtle sharpness of the opening. If things unfolded the way he was starting to hope they would, he'd love to see her in a boardroom someday.

Mr. Altaire's smile froze, leaving him hanging helplessly behind it, but he recovered enough to give the side of the wagon a solid hit that tried to masquerade itself as a neighborly pat. If he took even one more step toward Beauty, James decided, he'd have his claws around the man's throat in a heartbeat. "I was just surprised to see your . . . winning personality gracing the neighborhood with its presence on such a fine, sunny morning," Mr. Altaire replied, his voice syrupy sweet and his smile forced. "And you're keeping such . . . interesting company, too. Did you offer to help your sister with 'Bring Your Pet to School Day,' by any chance?"

A small part of James had wondered whether his assurance that he could deal with whatever strangers threw at him had just been bravado, and whether he could make it a full day without maiming anyone. That, thankfully, turned out not to be a problem, though

James was admittedly distracted by the sudden need to physically restrain Beauty from leaping over the side of the wagon and choking the man herself.

It was wonderfully touching, actually.

Arm still firmly across Beauty's chest, James gave the man the smile that showed off his fangs to their full advantage. "Oddly enough, you look *just* like someone a knight I know told me about recently." He used his smoothest, friendliest voice, the one he'd always enjoyed using when he told arrogant people that he now owned their entire lives. "I believe he'd just been hired to slay a creature who'd been terrifying a group of villagers. He'd said something about the thing being so impossibly unpleasant it was frightening the cattle." Beast furrowed his brow in mock thoughtfulness. "You do seem remarkably like the creature he described. Have you run into any knights lately, by chance?"

By this point, the man had gone almost completely white, his mouth hanging open as if he couldn't quite believe what he'd just heard. Unfortunately, he managed to rally, sucking in a sharp breath and trying to put color back into his face by sheer force of will. "I see you have a talent for finding associates with the same regrettable impulse-control issues, Miss Tremain." He cleared his throat, taking a very definite step back. "I'm afraid I need to insist that both of you tell me what you're doing here, and how long you intend to be doing it."

The temptation to shoot back the insult that hovered on the tip of James's tongue was extreme, but he'd noticed that Beauty wasn't entirely comfortable with his tendency to simply take charge of things. She'd been remarkably tolerant of the impulse so far, but it was probably a good idea to curb it while he could.

Besides, every shot he took meant one less time he could enjoy watching her get riled in his defense.

"Actually, I don't think you can insist on anything at all, Mr. Altaire," Beauty said sharply, now firmly settled back into her seat but still glaring daggers at the man. "Unless you've actually become important since last time I saw you, a couple can sit in the sunshine without being ordered around by a petty, small-minded man who's had three wives leave him because they couldn't stand to listen to him night after night."

Mr. Altaire's jaw worked for a moment without any sound coming out, but after a strangled noise he finally got things moving again. "They can't if they're in a temporary parking zone! If you're still here in twenty minutes I'm fully within my rights to call the—" Suddenly, the words cut off again, and you could practically see the gears in the man's head moving as his eyes narrowed. "Wait. Did you say *couple?*"

James tensed, already able to tell exactly where this was going. Now *he* was back to seriously considering choking the life out of the man, or at the very least making him bleed. Now wasn't the time to get arrested on assault charges, but if the fool actually hurt her, James didn't think there was anything that could stop him.

Clearly, some of this was evident in his expression, because the man went pale again and took another step back. Beauty, thankfully deciding she could once again take on the duties of being the calm one in the relationship, placed a firm, steadying hand on his thigh. "Yes, I said couple." She lifted her chin, sounding proud rather than defensive. "Sadly, there's a deficiency of intelligent men in this city, so I had to look elsewhere before I found someone actually worth dating."

"But he's a . . . a *monster!*"

She smiled a predator's smile. "And you're a frigid, unpleasant, narrow-minded moron. Clearly, I fared far better than whatever poor fool you may find to be wife number four."

The man blanched completely white, then spun on his heel and stalked off in whatever direction let him escape as quickly as possible. Once he'd disappeared from sight, Beauty let out a long breath that was shakier than Beast would have expected. "I am so, so sorry that happened." She squeezed his leg, apology in her eyes. "And I don't think you're a monster, even though it sort of sounded like I accepted what he'd said, but if I'd tried to argue semantics he would have just kept going and he'd already set up the *perfect* opening for my comeback . . ."

Chest tightening, he cut off the rest of the explanation by pulling her into a hug. "I wasn't worried," he said quietly, feeling the corners of his mouth sneak upward. "I was just trying to figure out whether or not it would be appropriate to applaud while he was still in earshot."

He heard her sigh, but it sounded more relieved than anything. "I should have warned you about the possibility that we'd run into him, but after I'd met you I didn't think my luck was quite that bad anymore."

James grinned, flattered. "So you think I'm good luck?"

"No, you're the result of my sudden good luck. There a difference." Beauty was grinning herself as she lifted her head to look up at him. "I loved your story about him terrifying a village. I thought you'd just knock him over and threaten to rip his head off, but that expression on your face when you'd asked him if he'd run into any knights lately was so much more entertaining." She chuckled a little as she laid her head back against his chest. "Also, Waverly and Grace didn't have to top off their morning by bailing us out of jail. Always a plus."

"I thought so." He rubbed a hand up and down her back, careful not to accidentally snag her shirt with his claws. "Besides, I was defending myself with words long before I ever got the claws." He paused, almost surprised at the thought. "I think I just forgot that for a while."

Beauty tightened her arms around him. "Well, you picked an excellent time to remember."

CHAPTER 19

Grin and Attack It

It would have been more efficient to split up at that point, with Beauty and James getting dropped off at the temp agency while Grace and Waverly went on to the school. But the school was close enough that they couldn't avoid driving past it, recess hadn't quite ended yet, and Grace had had no idea of how popular a teacher she was. As soon as they'd come into view some of the kids started running toward them, and it would have taken someone much more hard-hearted than her sister not to stop then and there.

They were mobbed almost immediately, with the older kids gathering around Grace to ask where she'd been all week and to tell her about various things they were working on in their classes. The younger ones only had eyes for James, and were crowding along the side of the wagon to pepper him with questions.

"Would you eat my teacher for me? She won't believe me that my brother got turned into a goat and ate my homework."

"Have you ever fought a dragon? I bet you could fight a dragon with claws like that."

"You're really tall. Do you bump into ceilings?"

James, wearing the stunned look of someone who'd just been

hit over the head, turned to Beauty with a pleading expression. "Tell me we can stay in the wagon again."

"I do wonder sometimes about your sense of adventure, James." Waverly's voice was warmly amused as he stepped down on the open side of the wagon, watching Grace and the children with an unabashedly tender expression. "If you're not willing to brave young people even in these temporary circumstances, it doesn't speak well for how you'll fare when you end up with a brood of your own."

James's startled gaze immediately shot over to Beauty, clearly considering what Waverly had just said, and Beauty immediately felt her cheeks flush. Not that the idea of having kids with James wasn't a wildly intriguing—and tempting—one, but she hadn't really let herself start planning out that far ahead . . .

Grace gestured toward Waverly, and the crowd of kids parted just long enough to let him through to join her. James looked back down at his own crowd, then back over at Beauty. "He does have a point." He smiled, a little crookedly. "Shall we, my lady?"

She met his eyes, feeling lured by a future she knew she shouldn't be trusting just yet. But when he looked at her like that, it was hard not to believe that anything was possible.

At her nod, he jumped down from the side of the wagon and into the mob of children. When he turned back around and held a hand out to her, she took a deep breath and joined him.

WHEN THEY ARRIVED at the temp agency, however, it was Waverly's sense of adventure that failed him.

"There's no need for all four of us to intrude," he said quickly, carefully ignoring that he'd had no such qualms at the school. "I need to pick up a few things in town, and I would be deeply grateful if Grace would be willing to keep me company."

He bowed a little in Grace's direction, very deliberately ignoring Beauty's suddenly knowing grin. "So this has nothing to do with not wanting Manny to meet your girlfriend just yet?" she asked innocently, making James smother a chuckle. "Because he already knows Grace, and I'm sure he's really looking forward to talking to her again. He probably has all *kinds* of stories he wants to tell her."

Waverly's pained expression nearly made Beauty burst out laughing. "I can only imagine," he muttered, shooting Grace a look that Beauty would have called pleading on anyone else.

Her sister fought back her own smile. "We'll pick you up in an hour," she told Beauty. "For Waverly's sake, try to remember to meet us outside."

As the wagon drove away, Beauty and James turned around to face the building. "Now that we've had our entertainment for the afternoon," he said, squaring his shoulders, "where do we start?"

She considered the question, trying to think about who might actually be there, when she heard a faint hammering sound from the far side of the building. Immediately making her decision, she took James's hand and led him around the corner. "Come on, Beast. I know the perfect person to have you meet first."

Steve had been fixing a bit of crumbled brickwork between the first and second floors, but he stopped when he caught sight of Beauty. "Manny said you were taking time off because of your dad," he said, hooking the trowel back on his belt and stepping away from the wall. "Want me to go shake him again?"

"Actually, I've kind of got people lining up to threaten him now. But thank you." Smiling, she held up her and James's joined hands. "Steve, this is my boyfriend James." Then she turned to Beast, trying not to worry about the surprised expression on his face. "James, this is Steve. He's a very good friend, and the guy I hoped you'd put in touch with your tailor."

James's brow furrowed, then cleared suddenly. "The pants?" He turned back to Steve. "Okay, I can see that." He held out his free hand to Steve. "Pleased to meet you. I'd apologize for the fact that we've clearly been discussing your wardrobe without you, but you seem to know Beauty well enough I can't imagine you're surprised."

Steve smiled slowly as he shook James's hand. "Not really, but

if you know a guy I'd be interested if you'd pass the name along."
Then he took a step back, settling his hands in his pockets as he gave
James a slow, measuring, up-and-down look. Then he met Beauty's
eyes. "So, he looks like he could bounce your dad pretty good, too.
He one of the people in line?"

Beauty grinned. "Oh, definitely. Sometimes it's hard for him to
remember he can't just kick everyone else out of line and take over."

James raised an eyebrow at her. "I'd be happy to stand aside and
applaud while you and Grace beat him up, but only after we've made
absolutely sure he's run out of last-minute ways to hurt you both."

Steve smiled. "Well, that's one way to solve the problem." At
Beauty's questioning expression, he tilted his head. "You needed a
guy who didn't wait for you to ask him for help."

She closed her eyes, just now remembering the conversation she
and Steve had had the last time her father had shown up at work.
When James nudged her shoulder in question, she opened her eyes
and shook her head. "Long story."

Steve, of course, was more than happy to add commentary. "Not
that long. She's not good at calling for backup, especially when it
comes to her dad."

James let go of her hand only to put his arm around her shoulders. "Believe me, that's not a problem anymore."

Steve nodded, seemingly satisfied. "Sounds about right." He
used his elbow to gesture back toward the front of the building.
"You'd better get inside, though. Manny'll be mad if he finds out
you've stopped by without telling him hello."

When she and James went back around to enter through the
front doors, James took her hand again. "I would tease you about
having a thing for tall men, but then I'd have to imagine the two
of you dating at some point," he rumbled, keeping his voice low as
they headed inside. "Now doesn't seem like the best time for me to
get insanely jealous, so I'll just say I like the guy."

Beauty grinned, both flattered and touched. It was a little too
embarrassing to admit, but the possibility of making someone

romantically jealous had never occurred to her. "If it helps, we never even thought about it." She squeezed his hand. "I was waiting for someone who could argue with me properly."

When they went inside, she smiled at the woman sitting at the front desk. "Is Manny in a meeting?" she asked, careful not to ask to see him until she was absolutely certain she wasn't interrupting anything. Doris manned the schedules of everyone in the building, and probably would have been referred to as the office dragon had Manny's existence not made the nickname unfortunately ironic.

Doris, looking up from one of the three mirrors she manned, gave James a long, speculative expression before moving on to Beauty. "New client?" she asked, the surprise in her voice not as offensive as it would have been from anyone else. During the one even semi-personal conversation she and Doris had ever had, they'd bonded over being the kind of people who were good at getting the job done. It wasn't a talent that made them very popular, but it helped them understand each other.

"It's more of a personal introduction, actually." She set James's and her joined hands down on the desk, hoping he wouldn't take Doris's inevitably chilly reception at all personally. If she didn't actively hate a person, that person had made the best impression on her they possibly could. "He didn't know we'd be coming today, but he's definitely expecting us."

It wasn't a lie, exactly. Manny had practically been the one to set her and James up, and by this point Beauty was sure Waverly had told him that they'd started dating. If she didn't give him his chance to enjoy the results, he'd just find a way to do it on his own later.

Doris gave them both another long look, and an imaginative person might have said that her mouth softened ever so slightly. "He's talking to someone, but you can wait for him in the back." She stuck her thumb in the appropriate direction. James, thankfully not at all offended, sketched her a small bow before they headed into the main office.

It was barer than a normal office building, since most of the actual work occurred at various job sites throughout the surrounding kingdoms. The main building was mostly for paperwork, and therefore there were rows of simple, mostly empty desks and rows upon rows of filing cabinets full of all of the information connected to every job the agency had ever worked on.

"Manny believes in having hard copy backup," she explained, noticing the attention James was paying to the cabinets. "The information itself is all input into the company's mirror system, but he feels that's too easy to erase or tamper with in case we ever need it to defend ourselves in court."

"Or need a little something to force an annoying client to be more polite?" James asked. Before she could respond, he nodded in what looked like satisfaction. "It's a good idea. Even thieves who won't bat an eye at six-headed sacred temple monsters tend to think twice about having to deal with a few decades of handwritten, only loosely alphabetized files."

Beauty raised an eyebrow at his supremely content look. "For my sake, please don't start Manny talking shop. I'm very happy you both seem to enjoy it so much, but I left all my books in the wagon."

His grin had more than a little smirk in it. "I'll try to restrain myself."

She introduced James to the few people there, and their responses ranged from polite good humor to the vague pleasantness of someone who has no idea why you're suddenly talking to them. All in all, it turned out to be mildly embarrassing, and ended just as Manny's door finally opened again.

Seeing it, Beauty eagerly stepped forward at exactly the same time that James jerked both of them backward around the nearest corner. Surprised, she looked up at him for an explanation, and he pointed toward the man walking out of the office just ahead of Manny. The two hesitated in the doorway, still talking. "Daniel Carlyle," James said, "He owns a shipping company based in the capitol."

The details were enough to trigger Beauty's memory. "He generally comes in for a merperson interpreter. I don't know why he doesn't just man up and finally hire one on a permanent basis . . ." The words trailed off as the rest of her brain finally joined the party. "He's one of the men you used to work with." She shook her head, annoyed at herself as she pushed them both back around the corner, a little further out of sight. "I'm so sorry, Beast. I can't believe that didn't occur to me . . ."

When there was no response, she looked back up at him. He was staring at Mr. Carlyle with an intensity that didn't look like either panic or longing for the old days, and after a moment he took a deep breath. "I'm still being a coward," he said quietly, then stepped away from the wall. When he felt her watching him, he straightened his shirt and tried to smile. "He's never seen me like this. I could be standing right in front of him and he wouldn't recognize me as James Hightower."

He had a point, but she also knew his eyes were saying more than that. "You're going to tell him, though," she said quietly.

James let the air out of his lungs. "Yeah." He squared his shoulders. "Back me up?"

She laid a hand against his arm, hoping her face showed how incredibly proud of him she was. "Of course."

The conversation between Manny and Mr. Carlyle was just wrapping up when James stepped forward, Beauty right next to him. Manny started to grin at the sight of them, then met her eyes and saw enough to know to even his expression out again. She gave him a tiny nod as James stepped toward the other man. "Daniel." His voice almost sounded easy as he held a hand out. "It's been a while."

Mr. Carlyle blinked. "I'm sorry, but I believe I would remember if we'd met before."

"James Hightower." In the silence that followed, the man's eyes went wide, and James's mouth quirked in an expression that didn't have a great deal of humor in it. "Don't tell me you didn't hear about the curse." He lowered his hand. "I thought you paid your secretary to keep you more in the loop than that."

It took a little while for the man to collect himself, and Beauty was grateful she was standing far enough away that she couldn't easily give in to her impulse to smack him. Finally, though, he was the one who held out his hand. "James." There was the trace of embarrassed laughter in his voice. "I would say 'the Beast' has been missed, but everyone's making a lot more money without you nipping at our heels."

James shook his head. "Enjoy it while you can." There was the briefest of hesitations, so short Beauty thought she might have imagined it. "I'm thinking about getting back into the game."

Mr. Carlyle couldn't quite stop his eyes from flickering a little wider, but he recovered much faster this time. Before the man could actually think of anything to say, however, James had turned back to Beauty. "I've been rude, though. My girlfriend Beauty Tremain is the entire reason I'm here, and I haven't even introduced her yet." He rested a possessive hand against her back as she stepped forward, though he might also have been providing some signal as to where on earth he was going with this. "Daniel, this is Beauty. Beauty, Daniel. He's provided me with a few memorable investment opportunities over the years."

"Pleased to meet you." Beauty held out a hand, trying not to be too obvious as she watched James's former business associate wage a brief but desperate struggle with his eyebrows. If the man always had this much trouble keeping his reactions hidden, it was a wonder he'd managed to survive any business deals at all.

Finally, he seemed to rally. "I'm pleased to meet you as well," he said, shaking her hand. "Are you looking forward to breaking the curse?"

She narrowed her eyes, more than ready to make the man regret he'd ever asked such a stupid question, when James smoothly cut in. "Actually, the experts I've consulted are fairly sure the curse is unbreakable." There was a faint edge to his voice she hadn't picked up on before, and as she looked up at him she saw a bit of grim pleasure in his eyes. "Luckily, she's decided she likes me anyway."

The conversation stumbled on for a few more minutes, at which point Mr. Carlyle finally made the appropriate excuses and fled the building. Once he was gone, Manny shot James his "I'm considering whether or not I should eat you" look. "If you just cost me a client, kid, I'm going to be expecting a very generous thank-you for setting the two of you up."

James smirked. "Don't worry about it. He's so embarrassed about sticking his foot in his mouth that he might actually start hiring you for more work." He met Beauty's eyes, his expression finally softening. "Thank you for letting me run with that, even though it will probably turn out to be a terrible idea in the long run."

She patted his arm. "Thank you for understanding that smiling and nodding was the closest I could get to being supportive. I'm still not entirely sure what your plan was."

James grinned a little sheepishly. "Neither was I."

Manny looked back and forth between the two of them, then flashed his own toothy grin. "There won't be enough gold in the kingdom to get me to babysit the kids you two are gonna produce."

THE VISIT WAS wrapped up without any verbal bloodshed, and in a great show of restraint, Manny was kind enough not to be waiting outside when Grace and Waverly picked them up. Neither Beauty nor James even teased him about it, since Manny had promised both of them they could have ringside seats when he finally cornered his old friend.

The good humor didn't survive the entire way home, however. The four of them could hear the elementals well before the house came into view, roaring like a midwinter gale even though the air around them was calm and still. As they got closer, they could see the small figure curled up in a protective ball on the lawn, golden hair and silken skirts being ripped at by the elementals.

Beauty's stomach gave a single, hard twist. A part of her brain tried desperately to convince her it was just another one of those idiot women lured here by the guidebook, but the elementals had never attacked any of them before this. Another, angrier part of her wanted to just sit back and enjoy the show.

That, however, would only have been delaying the inevitable. Juliana was back, and frightening her away wasn't going to solve the problem. "Waverly, call them off." She had to almost shout the words for them to be heard over the wind's anger.

For a moment he didn't respond, his eyes narrowed at the woman on the ground. "I see no need."

Beauty looked over at James, the knot in her stomach tightening when she realized she couldn't translate his expression. When his hand moved to rest on leg, her heart jumped. "Call them off," he said finally, meeting the other man's eyes. "We need to know why she's here."

Jaw tightening, Waverly dismissed the winds. Grace took his hand in silent support as they all stared at the figure on the ground, which still hadn't moved. Briefly, Beauty found herself hoping the other woman was dead, which *would* be enough to settle the matter. Surely Waverly had hidden a body at some point in his life . . .

Finally, James swore and jumped down off the side of the wagon, stalking towards the seemingly unconscious Juliana. Beauty hesitated, wishing she had something appropriately heavy on hand, then climbed down after him. She turned around just in time to see James crouch down over the woman, probably to check for a pulse.

Beauty hadn't even taken a step, however, before Juliana suddenly pushed herself upward and at James. When he fell backwards, surprised and trying to get out of the way, Beauty started running. Juliana fell forward, throwing her arms around James just as their lips made contact.

The magic started to swirl.

CHAPTER 20

Ch-Ch-Ch-Changes

Apart of him had hoped she'd died somehow, killed by a fear-induced heart attack when the elementals had decided she was the enemy. James suspected, though, that he would've just ended up even angrier at her, cheated out of his answers because she couldn't handle a measly little windstorm.

Taken together, it was enough strain that he should have asked Waverly to check Juliana's pulse for him. Or Beauty, who seemed like she might let Juliana live just long enough to get some answers out of her. But he'd gone himself, alone and so focused on brooding that Juliana had caught him completely by surprise. He barely had time to blink before she was practically on top of him, clinging to him like a gremlin and sobbing things that might have been words if he'd had any more interest in concentrating on them. He fell backwards, getting a hand between them to shove her away . . .

Their lips only made contact for a second before he managed to pry her off, scrambling backwards with a desperation that gave no thought to any perception of manliness. He was panicked enough that it took him a second to notice the sparkling light starting to swirl around him.

Sparkling, magical light. Just like what there'd been when he'd been cursed.

His first horrified thought was that Juliana had found some way to curse him again, or had thrown in an enchantment as some sort of graduate project for evil sorceress training she'd never mentioned. She was still on her knees, staring at him with her hand over her mouth and tears filling her eyes. He tried to stand up and attack her properly—if he survived this, he'd have to apologize for restraining Waverly's more violent impulses—but an incredible pressure kept him pinned to the spot as firmly as a giant who'd taken up wrestling.

The magic was thicker now, a wall of almost painfully golden glow that made him want to close his eyes. He could still see Beauty, though, halfway between him and the wagon. She was frozen mid-run, staring at him with wide eyes and an expression he couldn't make out with all of the magic getting in his way. She took another step toward him, clearly deciding to brave whatever latest disaster Juliana had cooked up in order to get to him, and he lifted a hand to tell her to stop.

Only to stare as his claws melted into fingertips, and his fur dissolved into pale skin in a wave that rippled painlessly down his arm.

James's brain refused to accept the information his eyes were taking in, shutting down completely and leaving him unable to process what was happening. His shoulders shrank, the world around him rushing upwards as he lost about a foot of height. He heard his legs pop, the sound painful even if the sensation wasn't, and he looked down just in time to see the ripple slide any traces of fur right off his feet. He didn't dare reach up to touch his face, but his tongue could already feel the definite absence of fangs on either side of his mouth.

The magic faded, having caused more than enough havoc for the afternoon. Taking that as her cue, Juliana threw her arms back around him and promptly began sobbing something about her father and how sorry she was. Too shocked to fight her off, James sat there frozen as the truth finally managed to sink in.

He was human again.

The sound of footsteps that were probably Beauty's kick-started James's brain back into some semblance of functionality. She moved toward him hesitantly, like she wasn't entirely sure of her welcome, and it hit him that he was currently letting himself be clutched by his ex-fiancée.

Well, that wasn't going to work.

James shoved her away as he staggered to his feet, realizing only as his pants started to slide down his thighs that his clothing hadn't magically received the memo. He yanked the waistband back up before any unintentional and extremely-poorly timed comedy could happen, then finished trying to stand in a body that had entirely forgotten where its original center of gravity had been. Not to mention that his feet were now only about two-thirds the size they had been five minutes ago.

Beauty crossed the rest of the distance between them in a run. Before she could get there, Juliana managed to stop crying just long enough to slide right in under his arm and pretend to help support him. Beauty, who had been aiming for that exact spot, skidded to a halt again. "Charlton, darling, can you ever forgive me for letting my father keep us apart so long?" Juliana pleaded. She'd always called him by his ridiculous middle name, insisting it sounded more dignified. Looking back, he had no idea how he'd ever been able to stand it. "As soon as I learned about the curse I tried—"

Deciding that shoving clearly wasn't working, James pulled away from Juliana and headed straight for Beauty. He was already feeling steadier on his feet, but he still put his arm around her shoulders and leaned just enough to make clear exactly where he wanted to be. Thankfully, she immediately slid her arm around his back. "Explanations later," he said firmly to Juliana, trying to think past the headache currently attempting to shove its way through the front of his brain. Apparently, one curse had been enough to make his body decide that it was allergic to magic. "Now, you *really* need to stop talking."

For a second he could have sworn that Juliana glared at him, but before he could be sure, the expression had slid into a wounded look that almost matched her earlier tears. "But . . . but . . . I came all this way!" Her voice wavered. "I *saved* you." All her calm composure that he'd remembered was clearly no longer part of the picture, which was probably for the best. After all, his tastes had changed.

"So it was your *father* who cursed James?" And there was Waverly's voice, sharp enough to draw blood at thirty paces. He and Grace had finally left the wagon and were stalking toward their little tableau, Waverly looking like he was ready to kill and Grace trying to keep an eye on everyone all at once. "And you inconveniently decided to disappear for a year before suddenly riding in to save the day?"

Juliana inhaled tremulously. "Like I tried to tell you, I didn't even *know* what Daddy had done until just recently. When we left a year ago, he just woke me up in the middle of the night and told me we had to leave the country, but I thought it was because his business deals had made enemies. I was afraid they were coming after us." She gave James a fragile look, then dabbed at her tears with her knuckle. "I thought we were about to be *killed,* so I helped gather the servants and then fled with him."

James watched her, wondering whether his instinct to disbelieve every word she said was due to a healthy sense of self-preservation or to old doubts and betrayals rearing their ugly heads. In the end, he wasn't entirely sure it mattered. "So your father, who apparently decided to flee the country because of dangerous business deals I had no part of, suddenly decides to *curse* me on his way out of town?"

"I don't know!" She started sobbing, making little shuddering sounds rather than doing something so indelicate as to scrunch up her lovely face. "All I know is that just before he died he kept telling me how sorry he was—"

"So that's one problem down," Waverly snapped, causing Juliana to start sobbing again and Grace to take his hand in a mildly restraining fashion. Beauty still hadn't said a word, her entire body as tense as an ogre's battle drum. James looked down at her, wanting to read her eyes, but she pressed her cheek against his shoulder and stayed resolutely silent and still.

Suddenly, all those questions that had been swirling around his head for so long seemed far less important than making sure nothing terrible was going through Beauty's head. The fact she was this deathly quiet couldn't mean anything good. "It doesn't matter," he said firmly, immediately drawing Grace and Waverly's attention and causing Juliana to go instantly silent. His ex-fiancée lifted her head, a dangerously hopeful light sparking in her eyes, and James glared at her as he tightened his arm around Beauty. "She's broken the curse her father supposedly laid on me, and is now welcome to go back to wherever she came from. I, personally, would really like to go inside and find a pair of pants that fit me a little better than these ones."

Waverly raised an eyebrow, his expression easing a fraction. "If I remember correctly, you shredded all your old clothing in a fit of self-hatred."

James closed his eyes a moment. He'd forgotten that. "Is there *any* chance you managed to save a few?"

Something close to amusement flickered across Waverly's face. "Perhaps we can find something of your father's that's not too horrifying . . ."

Juliana looked back and forth between the two men, eyes wide with horror at having been so easily dismissed. "But . . . but . . . My father is *dead!*" She stepped toward him, hand outstretched pleadingly. "My home was sold such a long time ago! I have no place else to go!" James's glare sharpened, and she dropped to her knees like a puppet whose strings had been cut. "Please, Charlton, I'm begging you! Don't leave me out here all alone!"

Clearly, getting rid of her quickly wasn't an option. Would the promise of a few days of shelter be enough to shut her up? There had to be more she wasn't telling them—Juliana's father had been just opportunistic and thoughtless enough to get involved with dangerous people, but James doubted that he'd had anything to do with the curse. Even if Juliana hadn't done it—and if she had, Beauty's presence would surely put an end to whatever she thought she would gain by undoing the damage—there had to be more that he could find out from her.

He met Waverly's eyes long enough to see that he was wrestling with the same questions, and hated all of the answers he'd come up with. Grace's gaze was hard, her eyes only for her sister, and James realized she would agree to anything that would end the conversation faster and get Beauty someplace away from all this. It was at the top of James's list of priorities, as well, and if he had to sacrifice those answers to make sure Beauty stayed, he would do it in a heartbeat.

"Don't let her do anything stupid, okay?" he told both Waverly and Grace, deliberately not looking at Juliana. "We'll be right back." He felt the wind pick up as he tightened his arm around Beauty, then let her go only long enough to take her hand instead and pull her toward the house.

Once inside, he had to let go of Beauty's hand to close the door behind him, since the other one was still occupied with keeping his pants around his waist. Thoroughly exasperated, he stole the tie off the nearest set of curtains and started threading them awkwardly through the belt loops of his pants. Tying the ends in an undigni-fied knot, he immediately took Beauty's hands again. "The fact you haven't said a word since this whole mess started absolutely terrifies me. Talk to me, please."

Beauty opened her mouth, hunting for the right words, then closed it again when nothing useful came out. James's stomach sank when she pulled her hands away from his, the pressure in his chest nowhere near enough to keep his heart held together. Thankfully, she immediately saved everything by throwing her arms around his middle and holding on for all she was worth. James closed his eyes, miraculously able to breathe again as he held on just as hard.

"I was so scared, Beast," she said finally. "I kept trying to tell myself that there are hundreds of ways to break curses, and it couldn't really be True Love's Kiss, but if she really wasn't the one who cursed you and you stopped being angry . . ."

"No." He pulled away just enough to meet her eyes. "Whoever cursed me doesn't matter, and whether or not I'm angry at her doesn't matter. Now that I've fallen in love with someone else, she's just an unfortunately colorful part of my past."

Beauty's eyes filled, and she pulled him down for a kiss that did wonders for everything ailing him. It was a little awkward—he kept trying to compensate for fangs he no longer had—but it was the first thing he'd done that felt completely, totally real since Juliana had shown up on his front lawn again.

When they broke apart, her eyes had their light back even though he could see tear tracks down her cheeks. "Just to clarify, I'd better be that 'someone' you mentioned."

James grinned, brushing away the wetness with his thumb. "I hoped you'd figure that out." He pulled her close again, thinking about how differently Beauty fit against him now that he was back in his old body. It still felt right to him—as long as Beauty was there, anything felt right—but with everything that had been thrown at them so suddenly, he needed to be absolutely sure. "What about me? Now that you've seen the non-furry version in person, are you relieved or disappointed?"

She moved away just enough to look up at him, staring into his eyes as if she could do it all day. Eyes, he remembered her saying, that hadn't changed no matter what the rest of him had looked like. "I'd love you even if you were a twenty-foot dragon," she said finally, stretching upward for another kiss. "Though it is nice not to have to worry about always having a chair handy."

"This is true." He tightened his arms around her, sobering as he remembered the emotional quandary still waiting outside. "I'm so sorry about Juliana. Even if we leave her sitting outside, I don't think she's going to go anywhere."

"I don't think she is either." Beauty leaned her cheek against

James's shoulder. "Do you think she's telling the truth about her father?" She sighed. "Because I still want to hit her with something heavy for abandoning you, but I of all people can understand about fathers."

He smoothed his hand over Beauty's hair. "Honestly? I have no idea. My instinct says not to trust her, but I don't see why she'd undo the curse if she were the one to hit me with it in the first place. She had me without it, and I'd already set up everything to revert to Waverly if I became incapacitated by enchantment. He didn't like her even then, which meant she'd have gotten a lot more money just by leaving me uncursed and going through with the wedding."

Beauty was silent for a moment. "And if we do manage to chase her away for good, we'll never get the chance to be sure one way or the other."

James found himself immensely comforted by the "we." "If we let her stay, it will give all four of us the chance to keep throwing questions at her. Either she'll stick to her story and give us some more details she might not even know she has, or she'll crack under the combined pressure and tell us the story of what really happened."

Beauty took a deep breath. "And *then* we can kick her out?"

James nodded. "Then we'll kick her out so hard that dragons will complain she's interfering with their flight path." He sighed, tightening his arms around her. "I'm so sorry about this, Beauty. I had no idea she was going to suddenly show up . . ."

". . . and break the curse." Beauty swallowed, looking up at him. "When I couldn't."

He pressed a kiss against her hair. "I told you, True Love's Kiss had nothing to do with breaking this curse. For all I know, she set it up so it could only be broken by her kiss, or her father set it up to only be broken by someone in his bloodline."

There was more silence. "So if her father had lived," Beauty said finally, "we might have ended up trying to peel a sixty-year-old man off your lips."

James couldn't stop the laugh that escaped his lips, the sound freeing enough to loosen some of the tightness inside his chest. "So things actually could have been worse."

"Always." She pulled back enough to meet his eyes, moving her arms away from his middle to rest them on both sides of his face. "And if you can deal with my insane father, then I should be able to deal with your insane ex-fiancée."

They kissed fast and fierce, as if knowing they'd be interrupted by the sound of the elementals achieving gale-force winds. Beauty wisely stayed behind James as he tried forcing the door open, and for a disorienting second, he found himself wanting his much stronger, cursed body back. Just before the door was about to shove him down, however, the wind died down. James pushed open the door to see Juliana huddled on the ground, her hair and clothing a complete wreck. Grace stood only a few feet away, a furious glare on her face and not a single hair out of place. Waverly's eyes were on the front doors, his hand still held out in the gesture he'd used to stop the elementals.

James looked back at Beauty, comforted by the light of battle he could see back in her eyes. Then, taking her hand, he pushed the door open all the way and walked down the stairs as if he knew exactly what he was doing.

They stopped a few feet away from Juliana, and she slowly lifted her head to look up at him. "You *left* me," she said tearfully, muscles tensing as if considering whether or not to leap at him again. She caught Beauty's glare out of the corner of her eye, however, and stayed where she was. "How many times do I have to tell you I'm *sorry?* Charlton, my love, can't you just forget all the—"

"No." The word dropped like a lead weight, absolute silence rippling outward in its wake. "You don't have the right to call me 'my love,' or to be hurt that I left you outside with people who have every right to hate your guts. I will allow you to stay here for a few days while you make some plan about what to do with the rest of your life, but as payment I'll need the full truth about the curse." Juliana opened her mouth to speak again, but whatever she saw in James's eyes cut the words off before they could form. "Either you're to blame and you're lying to me, or your father did it and you have enough information about the curse to know the real reason why it happened. You will tell us *everything*."

She just stared up at him with huge, wet eyes, as if shocked by what he was saying. Then she took a deep, ragged breath, and the characteristic calmness he'd remembered finally settled over her. "I accept," she said quietly, standing up without assistance. She took a moment to dab at her tears again, then met his eyes. "I'm aware of the wrong my father has done to you, and I can accept that merely breaking the curse isn't enough to earn your forgiveness." She lifted her chin. "I will make you trust me again, Charlton, and I'll show you by telling you everything I know about my father and what happened."

James met Waverly's eyes, and the older man gave a small, extremely reluctant nod. Beauty squeezed James's hand, and he met her eyes briefly before giving her a return squeeze. Only then did he refocus on Juliana. "You're earning room and board, not trust. Upset my home in any way and you'll be out the door before you can even blink."

He and Beauty turned, heading back to the house.

INTERLUDE

The Comforts of Tailoring

Waverly hadn't been so close to homicide in a very long time.

Even now, caught up in the mundane task of sorting through the closet in one of the spare bedrooms, he half expected to hear the elementals roar in response to the emotions running so closely beneath his skin. The fact that Juliana had broken the curse had done nothing to lessen the sharpness of his rage. Whether or not she'd laid the curse initially, her timing in removing it seemed too much like an attack on the life James was just now beginning to put back together. For that alone, he couldn't help wanting her to suffer.

But James needed the truth, whatever it turned out to be, and more immediately he needed clothing that didn't look as though he had stolen it from a giant's rag bin.

And Waverly . . .needed a moment alone with his boy.

"Have I bowed before your genius lately?" James asked, taking the shirt Waverly handed him with a relief that went far deeper than the surface joke. "Because if not, allow me to remedy that immediately."

"I would suggest waiting until you've changed to do any dramatic bowing." He kept his voice light as he added to the small, precisely folded stack of clothing on the bed. Though James had indeed destroyed all the clothing in his closet at the time of the curse, Waverly had discreetly hidden away his out-of-season clothes in case just such an eventuality ever occurred. "Though I applaud your appropriation of the curtain tie, I would rather not test the security of the knot you used."

James's smile had a faintly self-mocking edge to it. "I didn't get particularly good at the out-of-doors stuff until after the curse, did I?" He shook his head, as if chasing off the thought, then hurried into the clothes Waverly had handed him. Once he pulled the shirt on he stopped, staring down at himself as if something didn't fit quite right, then shook his head and began tucking it into the pants Waverly had given him previously. When he was done he squared his shoulders, then rolled them as if hoping to get the shirt settled properly.

Quietly, Waverly crossed the distance between them, resting a hand on one of James's shoulders to still the motion. He then began making minute adjustments to the shirt, straightening and smoothing it into some precise imaginary alignment. James tried to look relaxed, as if this were the perfectly normal routine it had once been, but his expression still carried the faintly unsettled air of a man who had lost something and couldn't quite remember where he'd put it. His eyes wandered over to the mirror positioned above the dresser, then looked away quickly before he could focus on anything that might be reflected there.

Waverly met his gaze. "It will seem familiar again," he said quietly, his voice promising the certainty that life often lacked. "But it won't happen immediately. You must be patient."

James let out a long breath, more than a little relief back in his eyes as he scrubbed his hands across his face. It was always easier, after all, when someone else understood without you actually having to admit anything. "You know I'm no good at being patient."

Then, quite suddenly, James caught Waverly in a brief, tight hug.

"Thank you." The words were a mere breath against his ear, but it was enough to make Waverly's throat tighten as his own arms went around James. He didn't trust his voice enough to form a reply of any sort, but thankfully James didn't seem to need one.

Then they separated, clearing their throats and taking a step back to collect themselves. "Grace is still with Beauty, right?" James asked, forcing his hands not to make another adjustment to his shirt. "And Juliana is nowhere near either of them?"

"I believe Grace and her sister are in Beauty's room." It took effort for Waverly to keep his own hands restrained. "I cannot be certain, however, as I was occupied with locking Juliana in the entryway closet."

The corners of James's mouth quirked upward. "You're kidding, aren't you?"

"I wish I weren't. Though I did . . . strongly *encourage* her to remain in her guest quarters. The elementals may be helping." Then he sobered. "I feel compelled to point out that a long-term plan would defeat the entire purpose of allowing her to stay in the first place."

James's jaw tightened. "I'll talk to her." His voice was dark, but as his expression sagged it became clear that he knew how complicated the reality would be. He closed his eyes. "Things had been going so well, too."

"I know." Waverly couldn't stop his own small, sharp sting of regret as he returned a hand to James's shoulder. "There's still time to withdraw your offer."

The younger man opened his eyes again, fixing Waverly with a look that was equal parts weariness and resolve. "I won't let her poison the life I have with Beauty."

That was what Waverly had thought, but it helped ease both the killing rage and the regret to hear him say it out loud. He wasn't certain he would have made the same decision, but he couldn't fault James's logic. "Then we will have to come up with the quickest, most efficient way to get the matter resolved." The words were crisp as he returned to the closet. "I'm not certain Grace will insist on being involved, but Beauty will."

"She says she's ready." James moved to the closet to help Waverly look, then hesitated. "It was hard for her to see Juliana change me back."

Waverly thought of the sisters' history, so briefly sketched out by Manny and given disturbing depths by some of Noble's ravings. He was impressed she'd taken Juliana's little show as well as she had. "Are you surprised?"

"Of course not." James's hand clenched his shirt, wrinkling it. "It wasn't True Love's Kiss, Waverly. You know that, right?"

"I should be offended you even asked me that question." Despite the words, there was no sting in them. "But I can see why Beauty's fears might have tried to get the better of her."

James's shoulders dropped. "I wish True Love's Kiss had been the thing to break it," he said quietly. "Then Beauty would have broken the curse, and Juliana would have been defeated before she'd even shown her face."

Waverly watched the younger man's face carefully. "Were you disappointed?"

James sighed. "Honestly? I'd decided it couldn't be done. It was easier that way." His fingers tightened again. "Besides, Beauty was the one who really took the curse away." He took another breath, expression firming as the truth of what he'd just said settled in. "Juliana just gave me my old body back."

Waverly lifted a hand, resting it against the younger man's cheek and forehead before lightly pinching his nose. It had been a year since he'd seen these features, the face he'd known almost better than his own, and he was a little surprised to discover he felt no real sense of shock upon seeing them again. James had always remained James in his mind, no matter how he'd looked. "It seems much the same as when I last saw it," he said gently. "But you might want to take a look for yourself."

James froze, his eyes the only sign of the internal struggle going on within. Then he closed his eyes for another brief moment, giving an almost imperceptible shake of his head. "After Juliana's gone." A pause, and this time there was no sign as to what was going through his mind. "Then I'll do it."

Waverly laid his hand back on James's shoulder. "Fair enough." Then he stepped back. "Now, I believe we should finish this and return everything to your room before Juliana risks trying to get past the elementals."

Expression easier now, James went to get the rest of the clothes. "At least we know Beauty and Grace won't be overwhelmed by pity and let her out."

Waverly could not stop the grimace. "Thank the gods for small favors."

CHAPTER 21

Sucker Punch

Beauty had laughed when she'd found out how the elementals had played guard dogs, half out of humor and half out of relief that she could still find things funny. They kept her to her room throughout dinner, long enough to start hearing gentle knocking turn into assertive requests, move into complete silence, and finish with steady pounding and shouting that kept to obnoxiously decorous language. Despite the background accompaniment, the meal managed to be oddly relaxing.

Finally, though, they had to let her out.

They'd decided as a group that Beauty should be the one to get the first crack at the woman, and she asked to do it alone so Juliana wouldn't have a chance to keep leaping at James. Her clothes ruffled as the elementals breezed past her, then she slowly pulled open the door so she would be the first thing the other woman saw. True, it also left her in a perfect position to get punched in the face, but if Juliana were stupid enough to start a fight, Beauty would be more than happy to finish it.

Juliana had leapt forward as the heavy wooden door had swung open, her lips puckered and her arms flung out in a way that suggested she'd definitely expected James to be the one standing there.

Beauty took a step back, not wanting to imagine the woman making contact with her lips, even accidentally, but Juliana caught herself and jerked backward with a horrified expression. Her fists clenched, her eyes narrowed into furious slits, and she immediately tried to pivot around and stalk out of the room without even deigning to speak to Beauty. Unfortunately for her, the arm Beauty had braced against the edge of the door was a surprisingly effective barrier—babysitting Steve's toddler cousins, all full-blooded giants, did wonders for a girl's upper-body strength.

Beauty stepped into the room after Juliana, closing the door behind her. Juliana went back to glaring at Beauty, nearly vibrating with rage. Personally, Beauty found it far easier to deal with than the sobbing had been. "Get away from me, you dirty little peasant! I have no idea how you tricked your way into this house, but rest assured—"

"No, *you* rest assured." Beauty's voice cut off the rest of Juliana's rant like a slap. "I don't care what happened between you two a year ago, or what possessed you to let him get cursed and then flee the kingdom for a year. But Beast is *mine* now, and I'm not going to be stupid enough to walk away from him, no matter what you say."

Juliana's eyes flared, but her lips thinned and she glared at Beauty in complete silence for what seemed like a long time. Beauty stared her down, equal fury radiating out of her, until finally the other woman lifted her chin. "I *told* him," she said quietly, every word covered with frost, "that my father and I were running for our lives. I didn't mean to leave him in such a horrible situation."

Beauty moved so that her face was mere inches from Juliana's. "You didn't care what state you left him in, even if by some miracle you *didn't* know about the curse." Her voice was pitched just as low, her fingertips tightening around the bedpost. "We both know you have enough brains to have gotten word to Beast at some point, and his protection would have been far more reliable than your father's hauling you off to the middle of nowhere."

Her lips thinned. "My father . . ."

". . . was old? Sick? Criminally stupid?" Beauty narrowed her eyes further, noting that the other woman hadn't given the slightest flinch at any of the less-than-flattering adjectives thrown at the man she was supposedly so devoted to. The anger in her eyes didn't even deepen, which was telling given how easy she was to upset otherwise. "No matter what bad decisions your father made, we both know you're too intelligent to have just let him drag you down with him."

Something shifted in Juliana's eyes. It looked uncomfortably similar to the way Noble's face had changed when he'd suddenly decided Beauty was a worthy enemy. "What about *your* father? From what I hear, you spent years letting him drag you any *number* of tawdry places."

She'd expected a hit from that direction. Sometimes it seemed like half the world had heard of Noble Tremain, and all of them had an embarrassing story or two they were more than happy to pass around like after-dinner mints. "Maybe, but I got out the moment I found something heavy enough to keep him unconscious for a little while." She eased back slightly, raising her eyebrow. "And I'm the first to admit just how stupid my father is. What's your excuse?"

A wall slammed down behind Juliana's eyes, leaving them so flat that she seemed more like an enchanted statue than anything else. Beauty wondered if this was what James had always mistaken for calm, and if such iron control made it impossible for them to trust anything the woman could say. "Things were complicated."

"Ah, 'it's complicated.' That magic phrase so good at explaining everything from 'a wheel fell off my carriage' to 'my therapist got eaten by an enchanted washboard.'" Sarcasm seemed to work a lot more effectively than rage against this woman, and Beauty was smart enough to make good use of the weapons at her disposal. "Conveniently, it also says absolutely nothing. I need details if you want even the slightest chance of anyone here believing you."

"I will give *Charlton* the details." The words were even colder before, little blocks of ice aimed directly at Beauty's head. She didn't point out that Juliana's insisting on using James's ridiculous middle name gave the words slightly less power than they might have had. "You don't deserve to hear them."

Beauty gritted her teeth and fought to keep the rage from overwhelming her shield of amused disdain. "You don't get to decide what I do or don't deserve. I agree Beast needs to hear all the intricacies of whatever sordid little explanation you come up with, but you won't keep me from being there as well." She raised an eyebrow again. "I believe I mentioned that I'm not going to be stupid enough to walk away from him, unlike some people I could mention."

Juliana's shoulders rose and fell with unnaturally deep breaths. "It was smart, bringing in your sister." Her voice was flat now, though that might merely mean Beauty had managed to get her *really* furious. "I imagine Waverly's easier to deal with when he's distracted."

Now that was interesting. She'd have to ask Waverly how much trouble he'd given Juliana—maybe there'd been a motive in it somewhere. "Actually, he was the one who invited me in the first place." Beauty smiled, wondering if this was how James had felt when he used to flash his fangs. "He's been nothing but encouraging and supportive since I got here."

That made Juliana's eyes widen a fraction, and a flash of anger escaped through a crack in the internal shielding. "How—" Suddenly her mouth snapped closed, swallowing the rest of the question, and she squeezed her eyes shut violently as tears started to leak out from beneath her eyelids. "Charlton!" she called out. "Darling, don't leave me alon—"

This time, a violent whack with a pillow cut off the rest of what Juliana had been about to say. It was a less than elegant solution, but one that Beauty found entirely satisfactory. She lost her balance and fell onto the bed. This time, Beauty could lean down to threaten her properly. "You have nothing left here, no matter what fantasies were spinning through your scheming little head when you finally decided to sashay back and clean up the mess you'd made. Beast is *mine,* and I will keep reminding you of that until you finally listen."

She took a breath. "Now, tell me a little more about Waverly. Did you try to curse him, and end up getting Beast by mistake? Or was it—"

Juliana surged up again, enough momentum behind her to shove Beauty a few steps backward. "That's all you're good for, you know," she bit out, grabbing onto the front of Beauty's shirt as if seriously considering some physical violence of her own. "Cleaning up the messes better women leave behind them. The *only* reason you've managed to win Charlton over like you have is because *I* wasn't here, and now that I am I will *make* him see what a tawdry little mess you and your family are. He may not have been everything I had wanted him to be, but you aren't even worthy to sit beside him at a dinner table. How *dare* you think you can stand beside him in front of his peers!"

The words hit exactly where they'd been aimed, cutting deeper than they should have. Not that she doubted James's feelings, or thought for one minute he'd be stupid enough to get sucked back into whatever game Juliana was trying to play. But Beast *would* go back out into the world, and whether furry or non-furry he'd end up drawing plenty of people back into his circle. She'd only brushed up against the world of high finance as part of her work with the agency, but in some ways it seemed almost a more elite realm than the nobility. Even if Juliana handled the rejection poorly enough to re-curse James—not impossible, given the depths of madness the woman was revealing—the time would come when he would realize he had other options who'd fit into that world so much better than she would . . .

Beauty pushed back, hating the brief light of victory in Juliana's eyes, and the other woman looked so offended for a moment that a memory triggered in the back of Beauty's brain.

She shoved Juliana back onto the bed, pinning her to the mattress. "If I'm so unworthy, why did the mere sight of me in James's mirror make you suddenly run out here after staying away so long?" The other woman's eyes flared, which was more than enough of a confirmation. "That sounds to me like someone who saw a threat and wanted to get rid of her as soon as possible." Though why bother even making the call after so long? Beauty's eyes widened as a thought hit her. "The rumors," she said.

She was distracted enough that Juliana managed to push her away and sit up again. "No matter how far away you are, the latest gossip is just a mirror call away." The other woman almost spat out the words. "I couldn't *believe* such ridiculousness, but here he is, fawning all over you."

Beauty very nearly laughed, remembering the woman in the forest who'd first told them that everyone was talking about her and James's at-that-point imaginary love affair. She really should apologize to her at some point. "You didn't have anything to do with his getting into the enchanted nobility guidebook, did you? Because if you did, I should probably thank you—I had all kinds of fun chasing the women off, and Beast *so* enjoyed watching me do it." She stretched the "so" out just long enough to start the other woman's mental wheels turning. Hopefully, Juliana had a cruel imagination.

"Enchanted nobility guidebook?" Hatred mixed with genuine surprise, then slid into a kind of thwarted fury. "Of all the idiotic . . ." The sentence trailed off as Juliana stood, glaring daggers at Beauty as she folded her arms across her chest. "I refuse to speak to you any longer."

"Okay, then have fun in here. I'm sure we could find a closet for you if this bedroom doesn't suit you." Beauty opened the door and stood in the doorway. "As much as I've enjoyed our little conversation, I'm more than happy to leave you alone with your thoughts until you come up with something more useful to say."

She stared at Beauty for a long moment, then huffed out a breath. "I'm surprised you're not more understanding." For just a moment, Juliana allowed herself to look almost tired. "You know exactly what it's like to have to listen to a ridiculous man who thinks he has authority over you, but who wastes all the family resources on absurd schemes and leaves you behind to pick up the pieces."

It was an obvious plea for sympathy, delivered with just enough familiar-sounding emotion there might actually have been a grain of truth in it. Beauty suspected the woman had no idea how much she'd just admitted. "So was Beast the scheme, or one of the pieces you had to pick up?" The question was quietly, coldly deliberate, her hands clenching the door handle hard enough to turn her knuckles white. She refused to let this woman try to use James as a pawn. "You certainly didn't rush out here until you thought there was some competition."

Juliana's eyes flared. "Don't try to imagine you're better than me."

"Don't even *think* about trying to put me in the same category as you are, you heartless . . ." Beauty took a step closer, so furious she could feel herself shaking with it. "Did you expect him to be waiting out here, missing you until he was so desperate he'd give you everything you want—"

Juliana leapt at her, knocking Beauty flat on her back in the hallway as she attempted to punch her repeatedly with tiny, delicate little fists. Beauty managed to roll her over, getting enough leverage for one pretty solid punch, but Juliana refused to do the decent thing and lose consciousness. Beauty reared back to hit her again, then caught sight of James's bare feet out of the corner of her eye.

When she met his gaze, he just smiled and shrugged. "Don't mind me. I'm just enjoying the show."

His mere presence, however, was enough to clear out some of the red rage filling her. She looked down at Juliana, who had tears in her eyes even as she glared up at Beauty with an expression that promised death. They were probably fake tears, true, but Beauty was surprised the other woman had managed even that much.

She looked back up at James. "How much did you hear?"

"Enough," he said quietly. "For the record, I think your guess is a remarkably good one." His eyes left hers to meet Juliana's. "So is Beauty right? Was I a patsy from the very beginning?"

"How can you think such terrible things about me?" Juliana's eyes filled completely, and she even managed to make her voice waver. "I should have told you before, but I think my father was blackmailed into cursing you by the men we ran away from. They'd hoped he could get some money out of you, but . . ."

James shook his head and the rest of the explanation died in Juliana's throat. Then he looked back up at Beauty, holding a hand out to her. She put her hand in his, letting him help her to her feet. "Sorry if I got any blood on the carpet."

That brought a small smile back to James's face. "As long as it's Juliana's blood, I suspect Waverly will forgive you." He tucked her arm underneath his, and a fierce love filled her as she held on to him tighter. Even if there were someone out there who would be better suited to his world, that was just too bad, because—she wasn't going to let him go.

James looked back down at Juliana. Her sobbing seemed genuine, now, making the sort of undignified mess she hadn't let herself give in to earlier that afternoon. Oddly enough, it made her seem more human than she had at any other point before this. "I'm so so-so-sorry, Charlton," she managed to get out, then rolled onto her side and dissolved completely into tears.

Silently, Beauty and James left the room together.

THE REST OF the evening passed relatively quietly, with Juliana joining the group a half-hour or so later and asking in a small, sad voice if she might possibly have something to eat that night. Waverly gave her unceremoniously prepared leftovers as quickly as possible before sending her back to her room, but it was clear he felt the same sense of unease about her that Beauty and the rest of them did. It was unsettling to have one's enemy so thoroughly shattered.

Juliana's room was silent by the time Beauty made her own way to bed, a clear course of action having been outlined for the following morning. James decided he'd come as close to getting an answer as he was likely to get, though his expression made it clear he couldn't decided whether it made him feel like more or less of a fool. Either way, Juliana would be escorted out tomorrow morning, by the local constables if need be.

Sleep came easier than Beauty had expected, which made it all the more annoying when a solid-sounding *thunk* woke her back up in the middle of the night. At the second *thunk* she'd sat up and narrowed her eyes at the window, and by the third and fourth she'd crossed the room to shove the window open.

It was hardly a surprise to discover her father standing there, his hand poised to toss another small rock. The deadly focus he'd had at their last meeting had dissolved into his old hapless fury, and she allowed herself the brief hope that whatever he'd been planning had imploded without her having to know about it.

He dropped the rock so he could wave a fist up at her. "Fine, you win." Noble had always had the loudest whisper she'd ever heard, capable of not-so-accidentally transmitting a secret to everyone for miles around. "At this point, I don't care if you marry a *plant*. Just call off your lawyers."

Beauty blinked, surprised, then curved her lips upward. "Why? I'm sure they're having fun."

Noble's hands clenched into fists, and he took a deep breath for what would have turned into a shout meant to shake harpies out of their nests. Already imagining the entire house waking up—and the multi-party fight that would undoubtedly erupt—Beauty waved her hands in a cease-and-desist gesture. "Making a scene isn't going to make me more agreeable, you idiot!" she hissed down at him. "If you'd ever spent five minutes actually *thinking* about how people really thought, you'd already know that."

"Then come *down* here." His teeth were clenched as he jabbed his finger straight down at the ground. "I'm not going to look up at you like you're some royal up in her tower window."

Beauty hesitated. He'd wake up the entire house if she didn't go down, but someone would also have to sacrifice their sleep if she wanted backup. Not Grace—no reason for them both to suffer—and

Waverly and his elementals would probably end up being even louder than her father. That would undoubtedly wake up Juliana, who might suddenly get her courage back if she realized all the stories about Noble were actually milder than the reality.

James . . . no. It was stupid, but she didn't want her father to know the curse had been broken. It wouldn't take him long to find out it had been broken by someone else, and he would be thrilled to jab at the ache that hadn't quite healed yet. She believed with all her heart it hadn't been True Love, but she didn't even want to imagine what her father could do with that information.

So she was going alone, then.

She hurriedly threw some clothes on, hesitating long enough to grab a decorative sword off the wall before heading downstairs and out the door. It wasn't sharp enough to stab him, and the glued-on mounting board made it look ridiculous, but it would still hurt when she hit her father over the head with it.

Beauty stepped around the corner, catching sight of him in the shadows. "Okay, now . . ." The words trailed off as she looked back up at her window, realizing far too late that her father shouldn't have known which room was hers. Had he been watching the house? Or . . .

She tried to turn around, but before she could, someone jabbed a sharp-tipped charm into the back of her neck. The sword slid out of her suddenly nerveless fingers, hitting the ground only seconds before her legs buckled and forced her to join them.

As the world went gray, she sensed her father moving to stand over her. "I should have done this years ago," he muttered.

Then there was only darkness.

CHAPTER 22

The Perfect Woman

After a day seemingly designed to give him a heart attack, James was a little surprised at how well he'd slept. Still, it was early when he opened his eyes again, the dawn light just slipping into the full morning and the rest of the house quiet and still. Without Juliana in the immediate vicinity, it would have been a wonderfully peaceful morning.

Well, he could do something about that.

He pulled on some of his newly reclaimed clothing, making a mental list of the necessary mirror calls to get his ex out of his life for good. It was embarrassing to think she'd tricked him from the beginning—he could usually spot a con better than that—but it was probably as close to the truth as Juliana was capable of getting. In a way, he almost felt comforted—if she'd always just seen him as a means to an end, the betrayal hadn't come from some fundamental flaw on his part.

James headed for his bedroom door, hesitating when he remembered that Beauty still had his mirror. Just because he'd had a restful night didn't mean she had, and he briefly considered whether yesterday had been traumatic enough to overcome her usual appreciation for mornings. A kind man would probably let her sleep, but that same man would also miss out on the company of the woman he loved.

Besides, she'd probably forgive him.

Deciding the hallway wasn't safe—with his luck, Juliana was lying in wait somewhere to sob at him again—James headed out the window and up to the roof. Beauty's room was around the corner and a floor beneath his, which meant some wall climbing. Though he didn't have quite the reach he used to, or the claws that had been so convenient for gripping, the old rhythms came back without too much trouble. Her shutters were open, conveniently, but he still knocked on the window frame so he wouldn't scare her and potentially make her throw something. After a moment's silence he knocked louder, and when there was still no response, he slipped inside.

She wasn't there.

Staring at the empty bed, James felt weirdly disappointed. She might be in the library or something—his hearing wasn't quite what it had been when he was big and furry—but if she'd been awake for a while he wished she'd come and gotten him. Especially after the mess with Juliana, he'd rather have more time with her than extra sleep.

He was heading for the door to hunt her down when he caught sight of the envelope sitting in the middle of the hastily tossed-aside covers. It was the most carefully placed thing on the entire bed, and when he took a closer look he saw his name written across the front in large, precise letters. He wasn't an expert, but the handwriting looked a lot like Beauty's.

Feeling something inside him go cold, James snatched it off the bed and ripped it open. There was a letter inside, written in the same hand.

My dearest Beast,

I'm so sorry to have to do this to you, but I'm afraid I can't bear to stay here a moment longer. I would love to be a part of your world, but now that your former fiancée is here I've come to realize I'll never be worthy of it. In time, you'll see that, too, and I can't bear to be here when you turn back to her . . .

It went on, bringing up more and more nonsense that he and Beauty had already discussed and rejected in person. He reeled for a moment, trying to process what he was reading. Why would she just . . .

Beast read them again, searching, and a sudden, horrible certainty started to fill him. The chill in his stomach became a ball of ice, not at all touched by the heat of fury spreading through the rest of him.

He crumpled the letter into a ball, his fingers white-knuckled, and hurried from the room. It was an effort to keep himself breathing as he checked all of Beauty's favorite places in the rest of the house. Everything was quiet, just as he'd thought, and at the confirmation of it all, the terror inside him broke free.

Someone had taken Beauty.

He stormed upstairs, his mind a tangle of fear, rage and self-accusation. Juliana's door was locked, so he kicked it open and yanked her out of bed. She tried to scream, a half-shriek that strangled itself into a paralyzed silence when she met his eyes.

Beast wasted no time. "Where is she?" He shouted the words at Juliana's face. Beauty had been stolen right out from under his nose, probably by a father who proved time and time again that he considered his daughters' lives to have absolutely no value. She could be anywhere by now, in any kind of horrific pain or trouble, and the only clue he had to finding her was a woman who lied as naturally as she breathed. "What did you do with her?"

She stared at him wide-eyed as she gasped for air. "Who? Charlton, I . . . I don't . . ."

"James." He turned to see Waverly standing in the doorway, Grace right behind him. "What happened?"

"Noble took Beauty." Grace hurried off, presumably to see the awful truth for herself. James turned back to Juliana, radiating violence. "This one helped somehow."

"How can you think that?" Voice quavering, she tried sitting up. In the distance, he heard the elementals start to roar. "Beast, I swear I was in here sleeping the whole night. I don't know—"

He cut her off with a growl, shoving the letter into her face. "Noble couldn't have made it past the wards to leave the letter. Someone already inside the house had to do it." She swallowed, and he quieted slightly. "I don't know how the two of you matched her handwriting, but you weren't smart enough to make it *sound* like her. Beauty obviously didn't write that letter. Why don't you tell me who did?"

Waverly approached, but it was only to carefully pry the note out of James's hand so he could read it himself. "The wards would have picked up on any magic strong enough to force Beauty out of the house," he said, his voice impossibly grim. "They must have lured her outside somehow."

"Charlton, listen to me." Juliana was pleading now, her eyes continually flicking over to Waverly as if afraid of another attack from that direction. "I had nothing to do with this, I swear. I've heard things about her family—maybe the stress of meeting the woman you used to love was too much—"

Whatever flared up in his eyes stopped her cold. "If Beauty ever decided to leave me, she would tell me to my face." The words were quiet, each one individually wrapped in threat. "She would shout. She might even throw things at me. But she would *never* sneak out in the middle of the night without at least telling me something was wrong." He leaned in closer, baring his teeth as if he still had fangs. "You should have found a partner in crime who knew her better."

She swallowed, eyes glistening. "Charlton, darling, please . . ." She leaned forward as much as she could, trying to close the rest of the distance between them, and James's stomach twisted as he realized she was trying to reach for his lips.

He pulled away, grip still tight. "I told you what would happen if you upset my house. Tell me where Beauty is *now*, or I'll let Waverly and his elementals finish the job they started yesterday." James turned to discover that Waverly had disappeared at some point, clearly trusting James to beat any necessary information out of Juliana while he started utilizing other channels.

"But—"

His eyes narrowed, letting his voice go dangerously soft. "And if you even *think* about calling me 'darling' again, I'll take care of you myself."

The panic in Juliana's eyes ebbed, burned away by something that looked remarkably like anger. "Did it ever occur to you that maybe *you're* the one who doesn't know her as well as you think you do? After all, you never stopped to think about what *I* wanted out of life! What *I* needed to be happy! Well, now you're going to *have* to!"

"Was that a threat?" he growled. "Are you really that stupid?"

"It's not just a threat. It's the truth." There was a gleam of something that looked like triumph in her eyes. "I made sure the curse had the special accessories package, which means that it reactivates unless you adore me properly. Either I'm your true love, or you're a big, hairy monster again."

There wasn't any more room for rage left in him. "If that were true, I'd already have my claws back and you'd be eating your words."

She blinked, as if she hadn't expected that answer, then looked almost petulant. "I couldn't risk having the kiss not change you back at all," she said sullenly. "But I *had* to. You were rude, stubborn, and intimidating even before you got cursed. I needed the extra insurance to make sure you treated me like you should."

Somehow, that was enough to make him believe her. Beneath the fury, he felt a brief ache that he'd never get that chance to become familiar again with the man he'd been. He'd just barely gotten used to having his old body back, and he wasn't quite ready to part with it.

But if he got Beauty back, it would be more than a fair trade.

"So you're really nothing more than a whining child," he concluded. Juliana couldn't seem to stop talking. Maybe if he pushed on her, she'd spill something useful. "You decided you didn't want me, but now that you know I'll never take you back, you choose to hurt the one woman who means more to me than you ever did."

"I did everything I could to make you fall in love with me!" Her voice kept climbing. "Everything!"

"I thought I *was* in love with you." Clearly, the woman he'd seen as the embodiment of serenity was really only a hair's trigger away from exploding. The sheer pileup of things he'd completely failed to understand during their relationship was starting to become horrifying. "I proposed to you. What else did you want?"

"What I *deserved!*" She was crying now, but it wasn't out of grief. "My father was some little nobody selling enchanted armor-warmer when he met my mother, and he loved her so much he threw himself into the business world so he could shower her with riches. He made his fingers *bleed* for her!"

"Along with the kinds of friends and stupid decisions that eventually got him killed," he said flatly. "Not to mention the fact that I made more on an average Tuesday afternoon than he did in a month."

"I *know!*" The words were almost a wail. "Why do you think I picked you out in the first place? You weren't fat or old like all of the other men Father worked with, and you had so much more money than everyone else. I studied you for weeks before I officially met you, trying to figure out what you wanted in a woman so I could be everything for you. And I *was!* I was perfect!" She tried to whack his arm again. "But you never worshiped me like you were supposed to! I was just window dressing!"

His jaw tightened. The gods help him, it almost made sense. "So you decided to get my attention with the curse."

"That, and to make you sorry you hadn't appreciated me properly." Her expression crumpled again. "And then I hear through the rumor mill that you'd *found* someone." The words were bitter. "Everyone said some penniless little servant had swept you right off your feet. She was *nothing,* and yet everyone swore she was all you saw."

James felt nothing but ice at this point. "What made you decide to start working with her father?"

"Everyone's heard about Noble Tremain, the pathetic social climber who threw his daughters at whatever nobility he could find. And when I called your mirror and saw *her* on the other end, I realized it was a thousand times worse than if you'd taken up with some innocent little nobody." Her eyes narrowed. "How dare you insult me like that?"

He'd kill her. He'd kill her and donate the body to the lunch program of a retirement home for dragons. No one would ever know. "So you contacted Noble and arranged to do . . . what, exactly?"

"I didn't even think I'd need the pompous windbag! I'd made sure no one else could break the curse, and I was certain that when I saved you from your horrible fate you'd *finally* understand everything you should have from the very beginning." She was pleading now. "There's still time. All you have to do to stay human is forget about her and make me happy enough that I kiss you every day. You don't really want to go back to being the horrible creature you were, do you?"

"When that clearly didn't work, what did you decide to do with her?"

"I don't know where he took her! I just said I'd introduce him to a duchess I knew if he got her out of the way—I didn't care what happened after that. I expected you to be grieving, not in a horrible rage like this, but I thought if I offered the kind of refined, genteel comfort I knew I could give that you'd forget—"

James's patience snapped. Whatever else she'd been about to say disappeared as he roared. "No more excuses! You have to know something!"

"I told you I don't! All he said was that he'd finally given up on squeezing a happy ending out of her!"

Swearing, James let Juliana flop back onto the bed and hurried back to find Grace. Noble hadn't had a lot of time—though if James hadn't been *snoring* during Beauty's kidnapping, he'd have had even less—and there were only so many unpleasant magical surprises in the immediate area. It also had to be somewhere their father or one of his connections was familiar with, and probably a new enough place that Beauty hadn't seen it before. Noble was a plotter—he'd want some time to gloat, and for her to hear every word while he did it.

James had to believe she was out there somewhere, thinking up increasingly complicated and painful ways to kill her father. Because if the man had decided on a quicker revenge . . .

No.

Grace met him in the hallway, holding up a small charm. "I found this wedged behind a doorframe in the room Juliana slept in. I recognize it as a house blessing charm for a family with a new baby in it, but it looks too new for your parents to have put it there."

"It is." Grimly, James took the small copper disc out of Grace's hand. It had the image of a mother and sleeping baby embossed on one side. "It's spelled to help everyone in the house have a deeper, more restful sleep. Waverly said thieves use them to make it easier to rob houses."

It was comforting in one way—magic had kept him from knowing something was wrong—and it was infuriating in another. No matter what Juliana had said, she had to have bought this in advance. She'd *planned* this, and he'd let her into his house.

Cursing, he threw the charm against the wall. "I think your father's put Beauty in the middle of another one of his fairy tales, but this time he's planning to leave her there forever. Does he keep notes about potential stories he runs across, or is there somewhere he gets ideas from?"

Grace pressed her lips together a moment, but it was fury that lit her eyes. "I think he set up an office in the bad part of town. If he's written anything down about wherever he has her, we'll find it there."

"Good. Call the constables, give them the address to the office, and tell them to search it." He bared his teeth. "When I'm through with him, he'll wish I'd only tried to sue him for everything he has."

Grace's jaw firmed as she met his gaze. "I was wrong," she said quietly, the words trembling with the need to hurt something. "You can kill him."

James gave her a small nod that said he understood. "Juliana's still upstairs in the room she slept in." He laid a hand on Grace's shoulder. "Once you've made the call, feel free to do anything necessary to make sure she doesn't go anywhere."

The spark that lit Grace's eyes would've been sure to terrify Juliana if she'd had any sense. As Grace headed back to her room to grab her mirror, James went back to Beauty's room to find his own. Waverly was probably working his informant network—most of the major organizations in the kingdom had at least one employee who owed him a favor—but there were a few routes the other man might not think to tap immediately.

He felt his muscles tense as he stepped through Beauty's door, and he was careful not to look at the bed as he moved aside a stack of books to make room on the desk. Pulling the mirror down from the shelf, he keyed in the mirror code for the company that had made the cursed nobility guidebook.

When the mist cleared, an obnoxiously cheerful-looking, young redhead was smiling up at him. "Welcome to Enchantments-R-Us! How can we help you this fine morning?"

"My name is James Hightower." The growl in his voice had been automatic, a warning that now was not the time for the woman to be practicing her customer service skills. "I need to speak to your information systems supervisor immediately."

Her expression slipped a little as her eyes widened. "Mr. Hightower?" She froze a little, and at the very edge of the frame he could see her swallow. Apparently, he was now part of their training procedure. "May . . . I say congratulations on having your curse broken? There . . . there are several useful coupons you're now eligible to—"

"If you don't get the information systems supervisor on the mirror this instant, I will find some way to get you fired."

This seemed to get through to her, because she immediately closed her mouth. "Yes, sir." The mist swirled again, fading away to reveal an older woman with a far more serious expression. "Mr. Hightower, I just double-checked the records myself and can assure you—" She blinked, as if it finally occurred to her that the face promising death on the other side of the mirror was no longer furry. "Mr. Hightower?"

"Don't even think about offering me coupons. I can promise you won't survive the experience." Clearly, whatever training they'd received in dealing with him had been appallingly ineffective. "Do you still publish those enchanted greenery and architecture tour guides?"

"I . . . well . . ." She cleared her throat. "We discontinued those a few years ago, but we've held onto the mirror files of the most recent version in case a limited-run reprint becomes profitable."

James cursed silently. A few years was a bigger window than he'd hoped for, but it would have to be enough. "Send everything from the most recent version to me, please. Now."

She stared at him for a moment, finally realizing she should probably be affronted by the whole thing. "Mr. Hightower, we expect you to order like everyone—"

"A woman's life might be at stake." Shock blanked out the woman's expression for a moment. "I'll have my lawyer send the necessary questing documentation to you after the fact, but right now time is of the essence."

She wavered. "I would have to check with my—"

"If I get the files in the next fifteen minutes, my lawyer will stop breathing down your neck every six months."

The woman gave him an evaluating look, clearly wondering if he was serious. "To the mirror I'm currently connected to?"

"Yes. I need everything."

She considered this, then nodded. "I'll need that questing documentation by the next shareholders meeting."

"Done."

"Then you'll get your files within fifteen minutes." She paused. "I hope you find her."

He'd long ago given up on being able to breathe properly. "I have to."

She nodded again, and the mirror went dark.

CHAPTER 23

Between a Rock and a Sharp Place

Beauty felt dirt against her cheek, a rock digging into her ribs, and an ache in her head as if she'd been jabbed at by an extremely pissed-off gryphon. She hadn't even opened her eyes yet, and she was already pretty sure that when she did, she wouldn't like what she saw.

Horrifically enough, it felt just like being a teenager again.

That thought dragged last night's memories along with it, from Juliana to her father's appearance to her spectacular idiocy of walking right into a trap. She forced herself to wake up, cradling her head as she pushed herself into a sitting position to get her first look at her father's latest terrible idea.

Unfortunately, opening her eyes didn't improve her vision much. She was in a cave, clean-smelling enough that it was unlikely anyone else was living there, and lit only by a faint greenish light she couldn't even try to pretend came from the moon. A few instantaneous, panicked explanations flashed through her mind—her father had left her trapped in a time spell, or had simply rolled a rock over the entrance and left her with nothing more than Hero's Fungus—but as her eyes adjusted to the low light she realized the truth.

The mouth of the cave was completely clogged with plants,

and the green was coming from the sunlight filtering through the thick tangle of leaves and stems. Narrowing her eyes, she gingerly stood up—the cave was just short enough she couldn't do it fully, just the kind of special touch that meant her father had put some real thought into this one—and moved toward the plants for a closer inspection.

Unsurprisingly, they were mostly covered in thorns, some almost as long as her thumb and all far sharper than should have been possible for a plant. Years ago, such plants would have been a pretty standard part of an evil sorceress's arsenal, but they started falling out of favor when the sorceresses realized it was *really* hard to change your mind after using them in lawn decor. Then the tree fairies had started complaining, saying the thorns were an invasive species that threw off natural ecosystems. These days, they only existed in the study gardens of some of the braver witches.

And, apparently, here. She didn't have the sword of her true love—even her father was intelligent enough to have taken *that*. Maybe she could find some flint and start enough of a fire to burn it all down . . .

"Like it? I admit it doesn't have the . . . grandeur of some of my best plans, but I thought it suited our current circumstances."

Flatly refusing to jump like he wanted, Beauty glared at her father's voice coming from the other side of the plants. He had to have been lurking nearby to time it so well, maybe even to the point where he'd listened for her breathing. Knowing what that meant, she turned around and started scanning the cave for the biggest rock she could comfortably pick up. He'd find some way to make an opening in the plants at some point—to gloat properly, if for no other reason—and she'd be ready to bash his head in.

"What? No argument for your poor, wise, long-suffering father?"

Beauty's head snapped back around at the sudden petulance in her father's voice. Clearly, she was ruining his moment by not railing against her fate loudly enough he could enjoy it properly. If she could keep it up, it might goad him into making the opening she needed that much faster. True, he might also give up and just wander off unsatisfied, but knowing when to cut his losses had never been one of her father's strong suits.

Catching sight of an appropriately sized rock out of the corner of her eye, she started making her way toward it as silently as possible while Noble huffed outside. "Don't bother pretending you haven't recovered from that sleep charm yet. I can hear your breathing."

Sometimes it was creepy to be proven right.

After another stretch of silence, he cleared his throat. "Fine. If you're going to be like that, you'll never know how I came up with your little prison."

She had to stop herself from making a disgusted noise. Odds were the only thing he'd managed to do was stumble across some evil sorceress's practice ground from who knows how long ago. Since it wasn't part of some princess's enchantment, no knights, traveling adventurers, or other potential fiancés had come along to stop it from growing wild.

"I hope you don't think your new friend will be along to save you. You know you lost him as soon as another woman broke his curse, right?" He snorted. "I'm aware you convinced the fellow to fight for you somehow, but I hope you weren't stupid enough to think you could keep him after that."

Beauty's fingers clenched as fury spiked, and she forced them open just long enough to bend down and grab a fist-sized rock off the ground. She'd already suspected that Juliana was the one who had stabbed her with the charm, and unless he'd suddenly gotten clever enough to duck Waverly's elementals for a few days and spy on recent events, that little comment had just confirmed it. Hopefully, Juliana was in the process of getting what was coming to her.

The thought of James made her chest ache. For all he knew, she'd suddenly disappeared in the middle of the night without a word of explanation or the sense to ask for help. Surely he didn't think she'd just run off. Not after everything they'd said to each other.

She closed her eyes a moment. If he didn't doubt her love for him, he'd be tearing the world apart looking for her while pretending he wasn't terrified. And . . . poor Grace . . .

"You willful little brat, say something! I know the spell I used to transport you in there didn't do anything to your tongue!"

A spell? Beauty cursed silently, and her hopes of angering her father into giving away the opening she needed slipped away. He'd probably bought a short-range, one-time use transportation spell from the same place he'd picked up the stupid charm. All you did was touch the item containing the spell to whatever you want moved, say where you wanted it to go, and it would do the job for you. People often bought transportation charms in large batches to rearrange furniture.

But you had to touch whatever you wanted moved for the spell to affect it. Even if he'd bought more than one charm, he'd have to go through the bother of transporting himself into the cave, then using two more to get them both back out. He hated using magic on himself, and he couldn't imagine he'd consider her worth going out of his comfort zone for.

Which meant he might not be planning to get her out of there at all.

Beauty tightened her grip on the rock as her stomach went cold. "How much did she pay you?"

"Aha! I *knew* you could hear me!" Noble had to stop then, clearing his throat as he tried for something more "Master of the Universe" and less triumphant child. "And I have no idea what you're talking about. You know I'm too dignified to worry myself over such things as base profit."

He'd truly never seemed to care much about money itself, which had always been one of the more frustrating and perplexing things about him. She might have understood a good old-fashioned get-rich-quick scheme, even if she'd still been stuck in the middle of it. But he'd never seemed willing to settle for anything less than the title, the recognition, and his dream of a world that spun entirely around him.

"So what did she promise you?" She tried hard to keep the panic out of her voice, knowing he'd enjoy it too much. "You know Juliana's no more titled than we are, right? Hopefully, you weren't stupid enough to trust that she would just pull out some magic wand and make you an earl."

"How dare—" He cut himself off, apparently deciding that being goaded into a shouting match was no more suited to his victory than the gleefulness had been. She pictured him collecting himself, smoothing his hands down the front of his vest. "If you must know, the girl promised she'd introduce me to a widowed duchess she became friendly with on her travels. While I admit that it, too, lacks the grandeur I'm so well known for, I'm not nearly as deficient as you and your sister in the necessary social graces. I'm sure I can charm her even without the trappings."

"Do you remember how many titled old ladies you've flirted with over the years?" she snapped back, weirdly appalled he'd bargained her away for so little. "Most of them had you dragged out of the building the second you stood still long enough for the guards to catch you."

"This will be different!" Clearly, dignity had already lost the battle. "I won't have you and your sister hanging around my neck like millstones!"

"You don't know if this mythical duchess even *exists,* you idiot, let alone whether or not Juliana will follow through. Every other word out of that woman's mouth is a lie." She was close to shouting now, but blind anger wasn't going to help. Beauty forced herself to breathe. "After all the years you spent trying to con your way into every castle you could find, are you seriously going to ignore a scam when it's staring you right in the face?"

"I never scammed!" The voice stormed closer, stopping abruptly what seemed like only a few inches away from the thorns. "I fought for the place I should have always had! Juliana *sees* my inherent distinction, even though you and your sister yet refuse to. She and I understand one another. She won't fail me the same way you did."

Beauty felt her eyes sting as sheer, helpless frustration threatened to swamp her. Instead, she waited to make sure her voice was steady and grabbed for the only option she could think of. "Listen, I know that money isn't enough for you, but it's something the nobility respects and understands. The rich nobles like to spend time with people who are comfortable ordering things like gold-crusted tortes, and the poor ones want friends who can order the torte for them."

"I—" He stopped, realizing she wasn't precisely arguing. "What are you trying to say?"

"Hold me for ransom." The idea sounded ridiculous when she said it out loud, the old voice in the back of her head mocking her for thinking she was someone worth paying to get back. She ruthlessly shoved the voice back down, holding onto the thought that a ransom contact would at least give James, Grace, and Waverly some idea of where she was.

Of course, her father would never believe anyone would be willing to sacrifice something to get her back. So she had to improvise. "Enough people know I was at the house that my disappearance will be noticed. Now that the curse has been broken, B—James won't want to be connected to something like that. But you can tell him that you were the reason he was reunited with his beloved Juliana, and that if he pays you enough you'll make sure I limp off into the distance in shame."

There was absolute silence from the other side of the plants, and at first Beauty was afraid that the cobbled-together idea sounded so absurd that not even her father would buy it. When Noble spoke again, however, his voice was a thoughtful mutter. "Your former pet didn't seem intelligent enough to listen to reason. He doesn't have those claws anymore, but I'm sure he'd be all too willing to sic that rabid lawyer of his on me again."

"Then talk to Juliana. Tell her she owes you more for all the work you did to get me out of the way." Beauty couldn't believe he actually seemed to be listening to her. At the same time, there was something disorienting about the way the moment had shifted into a warped mirror-version of her teenage years. If anyone had told her the day would come when she'd actually *help* her father plot . . . "That way, you'll have enough money to make sure everything is absolutely perfect when she introduces you to the duchess."

In the quiet, she could hear him scratching his chin. "You really are more intelligent than you always pretended to be," he said finally, that faint but awful note of regret back in his voice. "Why didn't you ever use it to take advantage of any of those opportunities I gave you? If you had, we both might have ended up someplace much better than we are now."

There were a dozens of answers she could give him, all of which involved some combination of shouting, crying, and needing years of therapy. But she knew none of them would get through to him at all.

"I don't know." She let the air out of her lungs, almost wishing she still felt deadly furious. It would be so much easier to deal with than her newfound understanding. "You'll want to send that mirror call to Juliana as soon as possible."

"True." He was silent again, as if considering whether or not to say something else, but then Beauty heard the sound of footsteps walking away. Even when they had faded into the distance, she stood absolutely still, waiting in case he'd stopped somewhere or had decided to trick her somehow. In some ways the man was as simple as an unenchanted frog, but he *had* conned her into letting down her guard enough to leave the protection of James's house, so she knew he was just cunning enough to be dangerous.

After a while, though, Beauty decided her father couldn't have held out that long without making some sort of snide comment. Accepting that even paranoia had to have a limit, she leaned as close as she dared toward a tiny scrap of sunlight peering in through the network of thorn plants.

All she saw on the other side, though, was greener. True, it was a different shade, probably a forest of some kind, but that didn't narrow down her location nearly as well as she'd hoped. Depending on how long she'd been out and how much magic her father had bought, he could have stashed her anywhere along the borders of the nearest three kingdoms or even as far away as elven territory. Even if she did get free, she'd clearly have quite a walk ahead of her.

She'd better get started.

Taking several steps back, she threw the rock as hard as she could at the thorns before immediately ducking and covering her head. Like she'd been afraid it would, the rock merely bounced off the plants and crashed somewhere in the darkness behind her. She narrowed her eyes at the thorns for a moment, then immediately started scanning the ground for a smaller, narrower rock.

When she'd found one, long enough to hold between her fingers and still have a few good inches left, Beauty stood up and headed back to the thorns. Wedging the rock underneath one of the plants, she hooked her fingers on both sides and pulled as hard as she could. She might not be able to cut through the vines, but maybe she could unpick them like one of those knitting projects she'd always been so terrible at.

Her thumb exploded with sudden pain, and she yanked her hand back with a curse and cradled it against her chest for a minute. There was a deep gash, bleeding heavily enough that it was starting to drip, and she pressed the bottom of her shirt against it in the hope that it would staunch the flow. Her gaze shot back up to the plants, narrowing her eyes at the red smear on one of the thorns near where the rock was still trapped. There was no way her hand could have slipped *that* badly . . .

Suspicious now, she lifted her injured hand and slowly moved her finger toward the rock. No matter how close she got she could never quite touch it, and she realized the thorns were actually pulling the rock away from her. When she pulled her hand back to her side, pressing it against the shirt, she could see the plants moving back to their original position. A second attempt with another rock had exactly the same response, with a smaller gash on her opposite hand.

Great. Not only was she trapped by evil sorceress thorns, but they'd somehow become semi-sentient when no one was paying attention. Residual magic contamination, maybe. Or perhaps they'd always been sentient, and heroes had always been so busy cutting them into pieces that they'd never noticed.

These particular thorns apparently didn't want her to get out.

Too tired to even insult the universe properly, she sat down and held her hand up to the sunlight to get a better look at the gash. The bleeding had slowed but not stopped completely, and she gave a test yank on the bottom edge of her shirt to see if she could rip off enough to use as a bandage. Unfortunately, all she did was confirm her suspicion that your average piece of fabric was a lot harder to tear than adventurers always made it seem. She would've tried using one of the thorns to start the process, but she only had so much blood to spare. If she'd offended it, she'd just made a very dangerous enemy. . .

Beauty stopped, her brain forcing her to examine the thought she'd just had. She lifted her head, studying the thorns. It was a stupid idea, true, but it wasn't like there was anyone around to watch her fail spectacularly or add unhelpful commentary. And if she didn't try it, it may later end up being the only thing that could have saved her.

She moved one finger to the base of one of the stems, close enough to the ground that the thorns would have to really reach to get to her. When she touched the plant's tough skin, she pet it as gently as she would a firebird or something else equally fragile.

Nothing happened.

Beauty sighed, feeling stupid. Still, she had to know for sure. "You're such a beautiful plant, yes, you are." It took her a second to get into the voice, the same one used for small, fluffy creatures and children too young to look at you like you're an idiot. "Poor thing, left out here all alone with no one to look after you. You don't even have a good, strong building to climb on or enough sunlight to keep you warm and well-fed. No wonder you're lonely . . ."

Just when she was about to give up, she felt the plant press against her hand like a baby gryphon looking for a good neck scratch. She used her nails, very lightly, and the other plants started leaning toward her fingers like they wanted a turn.

Beauty closed her eyes, breathing out a half-laugh at the sheer absurdity of the situation. It seemed like she'd managed to make a friend, but what was she supposed to do next? It still wouldn't let her rip it apart, and now that she knew it was sort of alive, she wasn't too thrilled with the idea anymore either. She might be able to get it to attack her father if he ever came back, though . . .

"I could get you out of here," she said quietly. "I don't have the tools I'd need to dig you up and transport you safely, so you'd have to wait for me. But I promise you I'll come back for you, and I'll find you a nice solid building with good sunlight and someone who will pet you whenever you want." Hopefully, the agoraphobe in the tower could be talked into thinking of it as a pet that didn't need to be walked. Even if she didn't, though, Beauty would figure out some way to keep her word. "You just have to let me untangle you enough to get out of here."

The plants didn't move for a second, then they slowly relaxed back into their original position. Carefully, she started working the plants apart, close to the base of the plants so there'd be as much separation between them as possible.

"Good plants," she murmured soothingly. "I'll try to be as gentle as I can."

CHAPTER 24

Multiple Choice Tests

The map was spread across the dining room table, one edge slowly being consumed by the pile of papers the constables had brought over. Grace sorted through those, looking for anything remotely resembling something useful, while James and Waverly narrowed down the list of enchanted places provided in the database. None of Waverly's contacts had heard anything yet.

Juliana had been locked in a closet and was sobbing loudly enough to be heard even a few rooms away. They'd searched her for any more unpleasant little surprises, but the only charm they'd found was a small five-pointed star doctors often used to put patients to sleep. Their sale was supposed to be highly regulated, and once he got Beauty back James promised to hunt down whoever had screwed up that part of their job description.

They hadn't even given Beauty the chance to fight.

James had to close his eyes a moment, forcing his brain back to the immediate, physical problem at hand. All of the towers in the nearest four kingdoms—that they knew about, at least—had all been checked for secret basements and tenants with officially validated identities. The same was true of all the castles, magic springs, dragon caves, and glass coffins they were aware of. James had contacted the leaders of the nearest dwarf clans, all of whom promised to scour their mines, and the constables had contacted most of the sorcerers, sorceresses, and witches within a hundred-mile radius. But there was one place they hadn't checked yet . . .

He opened his eyes, trying to pretend he wasn't close to cracking from the strain. "Grace, there's an abandoned gingerbread cottage about fifteen miles from here," he said briskly, ignoring the sympathetic look he could feel coming from Waverly. "Any chance your father might have access to it?"

She took the mirror he handed her, her eyes narrowing as she studied the picture. Far too quickly, though, she shook her head. "I think he dated the owner briefly because he hoped she'd hold us hostage, but she wouldn't work with anyone older than ten." Grace handed the mirror back, the disappointment evident on her own face. "If I remember correctly, the house went into receivership last year and was bought by Sprat's Bakery Chain. I think it's pretty much dismantled by now."

James's jaw clenched at the sheer frustration of it. "It's all dismantled. Or occupied, checked, haunted, eaten, or transported across the continent." He slammed the mirror back on the table, hard enough that its magical shock field wavered slightly. "What am I doing in here? I should be out there looking for her!"

"Where?" Waverly's voice was sharp, not unkind but meant to cut through the anger. "Even with the constables out in force, there is still mile after mile of area left to cover. She could be anywhere, particularly since our informants have yet to see any sign of Noble." He waited until James had met his gaze. "How will you help Beauty any by running around aimlessly?"

James had no response to that—he knew Waverly was right, and it did absolutely nothing to change his feelings—so he simply bent back down to the mirror. "Fine, but we're running out of options here. As much as I know none of us want to think about the possibility, there are a few dungeons—" He stopped, lifting his head at a faint sound he couldn't identify. A moment later he heard it again, a sound almost like a sequence of musical notes, and he saw Grace and Waverly's attention shift as they caught it as well. It was only then that Beast realized what he was hearing—the sound of a mirror getting a call. He and Waverly both used the elementals as their signal, and surely Grace would recognize the sound if it were her mirror. Which left one other person in the house . . .The realization seemed to hit all three of them at almost the same instant. When Waverly headed to the closet, James shook his head before hurrying up the stairs after Grace. "We don't have time to get Juliana." True, whoever it was might hang up if someone else answered the mirror call, but James suspected that his ex-fiancée would make the situation even worse if given the opportunity to answer it herself.

The notes chimed again as the three of them burst into Juliana's room, and after a moment of hurried searching, James found the woman's mirror in a drawer. He immediately moved to answer it, then froze and shoved the mirror at Grace. If a female face gave them even an extra second, they might see the caller . . .

Grace answered the call, and when rage instantly flooded her expression he didn't need to ask who it was. "Where's my sister?" She leaned forward, clearly wanting to dive through the glass and strangle her father. "Tell us now, or I swear I won't stop James and Waverly from killing you this time."

James moved around to see the front of the mirror just as Noble had finally managed to stop sputtering. "Don't you—" When he caught sight of the expression on James's face, however, his eyes went wide as whatever idiotic thing he'd been about to say was cut off abruptly. "Where's Juliana?" he asked finally, his voice as wary as it should have been from the beginning.

"Unavailable." He made sure the word dripped with every ounce of his desire for violence. "Tell me where Beauty is. *Now.*" Noble seemed genuinely stunned by the demand, simply staring at him as if he couldn't entirely comprehend what he'd just heard. James's temper flared. "Am I speaking Elvish?" He was almost roaring now. "Where is she?"

Noble gave his head a small shake, clearly scrambling to collect himself. "Twenty thousand," he blurted out, seeming unsure about the number even as he said it.

So it had become a ransom demand. Somehow, he didn't think this last-minute bit of cleverness had been Noble's idea—if nothing else, the man should have laid at least a little of the necessary groundwork. Still, he could use it to his advantage. "Done. I'll have Waverly meet you in front of Goslings Bank to make the delivery."

"Not Waverly," Noble said quickly, his brow furrowing at the effort of the mental calculation. He didn't question the meeting location, however, or notice that James was making the kind of decisions that would allow him to plan unpleasant surprises for Noble. "Have . . . Grace be the one to meet me. And I want the money in gold credit slips."

James had no idea what had possessed Noble to think that Beauty's beloved, protective big sister was the safer choice in this situation. After Grace had finished dealing with her father, it was entirely possible that there would be nothing left for James to do except keep her out of jail. As much as his own need for vengeance raged, she had as much right to it as he did. "Done. She'll meet you in fifteen minutes."

"Fifteen?" Noble's eyes nearly popped out of his head. "But I'm an hour away from Goslings, and that's if I hurry!"

"An hour, then. You'd better hurry." James ended the call before Noble could say anything else, then turned to Grace. "How close do you think he is to wherever he's keeping Beauty?" He'd seen a dense, deep green in the background behind Noble, the kind you found only in older sections of forest. And if this one was just an hour away from downtown . . .

"Well, he certainly doesn't hang out in forests for his own amusement, but I think I heard him walking before he had the surprise of seeing my face." Mirror still in hand, Grace followed him as he suddenly rushed out of the room and back down the stairs. "I can't imagine he's planning to walk the whole way, though, so he probably has a carriage waiting at the nearest road," she said.

"He's clearly got more than enough little magical tricks at his disposal." James heard the bitterness in his own voice. "Why didn't he just transport himself out?"

"Father doesn't have any trouble subjecting the rest of the world to whatever suits his fancy, but he won't use magic on himself. He doesn't trust it enough."

"If you find any charms on him, feel free to get creative with them somewhere the constables can't see you. Waverly and I are perfectly willing to bail you out of jail, but I'd rather have the local prosecutor focus her energy on making your father suffer."

Waverly was waiting for them at the dining room table, both his and James's mirrors in front of him as he worked. "I tapped into the mirror call and cross-checked the clues you got out of him with the information we had already gathered. Most of the likeliest possibilities had already been eliminated, but there's a tower owned by an evil sorceress that shows some definite promise."

James leaned over to look at the picture. "We already checked that one. The sorceress took the tower with her when she moved to Nearby to be with her aunt."

"True, but the company's guidebook entry warned travelers that she enjoyed regular walks in the surrounding forest while she lived there. It's entirely possible she could have left some trap or experiment nearby that Noble is taking advantage of."

It was the closest they'd come to an answer all morning, and more importantly, it let him get out there and actually start looking. "Let's go. Grace can take the carriage and horses into town to meet with Noble, while you and I use the wagon and the elemen—"

The word cut off at the sudden stab of pain in his mouth, as if he'd bitten his tongue. His instinct was to curse, but the memory of briefly feeling the curve of a fang in his mouth again kept him silent. So it was starting now, soon enough to slow him down on his quest to find Beauty.

"James?"

"Nothing." James swallowed blood, shaking his head at Waverly and Grace's questioning expressions. He knew he should tell them, and he would, but right now all their attention and worry needed to be focused on finding Beauty. He could wait. He had to. "We have to hurry. It'll take some time to get the vehicles ready."

DESPITE THE ELEMENTALS speeding things along far more quickly than horses could have managed, the drive still seemed to take an eternity. He'd given Grace everything she'd need to get the money out of his account, trusting her to deal with her end of the problem, but he knew he wouldn't feel easy until he had Beauty in his arms again.

If, of course, his body held on that long. The sudden prick against his palm had given him the second of warning he needed to stop clenching his fist just in time to watch fur and claws finish rippling across his fingers before disappearing again. Waverly, who'd been focused on keeping the elementals coordinated and on the road while moving the unfamiliar vehicle, thankfully seemed to miss it.

He did, however, notice James still staring down at his hand a moment later. "James?" His gaze returned to the road, then flickered back to the younger man. "You do know we'll find her, don't you?"

James took a deep breath, moving his hand out of sight. "I know."

Finally, the road curved into a deeper part of the forest. The trees grew denser, more tangled, with more and more visible signs of the effort it was taking to keep them from overtaking the road entirely. It was almost a surprise when the small crowd of people appeared, practically lined up along the small wedge of open space at the edge of the road. When James caught sight of Steve and Manny, however, it began to make more sense.

"I called them while Grace hooked up the horses," Waverly

explained, waiting for James to jump down from the wagon before following him in a far more dignified manner.

"You *should* have called us the minute she disappeared," Manny growled, glaring up at Waverly as flickers of flame licked out of his nostrils.

"Yes, we should have," James answered, catching the dragon's attention. "I'm sure once we find her, she'll yell at both of us for you."

Their eyes met for a brief, silent moment, then Manny nodded and turned his attention to the group gathered behind him. "All right, people, you've all done jobs near evil sorceresses before. Remember to keep an eye out for traps, watch each other's backs, and send the rest of us a charm signal if you see anything that looks like it might double as a prison."

As the group dispersed, Manny turned back to James. "You don't look so hot," the dragon said abruptly. "You doing okay?"

"Of course not." He was starting to feel faintly dizzy, in fact, but it was ludicrous to think Beauty's boss could see any sign of the faltering transformation. He hadn't looked in the mirror, but he had no doubt he'd looked ragged and ready to kill someone almost since the moment he'd woken up this morning. "Beauty's missing."

"Valid point." Manny climbed up on Steve's shoulders, bracing himself like a ship's captain facing rough seas. "Let's go find her."

As they disappeared into the trees, Beast turned to look at Waverly. "We'll cover more ground if we split up." He knew that Waverly had heard Manny, and that this wouldn't help ease any suspicions he might have of James's deteriorating condition, but they were so close . . .

For a moment, Waverly looked like he was prepared to argue. Then he simply nodded. "If you get lost in one of the sorceress's traps," he said firmly, "I will find you just to hear you admit that it was a terrible idea to split up."

They went into the woods, heading in opposite directions. James kept his eyes and ears open, pushing his emotions back so he could concentrate. There was an almost complete absence of the usual animal sounds, including the gryphons and unicorns that tended to frequent the wilder areas where less-armed animals feared to tread. The evil sorceress's tower had stood due east of where he was at that moment, and if the forest was still so quiet this far out, it probably meant she'd really embraced the "evil" part of her job title. The traps, if they were still out there, would likely be lethal.

He slowed his steps a little, forcing himself to be even more watchful. It wouldn't help Beauty if he let himself get caught in something dangerous, or if he was too busy worrying about her to miss some sign that her father had blundered through here earlier. It seemed doubtful the man would know how to cover his tracks, let alone think things through sufficiently to realize the need to do so. If James could find where Noble had been, he could follow the route back to Beauty.

As minute after minute slipped by, though, he found nothing. Another, stronger transformative wave hit him, rippling up his arm from his fingertips all the way up to the shoulder. It was normal again a moment later, but the newly ripped fabric of his sleeve left it impossible to pretend nothing had happened. Once he found Beauty, though, it wouldn't matter if everyone else asked him a thousand questions.

And if he didn't, nothing would matter.

James shook off the thought when he heard something, going absolutely still to try and get a better sense of where it came from. It sounded almost like branches moving, even though there was no wind . . .

He threw himself backward just in time to avoid the hardened leaves suddenly filling the air in front of him, shooting downward fast enough to make a dangerously solid noise as every one of them sliced through the undergrowth. When the onslaught stopped, he carefully went over and pulled a single rock-hard leaf out of the ground. James tested the edge, snatching his hand back when he discovered it was razor-sharp, then looked up at the now-empty branches of the tree responsible for the attack.

Interestingly, the branches of the tree next to it were bare as well. He checked the undergrowth and found the same magically-modified leaves, which meant someone else had to have walked by here earlier and triggered them. There were no animals, and this part of the woods clearly didn't get too many visitors. None of the other members of the rescue party had come this way . . .

A quick search found a spot where the undergrowth had definitely been trampled, probably when Noble had flung himself out of the way. His trail was easy to find after that, though it took James a minute to decide which direction to follow, since the trail didn't head directly toward or away from the road. Either Noble really had made a rudimentary attempt to hide his trail, or he hadn't thought to bring a charm to help him navigate.

As the trail progressed, James suspected it was more likely the latter. At one point Noble had made a sharp turn, as if deciding he was definitely going the wrong way, then had taken another sharp turn several feet later in almost the opposite direction. Of course, there was a bush full of crazed warrior frogs just before the first turn, and even someone more composed than Noble was likely to get flustered after dealing with that.

Pulling a tiny spear out of his shoulder, James hurried far enough away from the bush for the little maniacs to no longer consider him in their territory. It helped that another ripple had hit, his face transforming completely enough that the fangs had nearly gotten him into trouble again, and the frogs had all looked alarmed and started shouting at him in what he presumed was Frogese. If only the curse had held long enough to give him his extra-acute hearing back . . .

When he found the trail again, however, he still managed to hear something. It was a small noise, just the breaking of a single twig, but it was enough to make James go absolutely still. Noble should be in town by now, either thinking he was still going to get away with this or being beaten within an inch of his life by his eldest daughter. Whoever *was* out here had also gone quiet the moment he had, proof they were much more aware of their surroundings than Noble ever seemed to be.

Hope flared, quick enough to leave him breathless, and he closed his eyes and took a leap of faith. "Beauty?"

He heard a small explosion of noise, the kind people made when they cared far more about where they were going than about who might hear them. Then Beauty was there, safe and warm in his arms. She wrapped her own arms around his neck, like she wasn't planning on going anywhere for the foreseeable future, and he pressed his lips against her hair and let himself just hold on.

"I think I'll need more lessons on that whole 'not getting hopelessly lost in the forest' thing," she whispered, with both laughter and tears in her voice.

His own chuckle was more than a little damp. "We'll have the whole rest of our lives to help you practice."

Beauty went still, pulling away from him just far enough to see his eyes. "Was that a proposal?" she asked quietly, still holding on to him tightly enough she didn't seem at all opposed to the idea.

James lifted his hands to her face, knowing this may be one of the last times he'd get to touch her without having to worry about claws. Even when they did return for good, though, he knew nothing else would change between them. "That depends," he grinned at her, heart lighter than it had been in a very long time. "Were you planning on saying yes?"

She grinned back, bright and beautiful, and was just about to answer when James felt a ripple hit his lower leg. It briefly gave him back the height he'd lost, but only on the one side, and the sudden push threw him off balance enough to make them both stagger. Beauty, her eyes going wide, helped keep them both upright. "Beast?" He could hear the worry in her voice. "If you got hurt by one of those stupid traps and have just been too manly to tell me how injured you are . . ."

"No." He held on to her when she would have pulled away to check, then took a deep breath. "I'm transforming back, Beauty. Juliana had the curse altered so it only stayed broken if I became her adoring little pet."

"Ah." She looked up into his eyes, searching them, and she saw enough to make her reach up and steal the kiss he'd wanted her to. "I'll kill her for you later," she murmured, then grinned. "That was a yes, by the way."

"Then that was a proposal." He turned them back towards the road, mentally earmarking the frogs and killer trees so they could avoid them this time around. "As much as I'd like to stand here and just keep kissing you, we'd better let the rest of your rescuers know you're safe. Manny was already upset we didn't call him before this, and now that he's got his own mini-mob behind him he's a little scarier than I'm prepared to deal with."

"Manny's out here? And he brought people?"

There was such surprise in Beauty's voice that he had to kiss her again. "Co-workers of yours, I think. I only really recognized Steve."

Her eyes were a little damp as she gave him a quick, fierce squeeze. "Then I'll wait to mention that I need you to bring me back out here at some point. I kind of promised these sentient thorn plants I'd move them someplace sunnier, and I'm not even going to pretend I'll be able to find them again without your help."

James grinned as they both kept moving. "Anything, my lady."

CHAPTER 25

Center of Attention

Even after Beauty and James had made it back to the road, they were alone for a little while—James, it turned out, hadn't thought to grab one of the alarm charms Manny had handed out to use as signals. They both had so much to tell each other, however, that they hadn't even made it halfway through sharing their news when Dave from accounting had popped out from the trees. Once he used his charm to signal everyone, an entire group of people arrived with more hugs than Beauty had ever expected to give or receive in her life.

When it was Steve's turn, he lifted her off the ground completely. "Even if you don't ask," he said quietly, gently setting her back down on the ground, "we're going to help you anyway."

She nodded, swiping her fingers across suddenly damp eyes. It had happened more than once during the round of hugs, though everyone had kindly refrained from pointing it out. "You're coming to the wedding, right?"

He smiled, pressing a kiss against the top of her head. "I wouldn't miss it."

At the moment, though, there were more immediate things to worry about. Grace was back in town showing Noble just what a furious daughter could do with a whole host of constables behind her, and though they'd go there next, Beauty wished she could have seen her sister in action. James had finally told Waverly about the conditional nature of Juliana's fix, only moments before another ripple across his chest had finished wreaking havoc on the poor shirt. That had earned a death glare, unsurprisingly, and a searching look that Beauty understood completely. Waverly, though, hadn't seen any more regret in James's eyes than she had, and right now the two men seemed to be back to normal.

Beauty stayed where she was for a second, watching them. Both men had already yelled at her for leaving the house without backup, and she'd just laughed, kissed them both, and agreed with everything they'd said. They were her family now, just as much as Grace and far more than her father could ever hope to be. If he or anyone else ever tried to drag her away again, she'd fight them all off just so she could make it back home.

She grinned. If she said that to James, he'd probably kiss her again.

Beauty headed toward them, intending to get her kiss, when she saw both men bending over Waverly's mirror. She hurried over, hoping to see Grace, but when she'd gotten close enough to see the surface of the mirror, she was surprised to find their lawyer on the other side of the glass. When James caught sight of her, he hooked an arm around her waist and pulled her close. "Noble's finally on his way, and Oscar's kindly offered to man the mirror so we can see the whole thing."

She leaned against his side, keeping him steady when another ripple up his leg threw off his balance. He gave her a slightly embarrassed but grateful look before they both bent back down over the mirror.

Oscar, poking his head back into the frame, nodded at Beauty. "I am pleased to hear you are safe, Miss Tremain. Your sister was as well, but she won't have time to properly express that to you until she's dealt with your father." He hesitated, then cleared his throat. "I find myself reluctant to interrupt the moment."

Waverly shot the man a look that threatened an extremely painful death. "She's *taken.*"

Oscar blushed, ever so slightly. "Of course, of course. I didn't mean . . ."

Rather than finishing the thought, he held the mirror up to show the front of Goslings Bank. Grace was standing there, a bag over her shoulder and her eyes absolutely cold as she looked at someone approaching. A moment later, their father came huffing into view, and her voice proved to be as chilly as her eyes. "You're late."

He stopped, and though Beauty couldn't see Noble's face, she knew he was glaring. "Yeah, well, the lord of the manor didn't exactly pick the easiest location for me to get to, did he?"

Grace lifted her chin. "You don't get a single credit slip until you tell me where you've taken Beauty."

Noble took a step closer. "Don't even *think* about trying to bully me, girl. You don't have enough steel in your spine to be any good at it." He held a hand out. "Give me my credit slips now, or you'll never see your sister again."

Grace's eyes flashed. It was the sign for anyone who knew her well to start looking for exit routes, and out of the corner of her eye Beauty could see Waverly's lips curve upward a little in anticipation. "You lost the right to order me around a long time ago*, Noble,*" Grace replied, each word a verbal slap. "But I was enough of a fool to actually feel pity for you, and I didn't want to let you drag Beauty down into a lifetime of hate and revenge no matter how much you deserved it. So, wrongly, I let you think you were something more than the disgusting worm you've always been."

This time she was the one who took a step toward him, making Noble stumble backward. "But now you've hurt my sister. My *family.*" Each word got sharper, more dangerous. "And you were stupid enough to think I'd let you get away with it!"

Pulling the bag off her shoulder, Grace opened it up and dumped the old files that had been inside onto the ground at his feet. While Noble stared at the pile of useless paper, as frozen as if someone had put a spell on him, she walked right over the top of it and delivered a very precise, well-aimed kick that had their father doubling over in masculine agony.

Beauty grinned in fierce approval as Noble made a pained gurgling sound and dropped to his knees. Grace, still standing on top of the pile, looked down on him with the kind of disdain it generally took evil sorceresses years to learn properly. "Constables, arrest this man." Noble's head jerked up to face Grace, and in that moment Beauty would have given a great deal to see the expression on his face. Then the constables swarmed, lifting their father to his feet and dragging him away as they listed all the charges against him, and Grace hurried over to Oscar and took the mirror out of his hand. "Beauty?"

Beauty leaned closer so that she was easier to see in the frame, resting the tips of her fingers against it as if she could reach through and touch her sister. "You were . . . that was . . ." She felt her eyes start to sting again, and she had to blink tears back even as she kept grinning. "I am so proud of you."

Grace was a little teary herself as she rested her own hand against Beauty's on the opposite side of the glass. "Get here the *second* you can. And in case you're not sure, that was definitely an order."

Beauty laughed. "Yes, ma'am."

When the mirror call ended, James kissed her hair. "You heard the woman. We'd better get moving."

GRACE STOOD IN front of the jail, hurrying over the moment the wagon came into view. Beauty hesitated, the transformative ripples coming fast enough now that she wanted to stay near James, but when he practically pushed her off the wagon she gave in and ran over to her sister.

The hug was so tight she could barely breathe, but Beauty didn't mind in the slightest. "I am so sorry I didn't stop him before this," Grace whispered, her cheeks wet.

Beauty's throat closed. "You stopped him a hundred different times. You have *nothing* to apologize for."

It was only then that Grace pulled back, giving her little sister the "Is there anything broken or bleeding you aren't telling me about?" scan used by caretakers everywhere. Satisfied after her sweep, she gave a small nod and wiped her hand across her cheeks. "They have Father in a cell, but the guards said they'd be happy to take their dinner break if you want to go in and yell at him without an audience."

Beauty hesitated. "I don't need to, but . . ." She glanced back at James, who had dropped down off the side of the wagon. As he took a step forward, the transformation moved up one arm, then down the other. An instant later it was gone from both, only to flicker back across his fingertips. There seemed to be no rhyme or reason to the pattern, nothing James could use to anticipate what his body was going to do next, and his frustration as he fought his own body made her ache.

When Grace followed her sister's gaze, her eyes widened. "What's happening?" Her eyes shot back to Beauty. "Is he okay?"

Beauty scrubbed a hand across her face. "Juliana made sure there was a loophole in her breaking of the curse. It's reasserting itself in the slowest, most painful way possible, and he *still* insists that he needs a few seconds alone with Father before we can all go home."

Grace opened her mouth, no doubt instinctively prepared to argue for the most sensible option, when she stopped and closed it again. "He deserves to," she said quietly, her eyes dark. "Beauty, you should have seen him when we realized . . ."

She shook her head to stop her sister, briefly closing her eyes against the thought of what he'd gone through. "I know." Taking a deep breath, she headed back to James as Grace and Waverly took the opportunity to have their own reunion. "Okay, the guards said you can have a 'beat him up' break," she said firmly, holding onto him even as her eyes narrowed. "But I am going in there with you, and then we are going straight home and you are letting me figure out how to take care of you."

James's expression softened, though he winced when another transformative wave rippled across his face. He'd be fine when the fangs were back in for good, but they kept hurting him when they popped in and out like that. "Why are neither of the Tremain women generals? Clearly, you've both missed your calling." He started to take Beauty's arm, then stopped. "I'm getting sick of tripping you."

"Well, I'm not getting sick of holding on to you." She firmly took his arm, giving it a squeeze. "So you're just going to have to deal with it."

Though the constables' eyes went wide the first time any of them caught one of James's partial changes, no one tried to stop the party from going in to see Noble. Her father was leaning his head against the bars, staring blankly into the distance as if the entire world had turned into something he couldn't process, and Beauty realized she had absolutely nothing left to say to him. The anger that had suddenly deserted her in the middle of the woods hadn't come surging back like she'd expected, and she had no interest in picking through the tangle of sadness and pity that had been left in its stead. Even that had faded into almost nothing, swallowed up by the sheer happiness she'd felt the moment James's arms had wrapped around her.

Now, though, she let him go, staying by the doorway as James stalked toward Noble's cell. As he got closer, a ripple went over both his legs, briefly giving him back his extra height at just the right moment to make him loom that much more effectively over her father. Somehow, that was enough to penetrate Noble's daze, and his eyes went huge as he started trying to back away.

He wasn't nearly fast enough, though. James reached through the bars, grabbing a handful of Noble's shirt and yanking him forward violently enough to slam him against the metal. The hit was hard enough to reverberate through the soles of Beauty's shoes, but her father stayed conscious enough to keep trying to struggle away from him.

James leaned forward so his face was almost right up against her father's. Another ripple went up his arm, but it didn't shake his grip in the slightest. *"Now* do you understand?" Beauty would have expected a roar, but his voice was colder than she'd ever heard it. "Don't even *breathe* either of their names again."

Then he let Noble go, abruptly enough that her father fell down in his desperate attempt to scramble backward. Without another word, James turned and immediately headed out the door, leaving Beauty alone in the room with her father. Their eyes met, and Noble opened his mouth . . .

Beauty's eyes widened as she suddenly realized why James had felt the need to leave so quickly. Completely forgetting the man in the cell, she hurried outside after the man she loved.

James had almost made it back to the wagon. She saw him hunched over on the ground only a few feet away from it, the golden glow of magic starting to swirl around him again. If she waited too long, it would be almost impossible to even see him through it. Now, though, she could still clearly see that this change hurt him much more than the last one had.

If Beauty hadn't hated Juliana already, she certainly would have begun to then.

Her footsteps didn't even slow as she ran toward James, ignoring the magic entirely as she dropped to her knees and wrapped her arms around him. He looked up, meeting her eyes, then gave in and grabbed onto her. The magic swirled around them both as he transformed, growing and changing in her arms, but as long as he didn't let go then neither would she.

When the light had faded, he carefully disentangled his claws from a fistful of her shirt and tightened his arms around her. "Thank you," he murmured, lips against her hair. "And I'm sorry about your shirt."

Beauty gave him a fierce squeeze, pressing her cheek against his fur. "At the risk of scarring any small children who might be within earshot, you have the permission to rip my clothes up anytime."

"Um . . . excuse me?"

At the hesitant question, asked in a voice that most definitely didn't belong to either Grace or Waverly, Beauty and James froze. Slowly, they pulled away from each other just far enough to look up at the small crowd of oblivious citizens that had gathered around them, the usual mix of families and people on their way home from work who were normally out and about around this time. All of them were staring at James with varying degrees of perplexity, and Beauty felt James tense as she tried to figure out if there was any way to manage a graceful exit at this point.

The person who had spoken, a pleasantly round gentleman carrying a bag of groceries, raised a hand. "Sorry, but don't these transformation things usually happen the other way around?"

The equally round woman next to the man hit him quite firmly on the arm. "I cannot believe you just asked such a rude question. What if this is what he looked like to begin with, and he got cursed into looking like a human?"

Now someone from the back piped up. "Yeah. You're discriminating against non-human sentient beings just by asking him that question!"

That set everyone else off, the conversation bouncing back and forth among the various onlookers quickly enough that it became impossible to keep track of.

"Why would anyone curse him to be human? So he can't go howl in the woods without the other animals looking at him funny?"

"I swear, Doris, I'm going to make you read that species' rights pamphlet if it's the last thing I do."

"Cursed or not, his lady friend doesn't seem to have a problem with it."

"Can she curse me too, so I can get claws like that?"

"Hush, Lionel. You can't have claws. You might scratch the furniture."

It was at this point that Waverly and Grace pushed their way through the group, the alarm on both their faces melting away to confusion as they listened. The people themselves were completely caught up in the debate, having seemingly forgotten why they'd gathered in the first place.

"Maybe it's an illusion. My cousin opened a charm shop in Nearby and got a sorceress to come out and make the entire front of the shop look like it was made out of roses."

"Wasn't an evil sorceress, was it? You've got to be careful working with those."

"You need to be certified before you can be called a real evil sorceress. It's shocking how many of the new ones advertise like they've gone through all the evil training but don't have the paperwork to back it up . . ."

When Beauty and James's eyes met, they both burst out laughing. Waverly made a disgusted noise, then held out a hand to help them both up. "Clearly, we're no longer needed here. I believe this is our cue to make a discreet exit."

As they climbed into the wagon and headed home, not a single person noticed.

THE FIRST THING Beauty did when they made it back to the house was wait while James put on some pants. He'd been wearing some, technically, and though they'd held on through the transformation as well as could be expected, they'd been ripped to shreds.

The second thing she did was head back downstairs and yank Juliana out of the closet. She'd been in there most of the day, and had pretty much shouted herself hoarse, and nobody cared in the slightest. When Juliana had caught sight of James, however, she tried to scrape together what was left of her voice. "See? I told you what would—"

Anything else she'd been about to say was cut off by Beauty's punch, which connected solidly with Juliana's cheek and instantly knocked the other woman out. Beauty dropped the now dead weight, disgusted, then pulled out every Dwarvish curse she knew as she cradled her now extremely sore hand against her chest. "That *hurt*," she muttered, keeping her voice low in case Juliana wasn't quite as unconscious as she appeared to be. "Why didn't anyone mention how much punching someone in the face hurts?"

"Because we live to torment you," James said affectionately, kneeling down next to her before taking her injured hand and pressing a kiss against her knuckles. "Though I'm happy to swoon in awe, if you'd like."

From above them, Waverly narrowed his eyes at the unconscious Juliana. "Unfortunately, we still need something more permanent to do with the woman. Though there's an excellent case against Noble, the only things that tie her to the kidnapping are a single sleep charm and the words of her co-conspirator."

"We have to be able to charge her with *something*." Grace made an exasperated noise, turning to Beauty. "Tell me you saw her at least talking with Father."

Beauty sighed, shaking her head. "Sorry, no. She jumped me from behind after I was already outside, and though I'm sure it was her I conveniently don't have any way to actually prove it."

James eyed his ex-fiancée with a coolly predatory expression. "How many people do you think know she's even here?" he asked, meeting Waverly's eyes.

Waverly hesitated for a moment. "It's worth considering. I think Manny has some useful connections . . ."

The mention of her boss sparked an idea in Beauty's brain. "Wait." She looked up at both men. "I think I know something we can do with her that has a lot less risk of getting us arrested."

James's eyes stayed narrowed. "It should *hurt*," he growled.

"Oh, it will." Beauty grinned slowly. "Of course, it depends on your definition of pain."

EPILOGUE

Fitting

When Beauty had told the group of her plan to deal with Juliana, Waverly could admit privately that he'd been less than convinced. Manny, however, had laughed for a full ten minutes upon hearing the idea, which was enough to persuade Waverly there was more potential to the idea then he was currently aware of.

Now, standing in the sunshine listening to the ceaseless stream of chatter floating down from the open window, he wasn't entirely sure he was convinced yet.

"Are you *sure* the dwarf mines wouldn't be a better idea?" James asked, echoing Waverly's thoughts as he looked over at Beauty. The four of them were running a quick errand for Manny before heading into town for the day, and while even Grace seemed to catch the inherent amusement of the situation, neither man had quite seen it yet. "With that community service injunction Manny pushed through for us, we can shove her pretty much anywhere we want as long as we figure out some way to justify it."

Beauty shook her head, still focused on the circle she was drawing with the tip of a company wand around a pile of food and other supplies. "She could escape the mines somehow, but the only way in or out of this tower is magic. Rose makes sure there's nothing like that actually in the tower. She's an agoraphobe, which means she's scared of open spaces, and she's afraid if she keeps magic up there some prince will steal it and 'save' her whether she wants him to or not." She grinned evilly. "She pays Manny to send regular sacrifices up there to keep her company, but now that she has a *permanent* roommate . . ."

Grace, who had been petting the thorn plants they had replanted there the day before, looked over at Waverly. Their inherent magic helped them grow fast enough they were now nearly as tall as she was, and to everyone's surprise, deep red buds had formed at several locations. "Manny gave Beauty the assignment just after she started with the agency. She was completely mute for three days afterward. I was stunned."

"Beauty, speechless?" Waverly raised an eyebrow as Grace approached, sliding an arm around her waist to pull her closer. It was a habit he planned to indulge in as often as possible. "I'm afraid I can't believe in something quite *that* fantastical."

"Hey!" Beauty pointed a finger at him, brow lowered in her best mock-affronted look. Then her attention shifted to James. "Shouldn't you be defending me?"

James lifted a shoulder, looking amused. "Sorry. I was too busy being shocked at the possibility of you not talking." He truly seemed to be at peace now, even though he was once again seven feet tall and covered in fur, and Waverly knew it was a gift he could never properly repay Beauty for.

Beauty glared at James. "Fine. If you don't want an opportunity to have me show my gratitude, I'll take care of this myself." She then turned to her sister. "Please kiss your boyfriend for me so he stops talking."

Next to Waverly, Grace grinned and pressed a kiss against his cheek. Waverly turned to meet her eyes, his fingertips resting lightly against her jaw. "I don't think that's what your sister meant," he said softly, and when her eyes lit up he leaned forward for a sweet, lingering kiss that filled him with the sudden desire to write terrible poetry in her honor.

When they broke apart, Grace immediately snuggled back against his side. Beauty, grinning herself, turned back to her intended. "See, that's what *you* should have done."

"Kiss Waverly?" James asked, pulling her close for his own kiss. "Sorry, but I don't think either of us would have enjoyed *that.*"

Once that had been completed, they all returned to the task they'd come there to complete in the first place. Taking a step back, Beauty yelled up to the tower's lone window. "Are you ready?"

A very pale young woman leaned out, one hand completely covering her eyes. "Everything's ready up here." There was enough distance between her and the ground that it was hard to tell, but she seemed to be smiling widely. "And thank you *so* much for sending me someone long-term. She was kind of rude at first, but I started telling her *all* about my collection of dust bunnies and she really seemed to be paying attention. Ever since Morbidia died there hasn't been anyone . . ."

"I'm happy for you," Beauty said quickly, clearly hoping to cut off any more explanation. "But you've got to step back now, or there won't be room for everything you ordered."

"Oh, right." With that Rose moved away from the window, and Beauty used the wand to lift the supplies upward in a steady stream flowing into the window. When one case fell, a little too heavy for the lifting spell stored in the wand, the elementals caught it and helped the box complete its journey. Once everything was inside the tower, the woman leaned back out the window with her hand over her eyes. "That's everything! Everyone from the agency is always so nice and helpful. Wait right there while I put this away, and then I can tell *you* all about my collection . . ."

When she disappeared again, Waverly could see Beauty grab James's hand. "Save me. Now."

James glanced back up at the window warily. "Already on it."

The four headed back toward the wagon, hoping to be on their way before Rose reappeared, when they were stopped by the sound of a very different voice behind them.

"You can't leave me here!"

They turned to see Juliana waving at them desperately from the window. "This woman keeps talking about the most *ridiculous* things, and she will not shut up no matter how rude I am! It gets exhausting just waiting to be allowed to say a word!" It was hard to tell at this distance, but there seemed to be genuine desperation in her voice. "Please! I'll do anything! Just get me *out* of here!"

The four met each other's eyes, then grinned in perfect unison. "I should never have doubted you," Waverly murmured, giving Beauty a small bow as they continued on their way.

"I'll forgive you." Beauty's expression was of absolute contentment as she patted her fiancé on the arm. "You'll have a hard enough time staying with this one for his suit fitting this afternoon." She looked up at James, love in her eyes.

Grace raised an eyebrow. "Yes, but I'm the one who's going to have to stay with *you* for the wedding dress fitting. Which of us deserves a little sympathy here?"

As James laughed, Waverly gave in to his own smile. "Oh, I believe we'll all manage somehow."

ACKNOWLEDGEMENTS

I WISH I could go around and hug you all, but this will have to do. First, thank you so much to my fans. I'm overwhelmed every time I think about the love and encouragement you've given me. Eternal thanks to Jolly Fish Press for giving me this chance, and to Mary-Celeste Lewis for being the best editor a girl could ask for. My stories couldn't be in better hands. My mom, though, has always been my first editor, and her determination and insight were vital in helping this story become what it is today. Without you, none of this could have happened.

JENNIFFER WARDELL is the arts, entertainment, and lifestyle reporter for the Davis Clipper. She's won several awards from the Utah Press Association and the Utah Headliners Chapter of the Society of Professional Journalists. Wardell currently lives in Salt Lake City, Utah. Her first novel, *Fairy Godmothers, Inc.,* debuted in April 2013, marking the beginning of her brand of wit, fantasy, and romance.

Follow Jenniffer at facebook.com/JennifferWardell